# Draco

## THE IMMORTAL HIGHLAND CENTURIONS
### BOOK THREE

# JAYNE CASTEL

WINTER MIST PRESS

The centurion with a heart of stone. The lady who scorns him. A marriage that will end the curse. Enemies to lovers in Medieval Scotland.

**Draco Vulcan stopped caring about anything or anyone years ago.** Cursed to live forever, he only finds joy on the battlefield. But in order to break the curse upon him and his friends, he must wed a woman he can't stand.

**The lady in question has just escaped a loveless marriage.** The last thing she wants is to enter another one—especially to the cold, brutal warrior who fights at William Wallace's side.

When the English king hears that Wallace is hiding at Dunnottar Castle, and lays siege to the fortress—Draco and the widow must band together against this common foe. **But are they prepared to take things a step further and sacrifice their own happiness to break an ancient curse?**

Book #3 in The Immortal Highland Centurion series, DRACO is the dramatic conclusion to a high-octane romance trilogy about three cursed Roman soldiers and the brave-hearted Scottish women who love them.

# Historical Romances
# by Jayne Castel

**DARK AGES BRITAIN**

**The Kingdom of the East Angles series**
*Night Shadows (prequel novella)*
*Dark Under the Cover of Night (Book One)*
*Nightfall till Daybreak (Book Two)*
*The Deepening Night (Book Three)*
*The Kingdom of the East Angles: The Complete Series*

**The Kingdom of Mercia series**
*The Breaking Dawn (Book One)*
*Darkest before Dawn (Book Two)*
*Dawn of Wolves (Book Three)*
*The Kingdom of Mercia: The Complete Series*

**The Kingdom of Northumbria series**
*The Whispering Wind (Book One)*
*Wind Song (Book Two)*
*Lord of the North Wind (Book Three)*
*The Kingdom of Northumbria: The Complete Series*

**DARK AGES SCOTLAND**

**The Warrior Brothers of Skye series**
*Blood Feud (Book One)*
*Barbarian Slave (Book Two)*
*Battle Eagle (Book Three)*
*The Warrior Brothers of Skye: The Complete Series*

**The Pict Wars series**
*Warrior's Heart (Book One)*
*Warrior's Secret (Book Two)*
*Warrior's Wrath (Book Three)*

*The Pict Wars: The Complete Series*

**Novellas**
*Winter's Promise*

**MEDIEVAL SCOTLAND**

**The Brides of Skye series**
*The Beast's Bride (Book One)*
*The Outlaw's Bride (Book Two)*
*The Rogue's Bride (Book Three)*
*The Brides of Skye: The Complete Series*

**The Sisters of Kilbride series**
*Unforgotten (Book One)*
*Awoken (Book Two)*
*Fallen (Book Three)*
*Claimed (Epilogue novella)*

**The Immortal Highland Centurions series**
*Maximus (Book One)*
*Cassian (Book Two)*
*Draco (Book Three)*
*The Laird's Return (Festive epilogue novella)*

# Epic Fantasy Romances by Jayne Castel

**Light and Darkness series**
*Ruled by Shadows (Book One)*
*The Lost Swallow (Book Two)*
*Path of the Dark (Book Three)*
*Light and Darkness: The Complete Series*

All characters and situations in this publication are fictitious, and any resemblance to living persons is purely coincidental.

*Draco,* by Jayne Castel



ISBN: 978-0-473-55113-1 (paperback)

Published by Winter Mist Press

Edited by Tim Burton
Cover design by Winter Mist Press
Cover photography courtesy of www.shutterstock.com
Roman Imperial image courtesy of
www.shutterstock.com

Visit Jayne's website and blog: www.jaynecastel.com

***

To Tim—love you forever.

***

*"The only thing people regret is
that they didn't live boldly enough,
that they didn't invest enough heart,
didn't love enough.
Nothing else really counts at all."*
—Ted Hughes, Letters of Ted Hughes

# PROLOGUE

## CATCH ME IF YOU CAN

*Edinburgh*
*Scotland*

**Summer, 1135 AD**

THEY WOULDN'T CATCH him, not this time.

Draco fled through the warren of narrow streets below Castle Rock. A stitch stabbed his side—a reminder that, with a belly full of ale and mutton, he wasn't in the best state to escape the warriors who pounded the alleyways behind him. Nonetheless, the fear of being caught spurred Draco on.

His feet flew over the slick cobbles, damp after an afternoon shower of rain. Ahead, a wagon laden with baskets trundled out onto the street, blocking Draco's way.

Spitting out a curse, he leaped up onto the wagon, causing the mule pulling it to give a shrill, grating whinny.

"Hey, get off!" the man leading the mule bellowed.

Draco ignored him. Nimble as a hare, he clambered over the mountain of wicker baskets and then jumped, landing lightly on his feet on the other side.

Shouts echoed off the stone buildings behind him, but now Draco allowed himself a grin.

*Catch me if you can.*

The wagon would slow that lot down, giving him time to get away.

Emerging into the wider thoroughfare of Grassmarket, Draco sprinted east. He knew Edinburgh well; he'd visited the town hundreds of times over the centuries, watching it grow from a Roman fort to a thriving Scottish royal center. The tangle of fetid alleys around the fish market would be easy enough to lose those idiots in.

Still, despite that he was close to shaking off his pursuers, Draco regretted lingering in town on this visit. *The White Horse* was comfortable, and the serving lass there had shared his bed the night before. Instead of leaving that morning as he'd planned, he'd enjoyed a hearty noon meal before sauntering out to the stables to saddle his horse.

Henry and his lads had been waiting for him.

Henry, the king's son, had been after reckoning with Draco ever since he cuckolded him three years prior. It would probably have been wise for Draco to avoid Edinburgh for the time being—but he wasn't given to being wise.

He liked to push things to the limit, every time.

Losing his lover Magda had turned him reckless. He'd been part of the raid afterward that massacred those responsible for her death—but had learned first-hand that vengeance sometimes left a bitter taste in a man's mouth. The years since hadn't been easy, but he'd realized he had no choice but to move on.

Draco left Grassmarket, diving into a dark lane and narrowly missing being doused by the chamber pot someone emptied overhead. Still grinning, as the fear of capture gave way to the thrill of escaping, Draco rounded the corner.

And collided with a wall of leather-clad muscle.

Henry's thugs were on him in an instant. Heavy fists collided with his face, his stomach.

*Shit.* He was sure he'd out-smarted them. How had the bastards caught up with him?

Draco fought savagely—but to no avail. They had him cornered, and they weren't going to let him slip their net again. Grunts and the sound of fists pummeling flesh filled the lane. No one came to Draco's aid.

Eventually, he hung between two of them, his head throbbing from the beating he'd just sustained, spitting out blood onto the cobbles.

A tall figure stepped out of the shadowed recesses of a building that overhung the street. A thin, young man, with aquiline features and dark hair brushed back into a rakish widow's peak, stood before him.

Henry, son of King David of Scotland, had been waiting a while for this moment. "Finally ... we have the freak."

*Freak.*

The name made Draco's mouth twist. Of course, Henry had discovered Draco's immortality a year earlier, when he'd jammed a dirk into his guts in an Edinburgh ale house and seen his victim alive and well the following day.

He'd caught and tried to kill Draco twice more after that.

Really, Draco was a fool to come back to Edinburgh.

Over the centuries, he'd made a point of keeping who he was a secret. Folk didn't tend to respond well when they discovered an immortal walked amongst them. Draco was a Moor of Valentia, a town on Spain's southern coast, and he'd been born well over a thousand years earlier. He'd joined the Roman Ninth legion at twenty winters, and had ended up in Britannia a few years after that. And then when the Ninth fell in northern Caledonia, he'd been one of three survivors cursed by a Pict witch to eternal life.

Draco couldn't die, although that didn't mean he couldn't feel pain.

"How's Suisan?" he slurred. They'd smashed his head repeatedly up against the wall, and he was finding it hard to think. Even so, his question hit its mark like a well-aimed quarrel.

Henry's smile slipped. "I broke the betrothal, and she wed another," he growled. "Do ye think I wanted *yer* leftovers?"

Draco grinned at him, aware that blood was trickling down his chin. "I did the lass a favor … sparing her a life shackled to you."

Henry went still, his heavy brows knitting together. A dangerous silence settled in the alleyway, and Draco's skin prickled.

He liked to push things, but had he gone too far this time?

"I loved her." Henry choked out the words. "But to ye, it was merely a game."

Draco's goading grin slipped. He hadn't realized Henry had actually been in love with the comely Suisan Boyd. He checked himself then. But would it have stopped him anyway? Likely not.

Henry's gaze was wintry when it settled upon Draco once more. A nerve flickered under one eye. "Ye won't slip away this time, Vulcan. There are ways of dealing with a man who won't die."

And with these words, Draco felt the first flicker of fear tremble in his gut.

They dragged him through the streets up to Castle Rock. The guards at the gate cast the party curious looks but said nothing as the king's son led his men and their captive inside the walls.

Draco's ears were ringing, his legs stumbling, and yet he tried to fight off the two brutes who held him fast.

He was a rash man, but not a dull-witted one. The look on his nemesis's face had scared him. He needed to get free.

Unfortunately, he wasn't strong enough. They'd beaten him soundly. It hurt with every intake of breath, a sign that a few of his ribs were cracked.

That would be the least of his problems soon though. *Will they torture me?*

Folk had tried that with him over the centuries, and the unpleasant memories still returned to Draco in his dreams. Although he awoke healed with every new dawn, he felt each cut to his flesh, each blow.

Being burned alive was the worst.

His belly cramped, sweat beading on his skin. *Mithras, I hope it's not fire they've got in store for me.*

But it wasn't.

Henry led the way to a small chapel inside the walls— a rectangular, stone building with a peaked roof. They entered through a Romanesque arch, into a sanctuary lined with low stone benches.

"This chapel was built in my grandmother's memory ... Saint Margaret," Henry announced, turning to face Draco. He favored his captive with a tight smile, waving his hand toward the altar at one end. "She was a pious woman, who died a few days after hearing of my grandfather's demise in battle." Henry motioned to one of the men behind them. "Pull up the flagstones," he ordered.

The two holding Draco tightened their grip upon him as they dragged him toward the altar. They and Henry looked on while three others used their blades to pry up the heavy slate stones covering the floor.

And as he watched them work, Draco's breathing quickened.

He started to wish they'd planned to set fire to him after all.

They raised a number of flagstones to reveal a tomb underneath.

"Open it," Henry commanded.

The grating of stone against stone filled the chapel as the tomb eventually yawned open. Even from a few yards distant, Draco could see the dusty remains of a skeleton within it.

He swallowed, fighting the sting of bile in the back of his throat.

Henry caught his eye before flashing him a hard smile. "Scared yet?"

Draco stared back at him. For once, a cutting response didn't rise within him. Henry had outmaneuvered him, and they both knew it.

The king's son met the eye of the bigger of the two men holding Draco. "Put him in the ground."

Draco fought them. Dread rendered him vicious, and he gouged, kicked, and twisted in their grip. His reaction was so violent that in the end it took all five of the men with Henry to drag him into the tomb, and they had to stand on him to keep him down.

Snarling and spitting curses, Draco glared up through their legs at where Henry had moved close.

The young man's face was a pitiless mask, and through his rage, Draco realized that he'd made a grave miscalculation the day he'd cuckolded Henry. Some men never forgot a slight and wielded vengeance like a weapon.

Henry's hate had made him strong.

"It took me a while to devise this end for ye," Henry said while Draco panted and clawed at the sides of the tomb. "But now that I see ye lying there, I realize the wait has been worth it. Enjoy the long darkness ... it'll give ye ample time to think on how ye wronged me."

And with that, Henry motioned to his men. "Cover him up."

Panic seized Draco then—a wild madness that reared up within him. "No!" he roared. "I beg you ... no!"

But none of them paid him any heed.


Henry watched his men seal the tomb, muffling the cries of the man inside. They worked swiftly, their faces pinched and pale. It was an unsavory task, but a necessary one. They all knew what this man was. This was the only way to deal with the demon.

After sealing the tomb, the men dragged thick sacking over it, to muffle the captive's cries and beating fists further. And once they'd replaced the flagstones, and stomped upon them to ensure they lay flat, Henry could no longer hear Draco Vulcan's cries.

Sending his men away, Henry lingered in his grandmother's chapel for a few moments longer.

Silence settled over the sanctuary, and Henry drew in a deep breath, his ears straining to hear the trapped man beneath his feet. Perhaps, if he listened carefully, he could catch the faintest whisper. But no one else would.

The young man walked to the altar then and crossed himself. "Forgive me, grandmother," he murmured. "Ye may have died of a broken heart, but I'm not going to martyr myself. Instead I choose vengeance." He paused there, his gaze lingering upon the iron cross before him. "I didn't wish to sully this place ... but it was necessary."

And then, without a backward glance, he turned and left the chapel.

**166 years later ...**

# I

# THE DRAGON

*Dunnottar*
*Scotland*

**Summer, 1301 AD**

DRACO HATED KIRKS.

Even sitting there, surrounded by others, the place made his skin crawl. He suffered Holy Rude in Stirling only because he never had to linger in the kirk itself.

Dunnottar chapel smelled of damp stone and fatty tallow—odors that made Draco's belly churn. Several decades had passed since he'd been freed from his stone prison beneath the floor of Saint Margaret's Chapel. Long enough for the memories of that ordeal to fade somewhat. And yet the smells brought everything back.

It was an irony that today celebrated Saint Margaret—a further reminder of that vile prison and the smothering darkness.

It seemed as if the memories would forever torment him.

Pressure built in Draco's chest, and he closed his eyes, trying to still the mounting panic.

"Draco ... is something amiss?"

Maximus's whisper jolted him back into the present.

Eyes flicking open, Draco glanced at where his friend sat next to him upon the low wooden bench, with his wife, Heather, at his side. They were both watching him, brows furrowed, as Father Finlay droned on from the pulpit.

"Merciful God. Ye gave the holy Queen Margaret of Scotland great love for the poor."

Draco shook his head, favoring them both with a tight smile. "I'm fine," he whispered back. "I just find this tedious."

"Behave," Maximus replied, mouth twitching.

A few yards away, dressed in black robes, his prayer book held out before him, the chaplain of Dunnottar halted his reading a moment and flashed them a scowl. Then, clearing his throat, he continued his prayer. "Dearest Lord ... lend yer ear to the intercessions of this holy woman and help us to live after her example so that yer goodness and mercy become visible in today's world."

Bitterness flooded Draco's mouth.

*Goodness and mercy.*

He'd seen little of those things in the long years of his life. Indeed, the woman, as saintly and kind as she was reputed to have been, was the grandmother of Henry, Earl of Northumberland.

A man who buried others alive.

Draco's only solace was that Henry had sickened and died at the age of thirty-seven, around seventeen years after he'd entombed his enemy under the floor of Saint Margaret's.

Shifting uncomfortably on the hard bench, Draco cast his gaze around the rectangular-shaped chapel. High windows let in honeyed sunlight, which pooled on the stone floor—stone that still bore the charred marks of a fire five years earlier.

A fire that had incinerated the trapped English garrison.

Draco's attention shifted to the man responsible for the massacre.

William Wallace sat at the front of the congregation, large hands clasped together in prayer. During the past two years in which Draco had been part of the freedom fighter's band of loyal warriors, he'd been surprised to discover that Wallace was a pious man.

However, that hadn't prevented him from setting fire to a chapel full of soldiers.

Draco's jaw clenched. *Pity he didn't burn it to the ground.*

Draco worshipped Mithras, Lord of the Light. Barely a day passed when he didn't visit the tiny temple Cassian had built. Hidden away at the back of the dungeons, the mithraeum felt like the last remaining link to his old life. It reminded him that he hailed from a warm land far to the south, from a time before the Christian God held sway.

Drawing in a deep breath, Draco suffered through more of the chaplain's sermon. He had nothing against Father Finlay; he appeared a kind enough man. However, it was agony being inside this chapel. The walls felt as if they were closing in on him.

The darkness, the madness, clawed at the fringes of his mind.

Draco broke out into a cold sweat. *I have to get out of here.*

Mercifully, Father Finlay concluded his sermon, and those seated upon the rows of benches beneath the altar rose to their feet and slowly filed out of the chapel.

Draco was the first to venture out onto the steps. He descended them two at a time, sucking in lungfuls of air. Warm sun bathed his face, and the sound of industry—the clang of metal being forged, and the shouts of men upon the walls—greeted him.

Dunnottar was readying itself for war.

Draco stopped at the foot of the steps and waited for the others to catch him up. His gaze flicked to the smith's forge. They'd brought in two young blacksmiths from Stonehaven to replace Blair Galbraith.

The man had just upped one day and left, without a word to anyone.

Draco wasn't surprised. After his brother's disappearance in late spring, the man had turned bitter and vengeful. He'd grown to hate Dunnottar and everyone in it.

"It's time for the noon meal," Cassian announced, approaching Draco. Captain of Dunnottar Guard, Cassian wore a mail shirt and heavy leather braies. The big man with close-cropped brown hair flashed Draco a smile. "Lady Gavina wants us all to join her in the hall today."

Cassian was always smiling these days.

He and Maximus were like two grinning idiots.

Draco knew he was being uncharitable, but the lack of care Maximus and Cassian were taking—both wedding mortal women when the curse was still upon the three of them—astounded him.

Was he the only sane one among them?

"Always thinking of your belly," Maximus called out from behind them. He had an arm around Heather, and was steering her toward the postern door and the stairs that would take them all up to the upper ward.

"I'm not hungry," Draco muttered.

"All the same ... the Wallace will want you at his side," Cassian replied, still smiling. "Come on." With that, his friend turned to where Aila, Cassian's sweet-faced bride, hurried up to them after a brief discussion with her mistress. Despite her marriage to Cassian, Aila had remained maid to the Lady of Dunnottar.

The lady herself was now descending the steps.

Gavina De Keith held herself like a queen, one hand holding up her long skirts as she daintily picked her way down. The sun glinted off her hair—locks so pale they were almost white—and bathed her milky skin. Even dressed in mourning black, the woman shone like a torch in a misty winter's dusk.

She was a beauty. There was no denying it. Yet the sight of Lady De Keith made Draco grind his teeth. There was something about the woman that roused his ire.

Sheltered, spoiled, and superior—she looked at him like he was something she wouldn't deign to scrape off one of her fine silk slippers.

They'd had very little to do with each other in the time Draco had been at Dunnottar, yet every exchange made Draco's jaw clench.

The lady didn't bother to hide her disdain for him.

Likewise, he went out of his way to be boorish whenever they interacted.

The party made their way inside to the long hall, where servants were placing platters of spit-roasted hogget alongside wheels of tangy sheep's cheese, boiled carrots, and large loaves of oaten bread.

Once again, Draco found himself observing Lady Gavina, while she took her seat upon the laird's chair. It was a huge carven seat made of oak that swamped her tiny frame. Nonetheless, she sat upon it as proudly as a queen.

Noting the straightness of her back, the way she held her chin high, Draco felt a stubborn jolt of respect for the lady. She hadn't been laird of Dunnottar long, yet she'd taken easily to the role. Not only that, but the folk here evidently preferred Gavina to her late husband.

The day before, the Wallace—never one to hold back his opinion—had told Gavina so. "Ye are loved here, My Lady," he'd rumbled, holding his cup of wine up to her in a toast. "The folk of Dunnottar favor ye far more than they ever did David."

It dawned on Draco then that he was *staring* at De Keith's widow. Irritated at this realization, Draco shifted his attention from Lady Gavina to where a steaming platter of hogget sat before him. The greasy odor of the meat made him feel faintly nauseated.

It was a fine meal, yet Draco hadn't lied to his friends earlier. He had little appetite. Seated at the Wallace's side, he watched as the big man piled his platter with roast meat.

William Wallace had a big enough appetite for both of them.

Draco drew in a slow breath as he tried to regain his equilibrium. It wasn't just being forced to spend time in the chapel, and endure the memories it roused, that had closed his stomach—but also their most recent discovery.

They'd solved another part of the riddle that Pict witch had given them all those years earlier.

They'd learned the identity of the 'Dragon'.

Cassian was now convinced Draco was part of all of this. His name did mean 'dragon' in Latin, but Draco found the theory far-fetched to say the least.

Especially since, if that was the case, Draco needed to find himself a wife.

The riddle had mocked them for over a thousand years now. Just five lines, and yet their meaning had remained frustratingly elusive. Once more, the lines whispered in his mind.

> *When the Broom-star crosses the sky,*
> *And the Hammer strikes the fort*
> *Upon the Shelving Slope.*
> *When the White Hawk and the Dragon wed,*
> *Only then will the curse be broke.*

They knew now that the Broom-star was the fiery star that reappeared in the sky every seventy-five years or so, and that the Hammer referred to Edward Longshanks, 'The Hammer of the Scots'. The fort upon the Shelving Slope was the old name for Dunnottar—which just left the identity of the White Hawk and the Dragon to solve.

*Ridiculous.* Draco helped himself to some bread and cheese before holding his pewter goblet up for a passing servant to fill. *Desperation has made Cassian draw a long bow indeed.*

He glanced right then, at where Cassian was serving Aila some roast hogget. Cassian gazed down at his wife with such love that Draco felt a sting of embarrassment for him.

Where was his reserve, his caution?

Shifting his attention across the table, Draco watched Maximus and Heather laugh together, before she playfully slapped her husband's arm, grey-green eyes gleaming.

*What is it about these De Keith sisters?* Draco's lips thinned. Heather and Aila had indeed bewitched his friends. Despite all the pain both men had suffered in the past, they were still willing to throw themselves into the breach once more.

*Idiots.*

Draco took a deep gulp of wine. It was sloe—full-bodied yet with a sharp tang.

"Try not to look too miserable," Cassian interrupted his brooding. Draco had thought his friend was too distracted by the winsome Aila to notice him, but he glanced up to see Cassian had fixed him with that level look he'd come to know well over the centuries. "The sun is shining, and we have only one thing left to solve in the riddle."

Cassian had uttered this last line in Latin, lest anyone should overhear them.

Not that there was any risk of that. Men and women now filled the narrow hall, their voices echoing off the stone. The wide windows, which looked both north and south, had been opened, allowing the rumble of surf against the rocks below and the cry of gulls to enter.

"You make it sound so easy," Draco growled. "I just need to find a White Hawk, and then we'll fly off into the sunset together." Draco muttered a curse before taking another gulp of wine. "I don't want to wed *anyone*."

Cassian's gaze widened. "You've been in a foul mood ever since I shared the news with you," he observed. "Don't you want to break the curse?"

"Of course I do."

"Then why the sour face?"

"Because I don't share your optimism. We've always known what my name means ... but suddenly you think I'm part of the riddle."

"Aila pointed out we've been so focused on looking elsewhere that we ignored what was right beneath our noses," Cassian replied with a rueful smile. "And my gut tells me she's right."

*And, if the lass told you the moon was made of sheep's curd, you'd believe her,* Draco thought. However, he didn't share the words. They were too bitter, even for him.

# II

# THE LADY OF DUNNOTTAR

THE CHAIR WAS too big for her.

Made of oak with roebuck heads carved into the arm-rests, it had been crafted for a man; Gavina felt like an errant child perched in it. She was barely sitting high enough to eat her meal, although she resisted the urge to call for a cushion to be brought.

Such a request was hardly dignified.

Gavina cast a glance left at where her sister-by-marriage, Lady Elizabeth, sat. The lady looked so pale and tense these days. Since their return from Stirling, she feared for her husband's life. Robert De Keith, the true laird of the De Keiths, was currently residing in an English prison. If Robert never returned, his son would one day become laird—but since wee Robbie De Keith was only three summers old, that wasn't going to happen for a while yet.

At present, Gavina ruled here, and she would have to get used to being dwarfed by her seat.

Even so, she was surprised by how easily she'd stepped into her new role. For years, she'd waited in her husband's shadow. Yet David had shown no interest in the more mundane tasks involved in running the keep.

Gavina was already used to working closely with Donnan, Dunnottar's steward, when it came to ordering supplies for the castle and organizing servants.

But now, she was in charge of the more important decisions as well.

Cutting off a piece of hogget with her eating knife, Gavina took a small bite and chewed slowly, her gaze traveling around the laird's table—where she, her kin, and important retainers and guests sat.

Ever since his arrival, William Wallace had joined them at the laird's table. And as always, his right-hand sat with him.

*Draco Vulcan.*

Gavina's gaze rested upon the Moor, taking in his haughty features, tightly-curled, short black hair, and hooded gaze.

If the man wasn't so unpleasant, she'd have found him attractive. As it was, on the few occasions they'd interacted, Vulcan had proved himself to have the manners of a goat.

There had been that incident at Beltaine recently, when he'd dared reprimand her for asking Cassian to dance with Aila. The lass had been sick with love for Dunnottar's handsome captain, and Gavina had only been doing her part to bring them together. However, Vulcan had scolded her like she'd been a misbehaving bairn.

Although, now that she knew the three men's secret, she understood his reticence to her match-making. Cassian had possessed a valid reason for keeping his heart walled off.

She'd never forget that moment, a few weeks earlier, when she'd witnessed Cassian Gaius stab himself in the heart in that oak glade. He should have died instantly, yet he'd held on, and then as the sun rose, the light filtering through the trees, he'd miraculously healed before their eyes.

She didn't like it, didn't understand it—but the foreigners seated at this table were all immortal.

Honestly, despite that Gavina didn't begrudge Aila or Heather their happiness, she worried for both women.

*If the curse isn't broken, they will both have to leave Dunnottar eventually … or folk will notice their husbands never seem to age.*

Aye, she shared Draco's misgivings, yet all the same, the Moor had overstepped.

There had also been the occurrence on the journey home from Stirling—an incident that had cemented her dislike toward him. Draco and his men had come to their rescue, saving them from a group of King Edward's men who'd hunted them down.

One of the English soldiers—a youth barely old enough to grow whiskers—had thrown down his weapons, fallen to his knees, and begged for mercy. But Draco Vulcan had shown him none, and had killed the lad in cold blood.

And when Gavina confronted him about it, he'd dismissed her rudely.

Gavina's jaw tightened at the memory of how his mouth had twisted with scorn.

It was only out of respect for the Wallace that she suffered the man to sit at her table.

"No word from Edward yet." Elizabeth spoke up, intruding upon Gavina's introspection. "I wonder what game he's playing."

Gavina frowned. Like Elizabeth and everyone else in the keep, she'd been on tenterhooks of late, waiting for the English king to turn his attention north.

John Comyn, the current Guardian of the Realm, who'd been forced to surrender Stirling, had assured them that The Hammer of the Scots didn't plan to attack the northern strongholds as yet. But her husband's assassination attempt would most likely have changed Edward's plans.

*I can't believe David would do something so stupid.*

David De Keith had gone to Stirling under the pretense of bending the knee to the English king. He was supposed to play along, feign loyalty, and gather details about Edward's plans, as well as lobby for the release of his brother from captivity.

Instead, he'd organized a private meeting with Edward, during which he'd pulled a dirk on him, and had his own throat cut for his trouble. His brother was likely to never see daylight again.

Gavina shared Elizabeth's worries. Although she'd had no part in her husband's actions, for David had never shared his plans with her, Gavina could not help but feel a sense of responsibility for the whole mess. It now was up to her to defend this stronghold should Longshanks seek reckoning upon them.

"Perhaps he won't attack us," Gavina replied after a pause, injecting a hopeful note into her voice. "After all, he's busy keeping the south under his control."

"He'll attack," Elizabeth replied wearily. "Longshanks is well known for his vengeful nature." Her throat bobbed then. "I wonder if he's ordered Robert's execution yet."

Gavina reached out and placed a hand over Elizabeth's. "Don't say such things, Liz. Robert still lives."

"But ye don't know that. Edward will be looking to punish our clan now."

The women's gazes fused for a long moment, and Gavina's belly knotted. She wanted to assure her sister-by-marriage that wasn't the case, to promise her that Robert would be returned to them whole and healthy, but she wasn't one for empty words, so she held her tongue instead.

"Are we ready for another siege?" Elizabeth asked, deliberately changing the topic away from her husband. "The English breached our gates easily last time."

"The Wallace and his men have reinforced them with iron bars," Gavina replied. "We also have been amassing quantities of slate and lead should they try to scale the walls." She paused then, remembering the attack years earlier. Robert had been laird of Dunnottar then, but even though he was a skilled strategist and strong leader, the castle hadn't been able to withstand the might of the

English. "Remember … we were all taken by surprise last time. It won't happen again."

Elizabeth nodded, a little of the tension on her face easing. "Ye are doing a fine job of ruling, Gavina," she said after a pause, managing a faint smile. "Unlike David, ye don't let paranoia and pride cloud yer judgement."

Gavina smiled back, warmed by Elizabeth's words. Her gaze then flicked across to where William Wallace was deep in conversation with his right-hand. The freedom fighter, and the aura of calm authority he emitted, definitely made her new position easier.

Of course, the Wallace was a wanted man—Edward Longshanks could never learn that the outlaw sheltered within her walls. Even so, Gavina felt secure in the knowledge she had Wallace's loyalty.

However, the English weren't the only threat to the stronghold these days. Her brother, Shaw Irvine, had threatened her husband with war if he didn't cede land to him. Now that David was dead, it was up to her to smooth things with her errant brother. She didn't want to fight her own kin, and would try her best to take the route of diplomacy. Nonetheless, the threat Shaw posed made Wallace's presence here even more vital.

They'd strengthened Dunnottar's defenses considerably over the past weeks. The Guard had now doubled in size, and the clang and hiss of the forge was an ever-present sound in the keep these days as the smiths worked night and day to make enough weapons for them.

Gavina's jaw firmed, resolve igniting in the pit of her belly.

Aye, Wallace had defeated the English numerous times in the past, and he'd do so again.

"My Lady ... a message has arrived for ye!"

Gavina glanced up, from where she was seated by the hearth, her gaze alighting upon the guard in the doorway to the laird's solar. She didn't usually spend much time in here, preferring the softer, more feminine sanctuary of the women's solar, but the Wallace had wished to discuss Dunnottar's defenses with her after the noon meal.

She sat surrounded by men—big, leather and mail-clad warriors dominated the large chamber.

The Wallace, Draco Vulcan, and Maximus Cato stood near the window, while Cassian Gaius leaned against the mantelpiece. Donnan De Keith, steward of Dunnottar, sat on a high-backed chair opposite Gavina. The steward was older than the other men present, silver lacing his thick brown hair, yet he still exuded a masculine forcefulness.

Despite that she had stepped into the role of laird with relative ease, these conversations sometimes made her feel out of her depth.

Diplomacy and negotiation were her strengths. She didn't know how to talk about warfare and strategy. Violence made her queasy. Nonetheless, these men sought to include her in all the decisions regarding the defense of this fortress.

"Thank ye," she said, reaching for the scroll the guard now brought to her.

Looking down at the wax seal upon the missive, Gavina's breathing quickened. She recognized the Irvine crest immediately: a banded sheaf of holly leaves.

"It's from my brother," she murmured as the guard went on his way. She glanced across at the Wallace then. His brow was furrowed, his dark gaze upon the scroll she held. "I wrote to him recently, requesting that the two of us meet to settle things," she continued. "This will be his answer."

The Wallace's frown deepened to a scowl. "Ye don't want to be wasting time on the likes of him, My Lady ... not with Longshanks threatening the north."

Stubbornness rose within Gavina. "He's my brother, William. I will do what I can to mend things between us

… especially since we need to be friends with our neighbors at a time like this.”

Beside the Wallace, Draco Vulcan snorted. Maximus cast his friend a quelling look, but the Moor ignored it.

Gavina cut Draco a glare. She wished he hadn’t been invited to this meeting. However, Wallace rarely met with her without Vulcan at his side.

“Well, let’s see what your brother has to say,” Cassian said, breaking the tense silence that descended in the solar.

Shifting her attention back to the missive, Gavina broke the seal and unfurled the parchment. At the top, in her brother’s spiky handwriting, was the Irvine motto. *Sub Sole Sub Umbra Virens*: flourishing both in sunshine and in shade. Underneath it was a short message.

Gavina cleared her throat. “My dearest sister,” she began, her voice turning brittle at the empty words. It was a mere formality, for Shaw had never shown any affection for her, not even when they were bairns. “I thank ye for yer letter and am heartened that ye wish to meet with me to discuss our situation. Congratulations also on yer new position as laird. In the interests of both parties, it is best we meet in a neutral spot. As such, I will await ye on the eve of the twenty-first of June in the Strath of Muirskie, upon Gordon lands. Yer ever-loving brother, Shaw Irvine.”

Silence followed Gavina’s reading of the letter. She lowered the parchment to see that opposite her Donnan De Keith was now frowning. “What did ye promise him, My Lady?” he asked quietly, his voice laced with concern.

Gavina frowned. Did he really think she’d promise her brother anything, especially after he threatened to lay siege to Dunnottar? He’d even bragged about his new siege weapon, ‘The Battle Hammer’, which he threatened to bash down the castle gates with if land wasn’t ceded to him.

“Nothing,” she said, her tone sharpening. “I merely requested that he and I meet to see if peace could be

forged between the Irvines and the De Keiths once
more.”

“You do realize that the twenty-first of June is
tomorrow?” Draco Vulcan drawled, speaking up for the
first time since entering the solar.

Gavina ignored him, her gaze still upon the steward.
“I will not make an enemy of my brother unless I’m left
with no choice,” she continued. “Shaw is a potential ally
we shouldn’t ignore ... especially with Edward of
England focused upon us.”

“It’s not safe for you to be traveling beyond these
walls at present, My Lady,” Cassian spoke up, a pained
expression flitting across his ruggedly handsome
features. “I suggest you send me to speak on your
behalf.”

Gavina shook her head, determination rising within
her once more. “Shaw expects *me*. He won’t treat with
anyone else.”

“Captain Gaius is right, My Lady,” Wallace rumbled.
“This is not the time for a lady to be making such
journeys.”

“I will be perfectly safe,” Gavina replied, raising her
chin as she met the Wallace’s eye. “All I need is an
escort.”

# III

# TRAITORS AND PROTECTORS

"YOU HAVE COME from Dunnottar?"

Edward of England observed the man before him. With wild auburn hair and a thick beard, the newcomer's face was in a state—swollen and bruised. His nose was badly misshapen and both eyes blackened. One look at the Scot, with his heavily-muscled physique, and Edward could see he was a blacksmith. One didn't acquire muscles like that from working the fields or even wielding a broadsword.

The newcomer tensed, his gaze flicking to the big man with red hair who sat by the hearth. Of course, only the high-born Scots understood or spoke French.

"Mar sin tha thu air tighinn bho Dunnottar?" John Comyn translated.

The newcomer mumbled a response through cracked lips.

"He says 'aye' ... and he brings news," Comyn replied, his gaze returning to the English king.

Edward's gaze narrowed. "So I hear," he replied coolly. "You wouldn't have been allowed up here otherwise."

The former Guardian of the Realm translated that too, and the blacksmith frowned.

Edward stood near the window in his solar. He'd been taking a cup of wine with Comyn when one of his men had announced he had a visitor. Edward would have turned the lout away if he hadn't mentioned Dunnottar.

The De Keiths had been on his mind of late, especially after their laird had tried to cut his throat just a few short weeks ago.

Gavina and Elizabeth De Keith had both slipped his net, but in the end, he'd decided he cared little about that. David De Keith had most likely acted alone. The man had been a scheming weasel—Edward had realized that from the moment they met. But he'd never imagined the laird would pull a dirk on him.

Fortunately for the king, De Keith had underestimated him. He might have been getting on in years, but he was still lethal in a fight.

De Keith's brother remained an English prisoner, as Edward hadn't yet decided whether or not Robert De Keith should be executed for his brother's act.

Edward had considered marching up to the fortress immediately and laying siege to it, just to teach the clan a lesson. But once his initial outrage faded, Edward let pragmatism rule his decisions. He needed to strengthen his defenses at Stirling before he marched off to Dunnottar. Keeping hold of the territories he and his son had already taken was proving more difficult than he'd hoped.

The Scots were hardier than the Welsh, it seemed. The additional troops he'd ordered from Northumbria had just arrived the day before. He was almost ready to make the trip north.

"So, what news do you have?" Edward asked, impatience creeping into his voice. Even from a few yards distant, he could smell the man: the rank odor of stale sweat and unwashed clothing. It was all he could do not to screw his face up.

The smith spoke again, his words mumbling and incoherent.

Across the room, John Comyn stiffened.

"What is it?" Edward barked. He hated not being able to understand Gaelic, and sometimes wondered if Comyn *altered* some of his translations to suit his own ends. The Scottish baron had bent the knee to him, yet Edward was ever watchful of Comyn.

He was a Scot after all, and none of them could be trusted.

"William Wallace is hiding at Dunnottar," Comyn replied, his tone wary.

Edward's gaze swiveled back to the smith. "What's your name?"

"Dè an t-ainm a th 'ort?" Comyn translated.

"Blair Galbraith," the man mumbled back, before saying something else.

"He was smith at Dunnottar," the baron continued. "Apparently, the Wallace arrived nearly two moons ago and has been hiding out in the fortress ever since."

*William Wallace.* Edward went still, coldness seeping through him.

Long moments passed. When the English king eventually spoke, his voice was quiet, yet flinty. "Apparently? You don't believe him?"

John 'The Red' Comyn pursed his lips, but didn't answer that.

Edward ignored him for the moment, instead focusing his attention on Galbraith. Rage ignited in the pit of his belly. *De Keith was hiding Wallace. The bastard knew I was hunting him ... he must have been laughing at me.*

Nonetheless, Edward kept his expression neutral. He knew better than to reveal his reactions in front of the likes of Comyn. A month ago, he'd drunk too much one evening and been too open with the man; Edward had later regretted his candor, and had been tight-lipped around the baron ever since.

Anger pulsed through him, and he let it burn, catching alight in his veins. A rush of vindictive pleasure followed. William Wallace had caused him no end of trouble over the years—and now he had discovered his location. The man's days were numbered.

Wallace had murdered William de Heselrig, Edward's High Sheriff of Lanark. Then, after winning the Battle of Stirling Bridge, Wallace had desecrated the body of Edward's friend Hugh de Cressingham, the treasurer he'd put in Stirling. Wallace had fashioned Hugh's skin into a scabbard, hilt, and belt.

But worse than all that—and of far greater worry to Edward—was the fact that William Wallace was a symbol of Scottish hope.

Edward would enjoy seeing the Wallace suffer for his crimes. The man's death would crush the rebellion.

*With Wallace out of the way, Scotland will be mine.*

"Thank you for bringing this news to me," he said finally, meeting Galbraith's eye. "I will make sure you are amply rewarded."

Comyn translated for him, and then the smith answered.

"He asks for no silver from you," Comyn replied, a brittle edge to his voice now. The man's face had flushed. His blue eyes glittered as he watched Blair Galbraith. "He says that revenge is payment enough."

Edward favored the blacksmith with a cool smile. "Well then, it appears we have something in common after all."

"I should head your escort, My Lady."

"No, Captain ... I'd prefer ye remain here at Dunnottar."

Gavina rose to her feet, her fingers closing around her brother's missive. He'd arranged their meeting sooner than she'd anticipated. She had to ready herself, for the Strath of Muirskie was nearly a day's ride from

Dunnottar. They would need to leave with tomorrow's dawn.

Across from her, Cassian was scowling.

"Please ready a party of twenty warriors to accompany me," she continued. "And while I'm away, ye and Donnan are in charge of the fortress."

"Aye, but Captain Gaius has a point, My Lady," the steward spoke up. "Ye should have a personal guard as well for this journey ... men who can oversee the discussions."

Irritation surged within Gavina. Since she'd taken over as laird, the likes of Donnan and Cassian had supported her. But when it came to making more important decisions, they grew nervous of putting their fate in a woman's hands.

Gavina held the steward's eye. She'd always liked Donnan, yet the patronizing edge to his voice—his concern that as a woman she was incapable of taking the lead in talks with her brother—rankled.

It was time she regained control of this exchange. Squaring her shoulders, Gavina drew in a deep breath, her gaze shifting across to the window where the Wallace and Vulcan still reclined.

"William ... can ye spare some of yer men to join my escort?" she asked. If it made Donnan feel better, she would increase the numbers of her party.

Wallace nodded. "Of course, My Lady."

"If you wish me to remain at Dunnottar ... I would ask you to take two men I name as your protectors," Cassian interjected here. He wore a stubborn expression now, a look Gavina had already seen in the past.

She inclined her head, her irritation fading a little. It warmed her to know that Cassian was so protective of her. She'd grown up feeling like an encumbrance in a keep full of rowdy, dominant men. And even her own husband hadn't cared for her well-being. Yet Captain Gaius, a man doomed to continue living for eternity, was doggedly loyal to Dunnottar and those who ruled it. He'd proved his loyalty numerous times over on that perilous flight back to Dunnottar from Stirling.

"Aye, Captain," she replied finally. "As ye wish ... whom did ye have in mind?"

Cassian held her gaze a moment, before he smiled. The captain then jerked his chin toward Maximus Cato and Draco Vulcan. "Those two."

"Clod-head! Why didn't you ask me first?"

Draco rounded on Cassian the moment they were outdoors. A warm breeze feathered across the lower ward, bringing with it the briny tang of the sea. However, Draco paid the fair afternoon no mind. He was too busy being angry at his friend.

Irritatingly, Cassian merely smiled back at him. "There was no need ... I knew you'd agree."

"But I'm needed here."

Maximus, who had just joined them, snorted. "As are we all ... however, Cass is right. Lady Gavina needs protecting."

Draco snarled at Maximus. "Well, why don't you go on your own then?"

"Two sets of eyes are better than one," Maximus replied, maddeningly calm. His dark eyes glinted with thinly veiled amusement, which made Draco want to punch him. "Plus, I know how much you enjoy Lady Gavina's company."

Draco growled a curse. "I've got better things to do than play protector to *that* woman."

"No, you don't," Cassian replied, a bullish expression settling upon his face. "You might not be part of the Dunnottar Guard, Draco, but the Wallace has sworn to protect this fortress and those who rule it. He's agreed for you and Max to escort Lady Gavina ... and that's the end of it."

"Don't worry," Maximus cut in, still grinning. "It'll only be an overnight trip. We won't be away long."

"All the same, my time would be better spent here," Draco insisted. He wasn't letting this matter drop so easily. "The English could attack at any time."

"We have scouts out watching the approach from the south," Cassian replied. "Worry not. We'll have advance warning of their arrival."

Draco muttered a curse. "We should be focusing on that riddle … rather than trying to pacify Irvine."

Maximus cocked an eyebrow. "There's nothing you or I can do here for the moment. Perhaps we'll meet your 'White Hawk' on our travels."

Draco glared at him, although he realized there was little point in arguing with these two. He knew he sounded petulant, but the last thing he wanted was to become Lady Gavina's personal protector—even for a couple of days. The woman's haughty manner brought out the worst in him.

"This journey is pointless anyway," he muttered. "Shaw Irvine isn't going to drop his claim, just because his sister pleads with him. Surely, the lady realizes that?"

"I think you underestimate Lady Gavina," Cassian answered, his gaze narrowing. "The woman has a sharp mind … if anyone can convince that warmongering laird to stand down, it's her."

# IV

# A PATH OF PEACE

IT WAS QUIET in the chapel, so much so that the rasp of Gavina's breathing seemed to echo in the stillness. Kneeling before the altar, she shifted position, closing her eyes as she whispered the last of her prayers.

It was growing late, yet she'd wanted to pay the chapel a visit, for there would be no time tomorrow.

"God guide me with yer wisdom," she murmured. "Please discipline me with yer justice."

The words gave her solace, balanced her after a day of conflict and hard decisions. She'd been on edge all afternoon following the meeting in the solar.

In truth, she was nervous about seeing her brother again.

She hadn't set eyes on Shaw since before her wedding to David—over six years ago now—and wondered if he'd changed much. He'd always been a rash, out-spoken youth, and had bullied her when they were bairns. It worried her that as soon as he'd taken on the mantle of laird after their father's death, he'd set about causing conflict with his neighbor.

Gavina needed to make him see sense. She'd wed a De Keith in order to keep the peace. They all had to do their part, and Shaw had to honor the pact his father had made with Robert De Keith. While Scot fought Scot, they'd always be easy pickings for invaders. The thought of the De Keiths and the Irvines at war made a weight settle upon her chest.

She would do all she could to avoid that eventuality.

"Dear Lord," she whispered. "The time has come for me to lead ... to make decisions for the greater good. Help me keep those within these walls safe."

With a sigh, she opened her eyes. She dearly hoped that God was listening to her this evening. But even if He wasn't, her time in the chapel had allowed her to focus on the task before her. Men always seemed intent on drawing swords against each other—but it was a woman's role to weave peace.

Rising to her feet, she brushed off her skirts and turned to see Father Finlay standing behind her.

"Father!" she gasped, one hand flying to her breast. "I hadn't realized ye were there."

"Don't mind me, My Lady," he replied with a smile. "I've only just stepped inside ... and wouldn't have done so if I'd realized ye were praying." He motioned to the banks of tallow candles that flickered down either side of the chapel. "I like to check on the candles before bed."

Gavina nodded and moved toward the narrow aisle between the rows of wooden benches. "Then I shall leave ye to it ... Goodnight, Father."

"My Lady," he said, stepping closer then. "I apologize for my presumption, but I heard a little of what ye were just saying ... and I wanted to assure ye that ye do indeed have the wisdom to do what's right. The path of peace is always the right one to take, in my view."

Gavina's step faltered, and she turned to face the chaplain once more. Father Finlay was a kind man, a good one; she only wished she could say the same for her brother. "I certainly hope so, Father," she murmured. "The future of Dunnottar depends on it."

Gavina was in a pensive mood the following morning when she sprang up onto the back of her palfrey and adjusted her charcoal-colored skirts. Her time in the chapel, and her short conversation with the chaplain, had made her resolve to come to a peaceful resolution with her brother even stronger.

She'd risen from her bed just before dawn and watched the sun rise from her window over the sea, while she rehearsed in her head all the things she'd say to Shaw. However, her musings had been cut short when Aila had arrived to help her dress and prepare for the journey.

Her maid stood on the steps of the keep now, next to her husband, her face tense with worry.

"Ye shouldn't be traveling without a maid, My Lady," she'd murmured earlier as she braided Gavina's hair into a long plait and coiled it around the crown of her head. "Who will attend to ye this eve?"

"I will look after myself for once, Aila," Gavina had replied with a small smile. "It's only one night, and I'd prefer ye remained here with yer husband."

It was the truth. High-born lady or not, Gavina was sure she'd be able to survive without Aila for such a short trip. Nonetheless, it did feel strange to be riding out without her maid this morning. Her escort was entirely male.

Gavina glanced over at where Draco and Maximus were sharing a few words before mounting their coursers. Of course, she knew why Cassian had chosen those two to accompany her.

He wanted to provide her with an escort he trusted unreservedly. Clearly, despite Gavina's assurances, Cassian was concerned her brother would try and harm her.

She tensed then, her gaze settling upon Draco Vulcan's broad shoulders. Yesterday the man had looked as if he'd just been struck across the face when the captain announced that the two of them would be her personal guards.

He'd managed to hold his tongue, although she'd seen how he bristled.

However, orders were orders.

Gavina's mouth thinned. She wasn't looking forward to traveling with him either.

"Max!" Heather rushed across the cobbled bailey and threw herself into her husband's arms. "Hurry back ... I miss ye already."

Maximus grinned down at her. "I'll be back before you notice I'm gone, carissima." The pair kissed passionately then, oblivious to the crowd of horses and men around them.

Gavina glanced away, embarrassed. Heather wasn't usually a clingy woman, but this was likely the first time the two had been parted since their wedding. They'd been virtually inseparable since that day.

Loneliness twisted within Gavina, catching her by surprise. She clutched at the supple leather reins she held. If only she'd felt that way about David De Keith. Unfortunately, she never had.

His death had brought a strange storm of emotions—regret being the strongest, and guilt swiftly following after. Maybe if she'd been a better wife, he wouldn't have sought solace in the arms of other women. She'd been harsh with Jean, Lady Elizabeth's hapless maid. The lass had been hopelessly in love with David, and had lashed out at Gavina for being dry-eyed over his death.

Jean's grief was short-lived, however, for she'd died on the journey back from Stirling. Nonetheless, the lass's rebuke had stung.

David had never given Gavina much reason to love him. Perhaps she was as cold as Jean accused—incapable of love.

Swallowing, Gavina shifted her attention back to the happy couple, who were still kissing. Maximus and Heather had such a strong bond, as did Cassian and Aila. It was hard not to envy them their happiness.

And yet, the threat of that curse cast a long shadow over their joy.

"Lady Gavina." William Wallace approached then. "Take care on the road."

The wind tangled his long dark hair, the bright sunlight highlighting the leathery skin on his face.

Wallace was only in his mid-thirties, yet he looked older. He had the features of a man who'd lived—a man who'd known much joy and sorrow.

One evening a few days earlier, the pair of them had shared a cup of wine after supper, and he'd told Gavina of Marion, the woman he'd lost. "I'll never love like that again," he'd said, a faraway look shadowing his dark eyes. And Gavina had believed him.

Unlike Cassian, who'd grieved deeply after losing his love, but had centuries to recover, the Wallace's sorrow was still raw. Marion's death had unleashed something within him, a hatred for the English that couldn't be tempered. Wallace would give his life for the cause in a heartbeat, Gavina knew it.

"I will, William," she said with a half-smile. "And I do so knowing that Dunnottar is in safe hands."

He smiled back, the expression lifting years off him. "Aye, ye need not worry about that." His smile faded as quickly as it had arisen, shrewdness lighting in his eyes. "Be wary of yer brother, My Lady. He will seek to bend ye to his will, I fear."

Gavina tensed. Here was she thinking that the Wallace had merely come down to see her off. But like Donnan, who'd cornered her in the gallery earlier, he was concerned she might say or do something foolish. It seemed that only Father Finlay had faith in her ability to conduct successful negotiations.

"I'm a woman," she said after a pause, "but let me assure ye, William, that doesn't make me a fool. Dunnottar is my home … and I won't let the likes of Shaw Irvine, whether or not he is kin to me, threaten it."

The Wallace's gaze widened at her show of spirit, before a grin split his face. "That's good to hear."

They clattered out of Dunnottar in single file, down the steep path that descended to the bottom of the defile. The party then rode up the rugged slope to the cliff-top opposite. A strong wind caught at Gavina's cloak, snatching at the fine strands of hair that had come loose from her braid. However, she found that she was smiling.

Last time she'd been beyond these walls, the worst had happened. That trip to Stirling was supposed to have been a peaceful mission. But instead, it had transformed into a fight for their lives. She'd imagined to feel nervous upon leaving Dunnottar again, and yet her brief words with the Wallace prior to their departure had really lit a fire in her belly.

She'd show them all that she was a capable laird.

Her father would have called her 'unfeminine' for taking on the role. He'd have chastised her for filling her head with 'men's matters', and encouraged her to hand over rule to the steward.

But once she'd taken the laird's chair in the hall, something inside her had come alive.

David had shielded her from all the important decision-making, and since they'd spent very little time together, and hadn't shared a bed since the first years of their marriage, he'd confided very little in her. As such, she'd often felt frustrated and bored.

Her escape with Cassian and the others from Stirling had been terrifying, and yet at the same time oddly exhilarating. It had proved to Gavina that she wouldn't shatter at the slightest hardship.

She wasn't like her poor mother who'd suffered from 'nerve trouble' her whole life. Greta Irvine had possessed a pale, ethereal beauty, but her sickly constitution and fragile nerves sent her to an early grave at thirty winters.

Dunnottar had never before had a female laird, and Gavina wanted to be remembered for doing the role justice.

They reached the bottom of the path. She urged her palfrey into a brisk canter, taking up her position between Maximus and Draco. Two riders carrying the De Keith banner, which flapped and snapped in the wind, rode up front, while the remainder of the company brought up the rear.

The thunder of hoof-beats shook the ground, and Gavina's smile stretched out into a grin.

This morning, it felt good to be alive.

# V

# ASSUMPTIONS

DRACO CUT A look right, at where Lady Gavina rode next to him. She leaned forward, braced against the wind. There was something different about her this morning. Her cheeks were pink—an unusual sight, for her face was usually so pale, especially against the dull black of her mourning attire. She rode well, sitting easily in the saddle as her mount lengthened its stride.

And to his surprise, she was smiling.

*She actually wants to go on this journey*, he thought incredulously. Perhaps she was looking forward to seeing her brother again? Although from what Draco had heard of Shaw Irvine, the man had the personality of a pit dog.

*Maybe she's just happy to be free of David De Keith?* This thought made Draco pause. He hadn't paid close attention to the laird and his wife over the past couple of months, but even so, the unhappiness of their union had been clear to all. De Keith had been a shit-weasel—a man of weak character who'd made a poor laird.

Surely, his lady wife couldn't do a much worse job of leadership.

Dragging his gaze from Lady Gavina, for he was coming close to staring now, Draco surveyed the lush, green hills that rolled away in every direction. To the north-west, wooded mountains rose up against a deep-blue sky. It was the loveliest morning Draco had seen in a while.

He wanted to be able to smile back at it, the way Lady Gavina was. But the place inside his chest, where his heart thudded against his ribs, was cold and dead.

Digging deep, he realized he felt nothing at all.

*We have to break the curse,* he thought, bleakness flooding through him. *I need an end to this.* With the curse broken, death would eventually find him, and it was likely to be from misadventure rather than old age.

He'd sought oblivion for so long, but the curse was always there to bring him back to the living with the dawn. He was so weary of life. Every morning when his eyes flickered open, heaviness descended. He always shut his eyes once more then, and murmured a prayer to Mithras.

Surely, one day, the Bull-slayer would heed him?

Death would be such sweet relief after a life that had gone on for far too long.

Draco clenched his jaw then. He hated that dark thoughts dogged him wherever he was and whatever he was doing. He wanted to lose himself in the beauty of the sunshine and the lush landscape unfolding around him.

*I'll feel better once war comes to Dunnottar,* he assured himself as the party thundered down a slope and the horses leaped the narrow burn at the bottom. Few men craved war like he did. He couldn't die, but being surrounded by death made despair release its stranglehold. He didn't relish the pain of being injured, but at least that brought a welcome distraction from the mire of his own dark thoughts.

As the noon sun crested the sky, the party stopped to rest their horses and eat some of the bannock and hard cheese they'd brought with them. They'd left the rolling hills and wide skies behind now, and entered a landscape of wooded valleys interspersed by meadows. Their resting place was next to a trickling burn, so that the horses could be watered.

Draco took his food and sat down with it upon a mossy boulder, apart from the others. He ate quickly, taking little pleasure in the meal. And all the while, his gaze surveyed his surroundings, taking note of every detail.

The English had yet to come this far north, but it still paid to be wary. Shaw Irvine might have planned an ambush, and could be waiting for his gullible sister to ride straight into his trap.

Draco's jaw tightened at this last thought, his gaze narrowing when it rested upon the lady herself.

He didn't know why, but his attention was constantly straying to Lady Gavina today.

*It's just because you've been charged to protect her,* he told himself. Nonetheless, it was as if she were the shore and he the tide. Without thinking, his attention shifted to her again now, and as it did so, he found himself scrutinizing her.

As much as he hated to admit it, for the woman chafed him like a boil upon his arse, the Lady of Dunnottar truly was a beauty. She sat upon a rock, back ram-rod straight, daintily picking at some dried fruits she had brought with her. The braid wrapped around the crown of her head was an austere style that drew attention to the slender length of her neck—she had a neck like a swan.

Her cold manner must have been off-putting indeed, for David De Keith had appeared immune to his wife's loveliness. Perhaps she was just as icy in bed, Draco reflected. Not all beautiful women were lusty between the sheets.

"Enjoying the sunshine?" Maximus approached Draco, shattering his reverie. His friend winked then, for he'd caught Draco staring. "Or gazing upon something else?"

Draco pulled a face and shoved the last bit of bannock into his mouth, washing it down with a gulp of wine from the bladder Maximus passed him. He'd sat down upon the boulder next to him, his keen gaze scanning their surroundings as Draco had been doing.

Before Gavina had caught his eye.

"It's quiet out here today," Maximus observed. "We haven't seen any travelers on the road."

Draco shrugged. "I'm not surprised. The threat of war makes folk a bit nervous of venturing out." He cast Maximus a look then and saw he was frowning. "Don't worry, Edward will come north."

Maximus grunted, taking back the bladder of wine and raising it to his lips. "The Broom-star isn't going to remain in the night-sky for much longer," he replied. "We're cutting things close."

Draco heard the tension in his friend's voice. A rare pang of sympathy lanced through him. Draco cared about few people these days, but Maximus Cato and Cassian Gaius were his brothers. The three of them had weathered long years together in this northern land, and although there had been lengthy spells at times between when they'd seen each other, the tether that bound them had never been broken.

Suddenly, he wanted to break the curse—not for himself and the oblivion he sought, but so that Maximus and Cassian might fully enjoy the happiness they'd found.

The realization caused surprise to jolt through Draco then, and he looked away.

*Perhaps, I've a heart after all.*

The warmth of the sun on Gavina's face warned her that they were nearing their destination. It was mid-afternoon, and the sun was dipping toward the western horizon. Despite the nervousness that had stolen upon her as the day progressed, Gavina had enjoyed the journey. It felt good to be away from the encircling stone walls of the fortress. They protected her from the outside world, but sometimes felt like a prison.

Slowing their horses to a brisk trot, the company entered the Strath of Muirskie—a long, wide vale covered in clumps of gorse and broom, interspersed with tightly-packed hazelwood.

"Did your brother say where exactly he'd meet us, My Lady?" Maximus asked, reining his courser in next to Gavina. "This strath is a wide space."

She shook her head, her gaze traveling over the broad vale stretching out before her. Up ahead, two deer broke free of the trees and raced away. "If we ride to a central spot, he's sure to find us."

"When did you last see your brother?" Draco asked, addressing her for the first time since leaving Dunnottar.

Gavina cast him a sharp look. "Not since I wedded David ... why?"

Draco too had reined up his horse close, flanking her left side while Maximus protected her right. Gavina met his gaze squarely, and for a moment, he merely stared back. The pause drew out, and then he answered, "I'm just wondering how well you actually know him."

"He's my brother," Gavina replied, her tone clipped now. "We grew up together ... I know him better than most folk, I'd say."

"And how would you describe his temperament then?" Draco asked, seemingly oblivious of the fact that she found his questioning impertinent.

Gavina's lips pursed. The urge to lie, to say that Shaw had a good heart under a blustering, bombastic exterior, rose within her. However, Draco Vulcan held her with such a direct look that the words wouldn't come. The truth was far less pretty, yet her protectors needed to hear it before they met with the Irvine laird.

"Shaw is a pompous bully," she said finally. "He's proud of his lineage ... and is suspicious of all neighbors ... not just the De Keiths. Wound his pride, and he gets nasty."

"How did he react to your union with David De Keith?" Draco asked.

Gavina drew in a deep breath. Her gaze flicked to where Maximus rode silently beside her. He too was watching her, his brow furrowed. Gavina had confided much in Heather about her past, and she wondered just how much her companion had told her husband.

"He was furious that our father became a peacemaker in his later years," she replied, glancing back at where Draco still had her pinned under a fierce stare. This was the first time the pair of them had exchanged more than a handful of words, and the intensity of his gaze unnerved her. "As a younger man, our father fought all his neighbors, but as he aged, he lost the taste for feuding. When he announced my betrothal to David De Keith, Shaw stormed out of Drum Castle and didn't return for months." Gavina tensed then, remembering the fraught period. Her father had been angered by his son's belligerence, and when he finally returned to the stronghold, relations between them remained frosty. "Shaw spoke little to me afterward ... and didn't attend the wedding," she concluded.

"So, all that said ... you believe the man wants to treat with you?" Draco cocked an eyebrow.

His incredulous tone rankled, and Gavina's jaw tightened. "He may ... the situation with the English worsens with each passing year," she replied, her tone clipped, "and now that David is dead, he may see the De Keiths as less of a threat."

Draco snorted at this, and Gavina scowled, her temper rising. "Ye disagree with me, Vulcan?"

He favored her with a rakish smile. "You want to believe your brother has changed, My Lady. But in my experience, people rarely do."

Gavina glared back at him. The man's arrogance was goading. He didn't know her, and he'd never met her brother. How dare he make such assumptions?

Maximus cleared his throat then, shattering the tension between them. "We'll find out soon enough ... look ahead. Riders approach."

Tearing her gaze from Draco, Gavina focused her attention farther down the strath at where a company of men on horseback thundered toward their party, dust billowing up behind them.

Squaring her shoulders, Gavina ignored Draco Vulcan now. He was wrong. People could change. She had to give her brother the opportunity to join her against the English. Gavina was a far better negotiator than her late husband. Unlike David, she wouldn't stoop to insults and threats. Instead, she would use the wits God had gifted her to resolve the situation. Given a little persuasion, there could be peace once more between the two clans.

# VI

# MEETING IN THE STRATH

SHAW HAD CHANGED physically since Gavina saw him last.

The man who pulled up his courser before her was heavier than she remembered, his thick middle evident under a mail shirt, and a short white-blond beard now covered his pugnacious jaw. Like his father, Shaw had started to go bald early in life—something he'd dealt with by shaving off his hair. Only a silvery fuzz remained.

"Good afternoon, sister," he greeted her with a broad grin. His gaze then swept over the party gathered behind her before his attention finally lingered upon the two men flanking her: Maximus and Draco. "Look at these louts ye have brought with ye," he continued with a snort. "What's wrong ... don't ye trust yer own brother?"

"Of course, I trust ye, Shaw," Gavina lied with an answering smile. "However, ye can hardly expect a lady to ride out to meet ye unescorted, can ye?"

Shaw's smile faded just a little then, his cornflower-blue eyes—the same shade as her own—widening. "Ye still have a sharp tongue, I see," he observed. "I hope ye flayed yer husband regularly with it." He grimaced then. "I imagine being wed to a De Keith was trying for ye."

*Ye have no idea, brother.*

Gavina had gone willingly into the union with David De Keith. She'd been eager to please her father and do her bit for her clan. But she'd been shocked to discover that her new husband disliked her from the first. Initially, she'd tried hard to please David, but when he scorned her for her 'pitiful' efforts, Gavina had emotionally retreated from him.

"I have done my duty," she said after a pause. Her brother's comment was a warning. She needed to soften her tone or things wouldn't go well between them. "As was asked of me."

"And now ye are a widow." Shaw Irvine grinned once more. "Look at ye, dressed like a crow. Don't tell me ye really mourn David De Keith?"

Gavina's mouthed thinned. She and David hadn't loved each other, and yet her brother's derision chafed all the same. A little respect wouldn't go amiss.

Shaw's grin twisted. "All of the Highlands is talking about how De Keith tried to slit Longshanks's throat. The cur had more spine than I thought."

"My husband acted foolishly," Gavina replied, forcing meekness into her voice. "And I barely escaped Stirling with my life as a result. Edward of England now has an axe to grind against the De Keiths ... and I fear he will soon march upon Dunnottar."

Shaw held her gaze, his smile twisting into a sneer. "So that's why ye contacted me ... ye want my help?"

Lady Gavina sighed. "I merely wish for the peace our father made to be reinstated. We must band together against the English. Surely, ye can see that?"

Shaw screwed up his face and spat on the ground beside him. "I have no quarrel with Longshanks ... for the moment."

"Maybe not now ... but soon you will." Draco spoke up then. His voice was low, yet with a rough undertone. "Edward will march north ... you'd better know who your allies are when he does."

A chill silence settled over the warm afternoon at these words.

Gavina cast the warrior a look of censure before shifting her attention back to her brother. The last thing she needed was for Draco Vulcan to wade in with his tactless mouth. Shaw was petulant enough without the Moor ruffling his feathers further.

However, her brother wasn't looking at her. Instead, he was glaring at Draco. "What would ye know about the Scottish cause, cèin?"

*Foreigner.* Shaw spat out the word like a curse, although Draco merely grinned. Likely, he'd been called worse over the years. "More than you do, I'd wager," he replied.

"Shaw," Gavina interceded, panic rising in a hot wave within her. "We must band together. Ye and I are kin. Set aside yer claims, and let us focus on keeping the north free of the English."

The Irvine laird focused on her once more. "I don't want to 'set aside' my claims, Gavina," he growled. "As ye well know, they are rightful ones."

"Are they?" she asked. It was becoming a struggle to keep her voice soft. Frustration beat like a raven's wings within her. She felt like shaking her supercilious brother.

"Aye," he replied, his gaze spearing hers. "And I expect ye to give me back my lands."

"The De Keith cottars have worked that valley and the hills around it for generations now, Shaw," she replied, hoping to appeal to his conscience. "It would be cruel to displace them."

His face screwed up. "What do I care about that? Those lands are *mine*."

"Couldn't we share it?" Gavina held his gaze. "Why can't *both* Irvine and De Keith cottars farm our border ... in peace?"

Her brother growled a curse. "There will be no sharing, sister. Not now. Not ever. Just give my lands back, and let's be done with bandying words."

Gavina shook her head, disappointment washing over her. She'd forgotten how little conscience her brother actually possessed, yet she wouldn't give up. "The boundaries of these lands have shifted like the tides over

the years," she began, her voice low and firm. "The
Irvines have both *ceded* and *gained* lands of late.
Forcibly taking back what's long lost will only end in a
blood feud that will span generations."

Shaw stared back at her, his blue eyes contemptuous.
"What's this? So, my little sister has become a wise
woman now?"

The mocking edge to his voice made Gavina grind her
teeth. David had always heaped scorn upon her when she
voiced an opinion, and quite frankly, she'd grown tired of
being ridiculed whenever she had something to say for
herself.

William Wallace's presence in the keep had made a
refreshing change from her husband's derision. He
treated her with respect. The outlaw was gruff and
intimidating, and yet he quite evidently preferred
women with spine.

Six years away from Shaw had softened her memories
of him. But now unpleasant recollections resurfaced. She
recalled how he'd thrown a cup of wine in her face one
Yuletide when she'd disagreed with him over some
trifling topic, how he'd kicked her beloved puppy across
the hall when it had peed on his boot. The pup had died
of its injuries a day later.

He was kin, but she had never liked him.

"I don't need to be a wise woman to see what's right
before my eyes," she said, her tone cooling.

"So, ye are calling me a fool now?" he asked, his voice
roughening.

Gavina's temper frayed. "No ... although only a half-
wit would squabble over borders while Edward
Longshanks sits in Stirling deciding which of his barons
will rule our strongholds."

Silence fell once more. Shock rippled over Shaw's
bearded face, followed by anger. "Ye need to learn yer
place," he snarled. "I can see I must teach ye some
manners." With that, he urged his courser forward. The
heavy horse lunged toward her. Shaw raised a meaty fist
to strike Gavina across the face.

"Touch her and you die."

Draco Vulcan had moved fast. His own horse shifted forward to block the Irvine laird. Steel scraped against leather as Gavina's protector drew the sword at his side.

Gavina's gaze settled upon the blade. It looked very similar to the one Cassian Gaius had wielded when he'd defended her and the other women from English soldiers during their flight from Stirling. It was a shorter and lighter sword than the heavy claidheamh-mòrs her countrymen wielded, and had a wide, leaf-shaped blade.

"Get out of my way," Shaw snarled. "This is between me and my sister."

Draco didn't move, although now Gavina's heart was pounding painfully against her breastbone. She'd hoped to have an equitable talk with her brother, but she'd let her temper get the better of her.

*Some peace-weaver I've turned out to be.*

Fury burned in Shaw's eyes. He looked like he wanted to take his dirk to her now.

"This isn't the time to be fighting amongst ourselves," Gavina spoke up, attempting to salvage the rapidly deteriorating situation. "Please, Shaw. Cast aside yer rancor toward the De Keiths. We all need to be on the same side."

"The Irvines and the De Keiths will never be allies," he roared, spittle flying. "And ye have betrayed yer own blood by suggesting such." He broke off then, panting hard. A vein in his temple pulsed, and the tendons in his neck corded, such was his fury. "I came here in good faith, believing ye were loyal to my clan ... *our* clan ... but instead, ye have forsaken us."

"Shaw, please. Can't we—"

"Enough, woman!" He hauled on the reins so that his courser backed up. The beast squealed and tossed its head, objecting to being so roughly manhandled. "I'll not listen to more of this horse-shit. Prepare to meet my Battle Hammer." His gaze shifted to Draco then, and he spat on the ground for the second time since the ill-fated meeting had started. "Droch bhàs ort!"

*May ye have an evil death!* The irony of the curse wasn't lost on Gavina. A fine thing to say to an immortal.

"Ith do chac!" Draco shot back, favoring the Irvine laird with a goading, savage grin.

"Why did ye have to say that?" Gavina rounded on Draco the moment Shaw Irvine and his party had thundered into the distance.

The Moor had just told her brother to go eat his own shit. Shaw's face had gone puce at the insult, and he'd even reached for his dirk, his fingers curling around the handle.

"Laird," one of his men had cautioned. "Stay yer hand … they aren't worth the bother."

Breathing hard, Shaw Irvine had heeded him, although that hadn't stopped him spitting another curse at Draco as he whirled his horse around.

Infuriatingly, Vulcan didn't look remotely sorry. "I could have said much worse," he said evenly. "I know some insults in various languages that would make your ass of a brother choke on his own tongue."

"I don't doubt it," Gavina countered, heat rising to her cheeks as anger ignited within her. "But I brought ye along to protect me … not to bait Shaw."

Draco shrugged. "It wasn't going well anyway. I just helped trim the conversation down a bit."

"Draco," Maximus spoke up. His voice held a warning edge. "Careful."

"The conversation was going well enough," Gavina replied between gritted teeth, still glaring at Draco. It was a lie, but she'd not admit such to this man. He wouldn't get the better of her. "Until ye decided to run yer mouth off."

"Your brother was never going to agree to stand with the De Keiths against the English," Draco countered, ignoring Maximus's warning. "I could have told you that … and saved us all the trouble of this pointless journey."

Gavina stared at him, momentarily struck dumb by this man's rudeness. "How dare ye?" she finally choked out the words.

Draco shrugged, dismissing her anger. "You are welcome, by the way," he drawled. "I might be uncouth in your view ... but if it weren't for me, you'd be sporting a black eye right now, *My Lady*."

# VII

## THE WHITE HAWK

"DON'T LOOK SO worried, My Lady ... your brother could be all bluster."

Gavina glanced up from staring at the glowing embers in the fire pit before her, to see Maximus observing her.

"Unfortunately, I know that he's not," she replied softly. "Shaw makes a lot of noise ... but if he decides ye are his enemy, he'll never forget it."

Heaving a sigh, Gavina dropped her gaze once more to the fire. Maximus was only trying to reassure her, but since he hadn't spent much time with Shaw Irvine, he didn't realize just how vindictive and grasping her brother could be.

*What a waste of a trip.* Gavina tightened her fingers around the clay cup of wine she cradled. She hated to admit it, but Vulcan was right. *I was a goose to think I could sway my brother.* Shaw was even more intractable than she remembered.

After leaving the Strath of Muirskie, they'd retraced their steps until the dusk had forced them to stop for the day. They were back inside De Keith lands now, camped on the edge of a birch copse. If they set off at dawn the following day, they'd hopefully reach Dunnottar by mid-morning.

Gavina couldn't wait. Her joy at being out of the fortress, at taking charge of matters, had faded. Tonight she felt on edge, tearful even—although being surrounded by warriors made her swallow down the urge to weep.

She'd not give Draco Vulcan another reason to mock her.

"Maybe Shaw Irvine is the 'Hammer' after all?" Vulcan spoke up then, breaking the weighty silence. Mercifully, he'd held his tongue for the rest of the afternoon. He sat cross-legged now, on the opposite side of the fire, his features cast in shadow. He appeared to be whittling a chunk of wood with a tiny knife.

Gavina had been aware of his presence all evening, although she made a point of ignoring him. It was growing late now, and only the three of them sat by the fire. Her protectors had set a watch around the camp and erected a small tent for her.

"Perhaps 'The Hammer of the Scots' won't strike Dunnottar," Draco continued.

"Excuse me?" Gavina asked, frowning. "What's all this talk of 'hammers'?"

"Cassian's convinced Edward will be the one to strike the castle," Maximus replied, meeting Draco's eye over the flickering flames. "And I agree with him."

"Shaw Irvine might just get to us first though," Draco countered.

"What are ye two blathering on about," Gavina snapped, irritated that she still didn't understand.

Both men looked her way then, before Maximus inclined his head. "I thought Aila told you of the riddle, My Lady?"

Gavina frowned. "Aye ... she did." She paused then, her gaze flicking between the two men. Draco now wore a shuttered expression. He didn't welcome her inclusion in the conversation. Nettled, Gavina continued, "She never actually recited it to me though."

"It speaks of an assault on Dunnottar, My Lady," Maximus replied after a pause.

Gavina tensed. She agreed with Cassian that an English attack was imminent, but the thought of it being somehow 'preordained' made a chill feather down her neck. "Could ye recite the riddle to me?" she asked.

"You don't need to hear it, My Lady," Draco said curtly. "Such things needn't concern you."

Gavina bristled. "Perhaps not, but they still do," she replied, her own tone turning frosty. She recalled Draco's anger back on that hilltop, at dawn after they'd slain the English patrol. He hadn't wanted the women to learn their secret. But it was too late now. Gavina knew who these men were.

"What can it hurt, Draco?" Maximus's brow was furrowed as he met his friend's eye across the fire pit. "She knows the worst of it … Lady Gavina might as well hear the riddle too."

A muscle bunched in Draco's jaw. He respected Maximus, Gavina sensed it. In many ways, Maximus was the unspoken leader of the three men, despite that Cassian captained the Dunnottar Guard.

When Draco didn't voice another protest, Maximus cleared his throat and began to speak. His voice, low yet powerful, drifted across the fire.

> "When the Broom-star crosses the sky,
> And the Hammer strikes the fort
> Upon the Shelving Slope.
> When the White Hawk and the Dragon wed,
> Only then will the curse be broke."

When Maximus finished, Gavina pondered his words. The riddle fascinated her—so much so that she forgot the humiliation and disappointment regarding her brother.

"And so, ye have managed to solve most of it?" she finally asked.

Maximus nodded. He glanced up then, his gaze shifting to the star-sprinkled night sky above them.

"That fiery star comes every seventy-five years, My Lady … and the three of us wait impatiently for its arrival."

Gavina raised her chin, focusing upon the bright silver comet that streaked across the heavens. "The Broom-star," she murmured, before her mouth compressed. Her dead husband had been a suspicious man; ever since the star had appeared in the heavens, he'd muttered on about it being an ill-omen. Indeed, it might have signaled the end for him, yet to these three immortals, it remained a sign of hope.

"The Hammer refers to Edward," Maximus continued, casting Draco a pointed look. "And the fort upon the Shelving Slope refers to Dunnottar's old name."

Gavina nodded. *Dùn Fhoithear*. She remembered Donnan De Keith telling her about it once.

"And now we finally have our 'Dragon'." Maximus's mouth quirked as he gestured to Draco. "We have only to find a 'White Hawk' for him to wed, and, as the riddle says, 'the curse will be broke'."

Silence settled over the fire. Draco's shuttered expression had turned brooding. He whittled the piece of wood in sharp movements, tension rippling off his lean frame.

"The White Hawk and the Dragon," Gavina murmured, letting the words sink in. A chill slithered through her belly then, making the wine she'd been sipping churn. "And ye have no idea who the 'White Hawk' is?" Her voice sounded forced and a trifle shrill, as dread now wrapped icy fingers around her throat.

Both Maximus and Draco looked her way once more, their gazes narrowed.

"Not yet," Maximus admitted, his frown deepening. "Is something amiss, My Lady? Your face has drained of color."

Hysteria bubbled up inside Gavina, but she managed to swallow it down. "It's a shock … that's all," she choked out.

"What is?" Draco demanded, his voice sharp.

Heart fluttering against her ribs, Gavina turned her attention to him. She held his gaze steadily as she replied, "It's just that my name ... Gavina ... means 'White Hawk'."

# VIII

## GRASPING AT SHADOWS

SOME SILENCES WERE truly awkward—and this was one of them.

For a few moments, Draco and Maximus merely stared at Gavina. Both men wore poleaxed expressions, their lips parting as the weight of what she'd just revealed settled upon them.

Eventually, Maximus shattered the brittle hush. "Gavina means 'White Hawk'?"

Gavina swallowed once more, in an effort to ease the choking tightness in her throat. "Aye ... I remember my mother telling me once."

Her words fell heavily, reverberating afterward like iron upon stone.

The crackling of the fire filled the void, and somewhere in the surrounding trees, a lonely owl hooted.

And then Draco muttered something in a tongue Gavina didn't understand.

"It's merely a coincidence," she spoke up. The men's reaction to her comment unnerved her.

Maximus's dark eyes had gone wide, and they now gleamed with excitement, whereas Draco had stopped whittling his piece of wood and stared at her as if she'd just sprouted horns and a forked tail.

Gavina heartily regretted being so candid. *Why did ye tell them what yer name means?* she berated herself inwardly. Some comments were better left unvoiced.

"I don't think it is," Maximus replied. "Nothing that's happened in the past few months has been." His voice had tightened. "Everything is falling into place ... as it is meant to."

"You think this is fate deciding for us?" Draco asked, not bothering to hide his disbelief. Unlike his friend, he hadn't welcomed this news. "After all these centuries of struggle, you believe the stars have aligned in our favor?"

Maximus's mouth quirked. "They had to ... eventually. You and Lady Gavina are destined to wed."

Draco stared back at him, the expression upon his sharp-featured face a blend of disbelief and horror.

Another chill swept through Gavina. This time the sensation made her hands and feet prickle. Like his friends, Draco Vulcan wanted the curse broken—but the thought of being wed to her made him lose sight of that fact.

*Wed to me?*

Gavina's breathing quickened, blood now roaring in her ears. "I think ye are mistaken, Maximus," she heard herself say, although her voice sounded as if it were echoing down a long tunnel, almost as if it didn't belong to her. "I'm a widow in mourning ... and am expected to remain chaste for at least a year. I cannot wed anyone."

She glanced down at the drab woolen kirtle she wore—dyed a dull-charcoal. It served as a reminder to them all. A widow didn't remarry barely a month after her husband's death.

Maximus stiffened, a shadow crossing his handsome face. "We don't have a year, My Lady." He gestured to the sky. "The Broom-star will fade from sight in less than a month. After that, the opportunity will be lost forever."

Gavina's fingers clasped around the cup. She could see the panic in the man's eyes. He loved Heather and wanted to grow old with her. Although she sympathized with his predicament, anger spiked through Gavina's belly.

He was desperate. But he'd lost sight of the fact that the decision also impacted her life. He was wedded to someone he loved, but he'd literally throw Gavina to the wolves in order to break the curse.

She shifted her attention to where Draco's face suddenly looked hewn of granite.

Gavina's belly twisted. He might have looked horrified at the thought of binding himself to her—but she felt the same way.

*Draco Vulcan is the last man I'd choose as a husband.*

Setting aside the cup, she rose to her feet. "I'm tired," she announced. "I shall retire now."

Maximus's spine straightened. "Please, My Lady ... don't dismiss this."

"I'm not." A sharp note crept into her voice. "I just don't want to talk about it any longer."

"You have just given us all the answer we've been searching over a millennium for," Maximus countered. His handsome face had gone taut, his eyes dark in the firelight. "There's no good pretending you haven't."

"Aye, but maybe I shouldn't have said anything. This is folly ... all of it!"

His gaze narrowed. "Perhaps to you it is, My Lady." His voice was sharp now. "But not to those of us who've had to live with the curse."

"I'm not marrying yer friend." Her voice was hoarse with the effort it was taking not to shout. "I'm sorry for yer pain." And she was, although it was difficult to feel anything but anger right now. "But I've just escaped one loveless marriage, and I don't want another."

A strained silence fell then. An infuriated expression settled over Maximus's face, yet he said no more. Perhaps he realized he'd overstepped, and that to say anything more right now would just worsen the situation. Draco held his tongue as well, although he watched Gavina, firelight playing over the lean angles of his face.

Heart pounding, Gavina turned and walked stiffly across to the tent they'd erected for her earlier. Without looking back at her two protectors, she knelt down and crawled inside.

Draco returned to the piece of rose-wood he was whittling. He needed to distract himself, to think of other things besides the brief yet explosive conversation that had just transpired.

He studied the wood carefully, a crease forming between his eyebrows. He'd started carving it without knowing exactly what he was going to make. Often his carvings began this way. Usually, the piece of wood or stone whispered to him, told him what it wanted to be.

This one was starting to take the form of a woman—a siren maybe.

Draco's mouth twisted. *Ironic really.* Sirens were famous for luring their victims onto the rocks, but Draco's life was already foundering, he didn't need a mermaid to lead him astray.

"I don't know why you're smirking," Maximus muttered from the other side of the fire. "If Lady Gavina doesn't agree to wed you, we're all doomed to remain immortal."

Draco's chin jerked up, and he met Maximus's angry gaze. "You sound so sure of yourself, Max," he growled. "But you don't know *she's* the 'White Hawk' the riddle speaks of ... any more than Cass knows I'm the 'Dragon'. The pair of you have gotten so frantic of late you're now grasping at shadows."

A nerve flickered under Maximus's eye—a sign that those words had hit him where it hurt.

Remorse flared within Draco, an ache rising just under his breastbone. He didn't like to lash out at Maximus or Cassian. The pair of them were the only souls alive who understood him, who really cared about what happened to him. And yet, ever since his friends had found love and wed the women who'd brought them happiness, he'd felt oddly estranged from them.

Neither Maximus nor Cassian knew of those lost years he'd spent under Saint Margaret's chapel in Edinburgh. He'd planned on telling them, yet when they'd finally met up again, he found himself making up some other story about why they hadn't seen him in so long.

He'd felt lonely afterward. Lying to his two best friends had felt like a betrayal at the time. But oddly, now he felt as if he was the one betrayed.

Maximus and Cassian had found something to live for, and yet all he wanted was death. They wanted 'normal' lives—to be able to remain in one place without eventually becoming outcasts. They wanted to father children, and to age just like everyone else.

Draco just wanted an end to it all.

"This is it," Maximus replied finally, a rasp to his voice. "I can feel it in my gut. You and Gavina *must* wed, or the curse won't be broken."

Draco's fingers tightened around the bone hilt of his whittling knife. He'd spent the last millennium avoiding marriage. However, over the years there had been one or two women—one especially—who he'd cared for enough to consider it, if he'd been mortal. Magda had been dead nearly two centuries now, a spirited woman who'd died tragically young. He sometimes thought of her. But he'd never willingly choose a woman like Gavina De Keith.

*As beautiful as a winter's dawn, and just as cold.*

He'd witnessed the horror that darkened her large blue eyes when she'd told them what her name meant. She'd regretted her admission the moment the words left her lips—especially when she'd realized what it meant.

"You can't compel her to wed," Draco reminded him, his own tone cooling now. Maximus's urgency, his need to break the curse, burned so brightly, it risked consuming him. "Just as you can't force me."

Maximus stared back at him, his jaw tightening. "I know you've always been an arse, Draco … but I never remember you being *this* selfish."

Draco shrugged, the insults washing off him.

"Don't you want to break the curse?" Maximus pressed, leaning forward.

"Yes, as much as you do."

"Really ... well you're not acting like it."

Draco snorted, his own anger rising. "I knew this would happen. Once you and Cassian got yourselves entangled with women, you lost your perspective. We all know how dangerous it is to hope. How many times have we looked forward to the coming of the Broom-star, only to be disappointed? Again and again."

"I didn't lose my perspective ... I gained it," Maximus countered, a muscle flexing in his jaw. "And if it meant that I didn't end up like you, I'm relieved I did."

# IX

## CHASING ANSWERS

THE ENGLISH WERE leaving Stirling.

John Comyn, Baron of Badenoch, stood atop the castle walls and watched them go.

From this distance, Edward's force looked a great, slithering beast, its chainmail skin glittering in the morning sun, its back bristling with pikes and standards. The clear call of silver trumpets echoed over the wide strath below the castle, drifting across the waters of the Firth and reverberating off the rocky crag and fortress perched high above.

Comyn 'The Red' observed the departing army with a cool gaze. Edward had reacted swiftly following his meeting with Galbraith. As reinforcements had arrived the previous day from Northumbria, he immediately set about preparing to march upon Dunnottar. The king had also sent word of his movements to his son in the south.

The baron stood upon the walls a long while, enjoying the warm sun on his face. Eventually, his attention shifted to the keep itself, his gaze swiveling to the guard of six English soldiers behind him. The guards stared back at him, their helmed faces impossible to read, and their hauberks glittering in the sun. They were his own personal escort that Edward had left behind to 'watch over' Stirling's guardian while he was gone.

The English king had also left a sizeable garrison behind to keep the town and castle in English hands. Edward might have been focused on capturing William Wallace at present, but he was as sharp as ever. Despite that Comyn had minded his manners since the English had taken Stirling, Longshanks still didn't trust him.

Clenching his bearded jaw, Comyn glanced back at the view as the last of the horns faded and the army's rearguard stomped their way east.

*He's right not to.*

Comyn had a job to do—but it wouldn't be easy with this lot watching him.

Nonetheless, 'The Red' wouldn't be thwarted.

The baron threw back the plum-colored cloak he wore about his shoulders and climbed down from the walls. Ignoring his escort, he then strode back across the inner-bailey courtyard toward the keep itself. Pebbles crunched underfoot, and his attention flicked across to the rose-entwined archway leading through into the gardens.

It was barely a moon ago that David De Keith had attempted to cut the English king's throat in there.

*If only the fool had managed.*

Chaos would have ensued, but the Scots could have made good use of it. Scotland would have been liberated by now.

Comyn made his way up to the solar where he and Edward usually broke their fast together in the mornings—and where the pair of them often shared a cup or two of wine in the evenings.

Before Longshanks's arrival, this had been John Comyn's space, but now the Plantagenet banner—a field of golden lions on a crimson field—hung upon the pitted stone wall.

Comyn's mouth thinned. How he'd enjoy ripping that banner down and burning it. Instead of golden lions, he longed to see a pennant hanging there with just one golden dragon, holding a dagger in its claw. Underneath it would be the Comyn motto: *courage.*

Courage indeed. He'd bided his time long enough. The English had made him their toady for too long. He could stomach it no longer. Now was the time to act.

A platter of food awaited him, as he'd expected. The noon meal was approaching, and as Edward wasn't residing in the castle at present, the baron would take all his meals here rather than in the Great Hall.

Seating himself at the long, rectangular table, while three of the guards took up their places inside the solar and the remaining three in the hallway beyond, Comyn lifted the wicker cloche to discover a large bowl of still-steaming venison stew, accompanied by oaten bannocks and a large wedge of cheese.

Satisfied, Comyn began to eat in hearty mouthfuls. He was a big man who enjoyed his meals, and as such, the castle cooks did their best to oblige him.

He had just finished the last of the meal, and was sipping from a pewter goblet of bramble wine, when a comely form appeared in the doorway.

Comyn smiled at the sight of Fyfa Comyn. Wed to his cousin Hume—steward of this castle—Fyfa was a sight indeed. Sometimes the baron wondered how the staid Hume managed to handle his spirited, doe-eyed wife. Comyn thought then of *his* wife, waiting for him in Badenoch. Joan was horse-faced and blade-tongued. How had Hume—who was a dour individual—managed to capture Fyfa's heart?

Tossing her wild dark-auburn hair over one shoulder, Fyfa shot the guard nearest a saucy look and flirtatious smile. "Bonjour!"

"Bonjour, Madame Comyn," the guard replied, his gaze devouring her.

Fyfa—with her lovely pale Scottish skin, wild hair, and soft curves—was indeed an arresting sight today, especially in a low-cut lèine and kirtle. The latter was a deep blue that matched her eyes.

And as Comyn had hoped, the guards all gawked at her.

It was the moment he'd been waiting for.

The baron slid a scroll from the sleeve of his surcoat and deftly shoved it under the empty earthen bowl on the platter before him.

Fyfa swept across the solar toward Comyn, bringing with her the scent of honey-suckle. The guards' gazes tracked her hungrily. They'd been hired to keep watch on the former Guardian of the Realm at all times—but like most men, a beautiful woman drew their eye.

"Good day, John," Fyfa greeted him with a knowing smile. "Did ye enjoy yer nooning meal?"

"It was hearty fare indeed," he rumbled. "Please thank the cooks."

Fyfa's blue eyes glinted. "I shall." She picked up the tray, before tossing a sultry look at the guard behind her who was openly gawking at her shapely rear. "I do like a man with an appetite," she murmured.

Then, with a wink to Comyn, who was now biting his cheek to stop himself from grinning, she sailed out of the solar.

Three pairs of hungry eyes tracked her.

Comyn sat back in his chair and patted his satiated belly.

*Please thank the cooks.*

Their brief exchange was the only clue Fyfa needed that a missive sat under the bowl he'd just passed her. Actually, there were two messages wrapped up in that scroll.

The first was to his brother, who was looking after things for him at Badenoch. In the message, he gave Blair Galbraith's name and implored Gordon to send men to Fintry to 'deal with him'. The man was a traitor to Scotland. But the body of the missive instructed his brother to gather the full force of his warriors and march on Stirling.

And the second note was to be couriered by a fast horse to Lochmaben Castle in Annandale, where Robert Bruce currently resided. Comyn had a strained relationship with Bruce. Like Longshanks, he suspected his family of coveting the Scottish throne. However, in times like this, Scottish blood was all that mattered. This

was their chance to unite against the English, and
Comyn wouldn't squander it.

Both his brother and Robert Bruce, he now rallied to
his side. Although a sizable English garrison still held
Stirling, Longshanks's attention, and a large bulk of his
force, was focused elsewhere.

'The Red' raised his pewter goblet to his lips and took
a deep draft, in an effort to mask the smile that now
curved his lips.

It was time to take back Stirling for the Scots.

Gavina emerged from her tent with the first rays of the
glimmering dawn. She'd slept fully-dressed, and
although a few wisps of hair had escaped her tightly
wound braid, it was neat enough to leave for now. They'd
reach Dunnottar by mid-morning anyway. She could
bathe and change clothes then.

Rising to her full height, Gavina arched her aching
back; despite the thick fur she'd slept upon, the ground
had been hard and lumpy. It felt good to stretch the
kinks out of her spine now. Yawning, she swept her gaze
over the clearing where they'd made camp overnight.

The others were all readying to leave. A few yards
away, Maximus and two other men were saddling the
horses while Draco kicked dirt over the fire pit. Seeing
Gavina had ventured out from her tent, Draco stilled, his
gaze pinning her to the spot.

"Mac ... Finian." He motioned to two of the escort.
"Our Lady has arisen ... you can pack up her tent."

Gavina's lips thinned. From his tone of voice, you'd
think she'd lain abed for hours, wasting the day while
others toiled.

When he'd spoken to the warriors, Draco's gaze
hadn't shifted from Gavina's face. He was watching her
with a direct look that unnerved her—a stare that flayed

the flesh from her bones. In the morning light, his dark
eyes looked pitch-black.

Gavina tensed her jaw. There was no denying it; this
man put her on edge.

And last night's discussion hadn't helped things.

*When the White Hawk and the Dragon wed …*

Gavina heaved in a deep breath. It was ridiculous—a
fantastical notion that she needed to dismiss.

And yet, she knew the curse wasn't a lie.

She'd seen Cassian Gaius stab himself in the heart
and then heal with the rising sun. The man who stared at
her across the fire pit was the same.

Unnatural, immortal.

Nonetheless, the urgency she'd seen written over
Maximus's face the night before had pained her. She
knew what was at stake for him, Cassian, and Draco. But
he asked too much. His aggression had made her
withdraw and put up walls. She wouldn't be bullied into
this.

Tearing her gaze from Draco's, and breaking the spell
he had cast over her, Gavina picked up her skirts and
strode over to where Maximus had just finished saddling
her palfrey.

"Morning, My Lady," Maximus greeted her coolly.
Gavina noted that he avoided her eye. "Your gelding is
ready." He stepped back then, dipped his head, and
moved on to saddle his own mount.

Gavina watched him go, pressure mounting in her
chest.

She'd expected things to be awkward in the aftermath
of that discussion. Nonetheless, she hadn't expected
Maximus to be unable to even look at her.

"My Lady … some bannock and cheese to break yer
fast?" One of the escort approached her.

Gavina favored the man with a brittle smile. "Aye …
thank ye." She took the food from him and began to eat.
Around her, the rest of the party appeared almost ready
to depart. Mac and Finian had dismantled her tent
swiftly, and were now rolling up the hide and fur. She'd
been the only one to sleep in a tent; the rest of them had

taken turns keeping watch before stretching out in front of the fire. It made packing up easy.

The bannock was stale, yet she was hungry this morning. Traveling always gave her a hearty appetite. However, the dry griddle scone caught in her throat when she spied Draco Vulcan striding toward her.

He'd gone off to saddle his horse, but now reappeared.

Gavina coughed in an attempt to dislodge the bannock crumbs, before reaching for the bladder of ale tied to the back of her palfrey's saddle. She unstoppered it and took a gulp, blinking rapidly as her eyes watered.

And when she glanced up, Draco was standing right before her.

Like earlier, his gaze was searing. This close, Gavina was struck by just how handsome he was: the man had near perfect coppery skin, and his features, although sharp, were beautifully sculpted. His mouth mesmerized her. The man was usually sneering or scowling, but his lips were sensual. This close, he smelled of leather and wood smoke.

A groove creased between his finely arched brows as he watched her. "My Lady ... are you well?"

Gavina nodded, taking another gulp of ale. "Aye ... just a crumb went down the wrong way." She met his eye once more. There was a challenge in his gaze; he was daring her to look away, to take a step back from him. But she wouldn't give him the satisfaction. "Did ye want something?"

Draco inclined his head. "About last night ..."

Gavina tensed. She'd hoped he'd let the matter be—as Maximus had. She wanted to tell him she'd prefer not to speak of it, but her tongue wouldn't comply. She merely waited for him to say his piece.

After a long moment, Draco's beautiful mouth quirked. "It's not easy ... being immortal, My Lady."

Gavina cleared her throat. "I don't suppose it is."

"We were cursed in the year one hundred and eighteen of Our Lord," he replied. "I was twenty-seven winters old at the time." Draco shrugged then. "We've been chasing the answers to that riddle for well over a thousand years. Maximus finds it a strain at times … it's really taken its toll on him—on all of us, to be honest."

Gavina wet her lips. She didn't know what she'd expected him to say, but it wasn't this. The only exchanges they'd had until now had been cutting. Yet he was trying to explain things to her. "Surely, this … riddle has nothing to do with me?" she asked finally, her voice barely above a whisper.

His mouth twisted. "Maximus is convinced it does … just as he believes I am the 'Dragon' the riddle speaks of." His obsidian gaze shuttered then. "Sometimes desperation makes men believe anything if it'll set them free."

"So … ye don't think it's true?"

He gave a soft, humorless laugh. "No … it seems most unlikely. I'd put it out of your mind, My Lady. Forget last night's words were ever spoken."

With that, he stepped back from her, turned on his heel, and stalked away.

# X

# LOOKING IN THE WRONG PLACE

RELIEF SWAMPED GAVINA when the high walls of Dunnottar appeared on the south-eastern horizon.

*Home ... at last.*

It was ironic really. For the longest time, the stronghold hadn't felt like home. She'd missed Drum Castle terribly at first. She'd always been a little lonely at the Irvine stronghold, especially since her mother's death—for her brother was unpleasant and her father largely ignored her—but it was the only home she'd ever known.

At Dunnottar, she'd been an outsider. *An Irvine*. It had taken a while for folk to accept her. But with each passing year, they had embraced her a little more—and then when Robert De Keith was captured by the English a year earlier and David took his place as laird, Gavina became 'Lady of Dunnottar'.

These days, she felt more a De Keith than an Irvine. And the disastrous meeting with her brother had only widened the gulf.

Riding between Maximus and Draco, Gavina was careful not to glance at either man.

It had been an awkward morning. Shortly after Draco's brief exchange with her, they'd mounted their horses and headed south-east, back toward Dunnottar. Barely a word had been shared since.

A strong wind had gusted in from the sea as they made their way home, chapping Gavina's cheeks and making her eyes water. However, she'd welcomed its sting.

The wind, and the cracking pace her escort set, had distracted Gavina from her thoughts.

*When the White Hawk and the Dragon wed ...*

Once again, the riddle whispered to her. Draco had told her to forget it, but she couldn't. That line had repeated itself, again and again, throughout the morning. It was ludicrous. The 'White Hawk' could refer to any number of things, surely? And yet, Maximus had gazed upon her as if she were the answer to all life's problems.

Gavina's throat constricted. To him, she was.

She could still feel his frustration and anger; it was a cold wall between them.

Draco might have advised her to cast the entire incident aside, yet this situation wouldn't be ignored.

Her belly felt tied in knots, and she dreaded seeing Aila and Heather again. Would they react the same way as Maximus?

*They'll think me heartless and self-centered for not agreeing to wed Draco.*

If the curse wasn't broken, both women were doomed never to have bairns with the men they loved. Maximus and Cassian wouldn't age, and so, with the passing of the years, they'd all be forced to leave De Keith lands. It wouldn't matter for the next decade, at most. But then people would notice.

Heather and Aila would have to become outcasts if they wished to remain wed to their husbands.

Gavina's pulse quickened. She didn't want to be responsible for that.

*Ye aren't,* she reassured herself. *This is all nonsense. It has to be.*

Gavina stepped back from the loom, her gaze traveling over the tapestry she was close to finishing. It had taken her a long while—especially since she didn't have much time to dedicate to such tasks these days—but the scene of Dunnottar Castle overlooking the sea had finally taken shape.

"Ye have done a fine job," Elizabeth spoke up from across the chamber. She sat near the fire, winding wool upon a spindle, while her son, Robbie, played with his prized collection of wooden horses upon the deerskin rug at her feet. "I've never seen such detail in a tapestry before."

Gavina huffed, running a critical eye down her work. "My mother taught me everything I know," she murmured. "She was the best weaver in the Irvine clan."

"Then she taught ye well."

Gavina turned from her tapestry, her gaze settling upon her sister-by-marriage. They made a somberly dressed pair these days—both in mourning black. However, while Gavina's husband was deceased, Elizabeth's husband, Robert, was likely still alive.

Elizabeth didn't look right in black. She had a vibrant, earthy beauty and a lush figure that Gavina had always envied. Her dark-gold hair was usually swept back in a long braid, and she had sharp, midnight-blue eyes that missed little.

Gavina's attention strayed then to where Robbie was lining up his horses side-by-side. Her chest constricted. Robbie was such a sweet-faced lad. She'd so hoped to have a bairn of her own. Although she and David hadn't lain together in a long while, David had made frequent visits to her bed in the first years of their marriage. However, her womb had never quickened.

David had eventually told her that she was likely barren. After all, everyone knew about the bastards he'd sired in Stonehaven.

Humiliation closed Gavina's throat. The Lord forgive her, but part of her was relieved that man was dead.

Gavina realized then that Elizabeth was watching her with an expression she'd come to know well over the past six years.

Her sister-by-marriage knew something was amiss.

"Ye've been back nearly two days, Gavina," she said after a pause, "and ye've barely said a word to me. Does something ail ye?"

Gavina shook her head. She'd been busy since her return. With threats to Dunnottar coming from two directions now, she met with Cassian, the Wallace, and Donnan daily to discuss Dunnottar's defenses. Work on the ditch outside the landward walls had been completed—and they'd just received a wagon of rocks from Stonehaven to use in catapults.

Keeping busy was best.

Her thoughts turned then to Maximus and Cassian's wives. Heather had wanted to visit her this afternoon, but Gavina had made an excuse. Aila still attended her morning and evening, yet neither spoke of the disastrous peace mission she'd just returned from. Was it her imagination, or did Gavina sense a reserve between them now?

*She knows I am likely their only hope.*

Guilt squeezed Gavina's chest then. Of course Aila knew—and she wouldn't be surprised if her maid resented her for refusing to aid them.

"Surely, yer brother's reaction can't come as too much of a shock?" Elizabeth pressed. "Especially after that missive he sent David in late spring."

"It doesn't really," Gavina admitted. Her gaze went then to the open window, where the rumble of men's voices on the walls drifted in. Dunnottar was so crowded these days—more men had arrived this morning, stout-hearted farmers who'd come to help defend De Keith lands.

A sigh gusted out of her; she was tired of keeping her worries to herself. She trusted Elizabeth, and like her, the woman knew Maximus, Cassian, and Draco's secret—for she too had seen Cassian heal from that mortal wound. It was time to confide in her.

"It's not Shaw," she admitted finally. "Although our estrangement saddens me ... it was inevitable in a way." She paused then, turning back to her sister-by-marriage. "Do ye remember Aila talking of a riddle ... one that would free Maximus, Cassian, and Draco from the curse that binds them?"

Elizabeth's smooth brow furrowed, her shoulders tensing. She didn't like mention of the immortality of those three men. Unsurprisingly, it put her on edge. "Aye," she replied cautiously, "although I don't know the details of it."

"Neither did I ... until yesterday. Maximus recited it to me, and I really wish he hadn't. I learned something rather disconcerting."

Elizabeth's frown deepened. "Like what?"

"Like I'm supposed to wed Draco Vulcan, if the curse is to be broken."

Elizabeth's dark-blonde eyebrows shot up. "What?"

Gavina gave a tight smile. "That was my reaction too. The riddle refers to the White Hawk and the Dragon. It's the final piece in the puzzle." She paused there, her fingers tightening around the tapestry beater she was holding. "That's what our names mean ... Gavina and Draco ... the 'White Hawk' and the 'Dragon'."

Elizabeth didn't reply for a few moments. Gavina's admission had clearly stunned her. On the deerskin before her, Robbie gave a squeal of delight as he chased one of his wooden horses across the floor. "It sounds ..." Elizabeth said after a pause, before breaking off as she struggled to find the right words to continue.

"Preposterous ... ridiculous?"

"Aye," Elizabeth agreed, her frown returning. "Surely, ye haven't agreed to it?"

"Of course I haven't."

"Ye are a new widow ... in mourning."

Gavina swallowed the laugh that clawed its way up from her chest. That wasn't the half of it.

"And ye are the laird. Yer responsibilities are to this clan ... not to three men ye barely know," Elizabeth pressed on, her voice hardening.

Gavina nodded. Elizabeth didn't need to convince her. "Worry not, Liz. I told them it was impossible." She broke off there, just as a knock sounded on the door to her solar. Tearing her attention from her sister-by-marriage, Gavina turned. "Aye ... who is it?"

"Captain Gaius, My Lady," Cassian's low voice rumbled through the oaken door. "May I have a word?"

Gavina tensed, her pulse quickening. Although she'd seen Cassian a few times since her return, it had always been in the Wallace and Donnan's company. They hadn't been able to speak openly. She'd been wondering when he'd seek her out. The dogged captain of the Dunnottar Guard likely had some choice words for her.

"Aye," she replied, swallowing hard. "Come in."

The door opened, and a tall, heavily-muscled man entered, a cloak of turquoise, blue, and green cross-hatchings—the De Keith plaid—hanging from his broad shoulders. Like Draco and Maximus, Cassian wore his hair cropped short. His hazel eyes, usually warm and frank, were guarded this afternoon.

Immediately, Cassian's gaze swiveled to Elizabeth, before his attention snapped back to Gavina. "I'd hoped to talk to you alone, My Lady ... if possible?"

"Lady Elizabeth can stay, Captain," Gavina replied with a sigh. "She knows everything, so nothing ye are about to say will shock her."

In response, Cassian's expression tightened, while Elizabeth pursed her lips.

Silence filled the women's solar for a few moments, before Cassian eventually broke it. "I know all of this has come as a shock to you, My Lady."

"Aye, it has." Gavina crossed to the fireplace and sank down into a high-backed chair beside the hearth.

"Surely though ... now that you've had time to consider things, you have—"

"I believe this 'White Hawk' and 'Dragon' thing to be a coincidence," Gavina cut him off. "Ye are looking in the wrong place for yer answers, Captain. Draco doesn't even believe it."

Cassian's strong jaw tensed. "Sorry, My Lady ... but I don't think we are. For years, I have tirelessly searched books and clan histories, believing that the clues to solving the last lines of the riddle would be complex and hidden deep. As for Draco, well, I'm afraid he hasn't been himself for some time, and this has come as a shock to him too."

"A shock to *him*? Ye do realize what ye are asking of Lady Gavina?" Elizabeth spoke up now. "She can't wed one of the Wallace's men ... even if the church allowed a widow to remarry so soon, she'd bring scandal upon herself and the De Keiths."

Cassian stared back at Elizabeth, his rugged face going taut. "Do you think I don't know all of this?" he replied, a rasp to his voice. "Do you think I'd ask, if there was any other way." His attention shifted back to Gavina then. "Believe me, My Lady, I understand what it is we are requesting of you."

She held his gaze. "Yet ye ask me, all the same."

"I have no choice. If your and Draco's union is the last part of the riddle, I *have* to ask you."

"Ye understand that Gavina would have to step down as laird if she was to wed Draco Vulcan?" Elizabeth cut in, her cheeks flushed now.

Cassian swung around to her, his hazel eyes narrowing. "A breach that *you* are more than capable of filling, My Lady."

Elizabeth sucked in a shocked breath at his presumption, while Gavina stared at him, her lips parting in surprise. She'd never seen Cassian like this before. Urgency rippled off his big frame, and his hands clenched at his sides. He was holding himself on a short leash.

Gavina's chest started to ache. How could he put her in this situation? She understood why Elizabeth was angry with him. He had overstepped in coming here and making such demands. However, dire need had made him act that way, and so she bit back the sharp retort that rose within her.

"Look, Cassian," she began, searching for a way to explain her position without upsetting him further. "I'm sorry, but—"

The boom of a horn cut her off. The blast was so loud that it caused the stone walls of the keep to shudder.

Whatever Gavina was about to say was lost then. Lurching to her feet, she put one hand to her galloping heart. She'd heard that horn once before, just after coming to live at Dunnottar—when the English had laid siege to the fortress.

Across the solar, Cassian had gone still, although his gaze now gleamed. "It seems our scouts have brought word from the south," he said when the horn's wail died away. "Edward approaches."

# XI

## THE HAMMER STRIKES

"THE HOUNDS OF Hell bite my arse," William Wallace muttered. "It looks as if Longshanks has brought the entire English army with him."

Draco scowled. He wished he could contradict his leader, but from their vantage point atop the walls of the guard tower, it certainly appeared as if a vast force marched toward them.

"The Lady of Dunnottar is making her way up the stairs, Wallace," one of their men called. "She wishes to see the army for herself."

Draco clenched his jaw. After arriving back at Dunnottar, he'd deliberately stayed away from Lady Gavina's meetings with Cassian and the others. It had been a relief not to see her for a couple of days. Their last few interactions had been awkward, especially in light of recent discoveries, and he'd been on edge ever since. But now, with the English army approaching, his reprieve would come to an end. He'd need to face the woman once more.

The Wallace stepped back from the walls, and the two men turned to see a small figure, clad in black, emerge from the stairwell. Although it was now high summer, there was a brisk sea breeze up here this afternoon. As such, Lady Gavina had wrapped a charcoal-colored woolen shawl about her slender shoulders. Despite the wave of noise echoing through the late afternoon air from the south, her heart-shaped face was composed, her blue eyes steely.

Watching her, Draco was surprised at her composure and the determination that rippled off her small frame. Whatever problem he had with this woman, he couldn't accuse her of being a coward.

*What exactly is your problem with her?* A voice whispered to him then. *Why does the sight of the lady make your hackles rise?*

A fine question indeed. When he'd first arrived at Dunnottar and caught a glimpse or two of De Keith's lady wife, he'd noted her beauty. However, on the brief occasions they'd actually interacted over the past months, it was her haughtiness that had vexed him, the way she looked at him as if he were a piece of hedgeborn scum.

Draco might have been a foreigner in this cold northern land—a foreigner who now followed an outlaw—but he'd been born to a wealthy Moorish family in Valentia, a town upon Spain's southern coast. Few women of this land bestowed him with such a jaundiced look as Lady Gavina De Keith, and her attitude nettled him.

And the fact that it got on his nerves at all angered him further.

What did he care for this woman's opinion?

Lady Gavina approached the walls, her blue eyes growing wide when she saw the rippling carpet of shields, standards, and pikes that approached from the south.

"The Lord save us all," she breathed. "It looks as if he intends to tear down Dunnottar, stone by stone."

William Wallace snorted at this.

Lady Gavina's attention swiveled to the outlaw. "I'm sorry, William," she said, her voice soft yet steady. "This is the worst place to be right now."

Wallace flashed her a wolfish grin. "My nemesis approaches," he replied. "The man who'd bring the lairds of Scotland to heel. There's no place I'd rather be at present."

Gavina shook her head, clearly bemused by the Wallace's eagerness to clash with Longshanks. Her attention then shifted to Draco—and for a heartbeat, their gazes fused.

"So, the Hammer strikes?" Her voice was barely above a whisper, yet he heard her all the same.

Draco cocked an eyebrow. "And the fort upon the Shelving Slope is ready for him."

The moment drew out, and Draco was aware that the Wallace was now giving both him and Gavina a bemused look, wondering at what passed between them.

For the moment, the pair ignored him.

Excitement flickered to life in the pit of Draco's belly. The riddle was playing out, as Cassian had insisted it would. But then the excitement doused, a chill following in its wake.

If he was right about the Hammer of the Scots—was he right about everything else as well?

Gavina stared down at the swelling tide of men and horses that surged over the hills and gathered upon the cliff-top west of the stronghold. Her belly churned at the sight. Reaching out, she gripped the edge of the battlements, her fingers biting into rough stone.

That was better. The sturdy stone anchored her.

"My Lady?" Draco Vulcan was at her side, his hand grasping her arm as he steadied her.

"I'm well," she assured him, resisting the urge to pull away. His fingers around her upper arm burned through the woolen sleeve of her kirtle, scorching her skin. "I knew Edward was on his way ... but *seeing* such a force gathering on our doorstep is another matter. I'm glad we have made such thorough preparations."

"Aye, My Lady," the Wallace agreed from behind her. "Longshanks never does anything by halves ... but we are ready for him."

"He wants to make an example of us," she replied, her gaze riveted upon the bobbing heads of men and horses that now covered the cliff-top opposite. "After David's actions."

"Perhaps," Draco replied. "Or maybe he's decided to take the north this year after all … and Dunnottar is his first step."

Gavina tore her attention from the English army, and she twisted to Draco. He stood so close to her now that she had to tilt her chin to meet his eye. "Do ye believe that's the case?"

His mouth lifted at the corners. "He's making a lot of effort just to teach you a lesson … don't you think?"

"Look," Wallace interrupted them. "He's sending out a rider."

Gavina shifted her attention back to the scene unfolding below. However, she was aware that Draco still gripped her arm. Initially, his touch had felt like a brand, but now it caused an odd tingling sensation to run up and down her arm. Her quickening breathing wasn't just because of the gathered force beneath these walls.

The man at her side had a disturbing effect upon her.

But at present, she had to focus. As Wallace had said, a lone rider had left the ranks and was making his way up the narrow, winding path to the gates.

"My Lady?" Cassian's voice rang out from farther along the wall. Gavina twisted to see that her captain stood atop the guard tower that flanked the far side of the gates. "Do you want us to fire upon him?"

Gavina saw then that a row of archers had readied themselves along the wall, bows raised.

"No," Gavina called out without hesitation. "He'll have word from Edward." She paused then, her spine stiffening. "Let us hear what he has to say."


A small party gathered before the gates in the lower ward. The Wallace and his men kept out of sight, while Donnan, Cassian, and ten of his men formed a semi-circle around Lady Gavina. All gazes now focused upon the lone rider that clip-clopped inside through the gap that had been opened for him.

The newcomer was a huge knight upon a bay destrier. And when he pushed up the helm of his helmet, Gavina felt a flicker of recognition. The man was Hugh De Burgh, Edward's right-hand. She'd seen him in Stirling's Great Hall when they'd banqueted with the English king.

"Good day, Lady Gavina," the knight greeted her in French. "The king wishes for a parley. Will you come down to the base of the fortress and speak openly with him?"

"There won't be a meeting," Cassian answered. His voice held a threatening note. "You tell us what Longshanks wants, and the lady can give her reply now."

Hugh scowled, although his attention remained upon Gavina's face. "He will only speak to Lady Gavina," he replied, his voice roughening. "No one else."

"I can go in Lady Gavina's stead." Donnan spoke up then. He too was scowling. "I am Donnan De Keith, steward of Dunnottar."

Hugh shook his head. "I repeat ... Edward wishes to speak to the lady herself. There will be no substitute."

"I will go," Gavina replied in French, forestalling Donnan as he opened his mouth to argue. "Edward has met me at least ... and it was my husband who brought him to our gates. If I can convince Longshanks that David acted alone, perhaps he will leave us in peace." She turned to the guard standing behind her. "Ready my horse, please."

"My Lady," Cassian growled. "You can't go down to him. This could be a trap."

Gavina shook her head. She knew her captain and steward were only trying to protect her, but Edward had made his terms clear.

Both men seemed to forget who was in charge here.

Meeting Cassian's eye, Gavina favored him with an arch look. "Ready yer horse too, Captain. Ye shall escort me."

"This isn't wise, My Lady." Tension rippled off Cassian's big frame. "You shall be in danger."

"Edward knows the rules of a parley, I'm sure," Gavina answered, squaring her shoulders. "And ye shall ensure I'm kept safe."

"My Lady ... King Edward said only you can—" Hugh began.

"Either I bring my captain with me, or we don't speak at all," Gavina cut him off, her tone turning steely. "You decide."

# XII

## THE PARLEY

"SHE'S A BRAVE lass, our Lady of Dunnottar," Wallace murmured, his gaze riveted on the steep path the three riders now picked their way down. "Her husband wouldn't have gone down to speak to Longshanks with only one guard as protection."

"Brave or foolhardy," Draco muttered. His attention fixed upon the slight figure, cloaked in black atop a mincing palfrey. As the day lengthened, the sky had grown overcast. And yet Gavina's pale hair stood out. Even at this distance, he knew it was her. "I wouldn't trust the bastard."

"Neither would I," Wallace replied. "But the fact she's a woman might make him go easier on her. It might work to her favor."

Draco frowned. He wasn't so sure. Watching Cassian and Gavina follow the English emissary down to the front ranks of the waiting army, he was surprised to find his jaw clenched. Worry twisted under his ribcage.

*Are you actually concerned about that woman's welfare?*

Draco's mouth twisted. Was it that, or merely his over developed sense of chivalry? He'd always been a bit of a fool when it came to defending women's honor.

It was such a gesture that had started the feud with Henry all those years earlier.

He'd been a guest in Edinburgh Castle, and had come upon the king's son cornering a frightened woman in a stairwell. It didn't matter that the woman was Henry's betrothed; she'd clearly not wanted his attentions. Draco had flattened Henry's nose and plucked Suisan from his clutches. Suisan Boyd was a lovely creature and had been grateful to him. During the rest of Draco's stay, they'd spent time together. One thing had led to another, and the pair of them ended up as lovers.

That had been the beginning of Henry's campaign against him.

Draco unclenched the hands he hadn't even realized he'd been fisting. He really didn't want to start getting protective over Lady Gavina. That would muddy things completely.

Draco watched Cassian and Gavina draw their horses up a few yards distant from the front ranks. A few moments later, a man upon a magnificent grey warhorse emerged from the vanguard. Clad in a rippling red and white surcoat, his hauberk and helm glinting despite the dull afternoon, Edward of England cut a regal figure— even at this distance.

The Wallace snarled a curse. "There ye are, filthy whoreson. Finally."

Draco cut his leader a warning look. He sometimes worried about the man he followed. Draco was committed to the Scottish cause; he too wanted to see the English chased from these lands. But for Wallace it went far deeper. He bore a hatred that gnawed at him like an ulcer in the belly. It fueled him, drove him, and yet at the same time, it also blinded him.

When it came to Edward of England, William Wallace lost all reason.

It wasn't just a fight for Scottish freedom, but something far more personal. Wallace blamed Edward for the death of the woman he loved—a slight he'd never forget.

A damp wind gusted in from the sea, stinging Gavina's cheeks. She was glad of the heavy woolen mantle that shrouded her, for when she gazed into Edward's ice-blue eyes, a chill washed over her.

In Stirling, before David tried to kill him, the English king had been welcoming, polite even. He was a man who enjoyed female company. He'd spoken to Gavina and Elizabeth during the two banquets they'd been invited to, and she'd seen that he was both articulate and intelligent.

But she hadn't seen him angry.

His face, handsome despite his age, was now set in grim lines, his gaze wintry as he met her eye. Gavina swallowed. She wasn't sure how she was supposed to greet him. After all, this man had tried to kill her. He'd sent a party of men out to hunt down her and Elizabeth after they'd fled Stirling—and now he'd brought an army to her gates. However, it was Edward who spoke first, saving her the trouble.

"I hear that you shelter William Wallace within the walls of Dunnottar."

The accusation fell heavily in the air, and it was with great difficulty that Gavina prevented herself from drawing in a surprised gasp.

*How does he know?*

Beside her, Cassian didn't move atop his horse, didn't utter a word. She hoped that he'd managed to keep his expression neutral.

She hadn't wanted Longshanks to know about the Wallace's presence within the stronghold. But seeing the murderous glint to his eye now, she realized it was vital he never learned of it.

His reckoning would be terrible if he knew she'd been hiding the man he'd been hunting for years.

It was time for some denial.

Drawing in a deep, steadying breath, Gavina continued to hold Edward's eye. "You have heard wrong,

Edward," she replied in French. She deliberately didn't address him as 'Your Highness' as she had back in Stirling. They'd been on a diplomatic mission then. As part of the ruse, David had been required to feign fealty. But she'd not toady before this man today.

He wasn't her king. He'd never be her king.

Edward inclined his head. Her lack of honorific hadn't been lost on him. His mouth curved into a smile then, although his eyes remained frosty. "Excuse me, *My Lady*, but I beg to differ. You're lying to me. I know this because Blair Galbraith paid me a visit in Stirling."

Gavina's pulse started to race.

*Traitorous bastard!*

With great difficulty, she continued to hold Edward's eye. Lying didn't come naturally to her, especially before a man with such vulpine intelligence.

*It matters not,* she counseled herself. *Ye cannot betray William to him.*

"Galbraith is a liar with a grudge," she replied after a pause. "It is *I* who speaks the truth."

"Well then ... allow me to enter your stronghold. I shall check for myself."

"You don't rule here, Edward," Gavina reminded him, her voice hardening as anger quickened within her. Her simmering temper made the French flow easily from her lips. "And since you have brought an army with you, I shall not be welcoming you within the walls of Dunnottar."

He stared back at her, and for an instant, Gavina felt a thrill of victory. Surprise had flared in those ice-blue eyes. He hadn't expected such a response from her.

Edward's mouth pursed. "I tire of Scottish women and their sharp tongues," he growled. "Your husband must have found death a welcome escape."

Gavina swallowed a laugh. Indeed, she'd seen the simpering women among Edward's retainers in Stirling. It appeared English men liked their women even meeker than Scottish men did.

The urge to argue reared within her, yet Gavina swallowed it down. She'd won a small victory in this barbed exchange, but she'd not press her advantage.

"It seems that we are at an impasse, My Lady," Edward said when the brittle silence between them drew out. Beside Gavina, Cassian wisely continued to hold his tongue. Nonetheless, he was a solid, steadying presence at her side. "If you won't let me see for myself whether or not you're shielding that enemy of the English, I have no choice but to name you my enemy as well."

Gavina stared back. She didn't break his stare, even if his words made her belly tremble.

*Be strong,* she counseled herself. *Don't let him intimidate ye.*

It was hard though. Edward's tone was now as icy as his gaze. Although he spoke with a slight lisp, his voice was powerful. There was a reason this man had managed to take half of Scotland, why he'd even taken Dunnottar in the past. He was a warrior king, and he didn't take kindly to being defied.

When she didn't answer him, Edward continued. "However, since I am in a merciful mood, I will give you one last chance. You have until sunrise tomorrow to deliver William Wallace to me." He paused there, letting his words sink in. "But if you don't, I will lay siege to Dunnottar. I swear I will smash this fortress to dust and burn every last one of you alive."

His words, uttered without a trace of emotion, made Gavina start to sweat. Nonetheless, her gaze didn't falter.

Another frosty silence stretched out between them, and Gavina realized that the parley was indeed at an end. There was nothing left to say.

Pulse racing, Gavina reined her palfrey around and urged it back to the path up to the gates. Wordlessly, Cassian followed her.

And all the way up to the gatehouse, she felt Edward Longshanks's gaze boring into her back.

Gavina's palfrey clattered into the lower ward bailey. Drawing up her mount, she swung down from the saddle to see a crowd amassing before her. Men and women—mostly guards and servants—watched her, their faces both pale and hopeful.

The Wallace was among them, a fierce presence towering over those standing by him.

Elizabeth pushed her way to the front, Robbie perched on a hip. "What happened?" Behind Elizabeth, both Heather and Aila approached, their faces strained.

Gavina didn't reply immediately. Instead, her gaze shifted to where William Wallace now drew close. The crowd parted to let the big man through.

Swallowing hard, Gavina tried to shake off the dread that now pressed down upon her ribcage. Edward was terrifying when riled. And when he'd uttered his threat, she'd believed every word.

When the English had taken Dunnottar in the past, they'd only laid siege to the fortress until the gates were breached, only killed those who fought them. Everyone else had been spared. Gavina remembered David railing at his brother as the English rounded them up like sheep. They'd locked Robert, David, and Donnan in the dungeons for a spell, until all three swore that they'd cause no trouble for the garrison that was now in place.

Looking back, they'd been relatively merciful. But there wouldn't be any mercy shown this time.

In defying Edward, she'd made an enemy of him.

Her gaze settled on the outlaw when he stopped a few feet away.

*Ye can't stay here, William.*

"My Lady?" Wallace's gaze was narrowed when it met hers. "What did Longshanks have to say?"

# XIII

## BLOOD WILL BE SPILLED HERE

"I'M NOT LEAVING Dunnottar." William Wallace's voice thundered across the laird's solar. "Especially with Longshanks within my grasp!"

Gavina took a sip of wine from the cup she clasped, welcoming its comforting heat. After her meeting with Edward, she felt in need of something to steady her frayed nerves. "He knows ye are here, William," she replied. The calmness of her voice belied her rapidly beating heart. "And he'll not stop till he captures ye."

"Let him come!" Wallace snarled. He started to pace the solar, his long legs eating up the space. The chamber was a spacious one, but the man's presence suddenly made it confined. "Let him beat on the walls. I'll happily put my dirk through his throat if he dares face me!"

They weren't alone in the solar. Elizabeth sat beside Gavina by the hearth, and Donnan stood next to her. Draco, Maximus, and Cassian had also joined them. The three friends stood by the window, their faces grim.

"William, please listen to me," Gavina said, making another attempt to penetrate the cloak of rage that shrouded the Wallace this evening. Outdoors, the light had faded, and the English army now crouched upon the cliff-top, waiting to strike with the coming dawn. "This isn't just about ye. The lives of everyone within these walls are at stake now. If ye leave Dunnottar, then maybe I can allow Edward to enter the castle and check that we aren't sheltering ye. Just maybe, he will spare us. I shall to do everything in my power to avoid bloodshed."

The Wallace wheeled around, his dark gaze spearing her. Despite that he wore a thick beard, she could see the muscles of his jaw working. "Do ye really think he'll spare Dunnottar, Gavina?" he asked roughly. "Longshanks already had his sights upon this fortress, long before he discovered my presence. Whether or not ye wish it, blood *will* be spilled here."

Gavina's belly dropped at these words. "William, I—"

"I'm not going," Wallace cut in, his voice lowering to a growl. "Besides, how would ye expect me to get past Edward's army?"

"I can't believe Galbraith betrayed us," Donnan spoke up, his grey-green eyes smoldering with anger.

"I can," Cassian cut in, his voice tight. "The man is bitter to the core. This is his way of taking his reckoning upon us all."

Gavina drew in a deep breath, focusing her thoughts. She was shocked and angered by the smith's treachery, but Galbraith couldn't be their focus right now. Instead, she wasn't finished trying to convince the Wallace to leave. She wouldn't give up hope of ending this peacefully—not yet.

"Stirling isn't the only castle with a secret exit," she said, her gaze seeking the outlaw's. "There is a boat below the cliff ... accessible via a rope ladder beneath the dungeon entrance. David may have been hot-headed, but he was no fool. He insisted Cassian ready the boat for him ... should the need ever arise for him to leave in a hurry." She paused there, letting her words sink in. "I suggest ye take it ... while ye can."

The Wallace's eyes widened further. "That craven," he muttered. "Why aren't I surprised that he'd give himself a way out, while the rest of ye burned?"

By the hearth, Elizabeth's mouth thinned. "Robert would never have sanctioned such a thing," she assured him. Next to her, the steward was scowling. David hadn't told Donnan of his boat. A few yards away, Cassian wore an uncomfortable expression.

Frustration spiraled up within Gavina. She understood their anger, yet once again the conversation was veering off course. Ignoring Elizabeth and Donnan's responses, she focused on the Wallace once more. His scowl was fierce enough to frighten bairns, yet she pressed on. "Whatever the reason for David's actions, the fact remains that wee boat is sitting there, William … ready for ye."

A heavy silence fell in the solar then. Gavina waited patiently for the outlaw's response, and as she did so, the banner that hung on the wall opposite caught her eye. It was the De Keith motto. Veritas Vincit—*Truth conquers.* She hoped her directness would be victorious in this instance, although judging from the thunderous look on Wallace's face, she feared it wouldn't.

"No man of honor would slink away at a moment like this," he finally growled.

Gavina swallowed hard. "Not even to save the rest of us?"

His mouth twisted. "I repeat, Edward of England won't show anyone here mercy, even if ye rid yerself of me and throw open the gates to him." His gaze narrowed. "Ye have managed Dunnottar well since David's death, My Lady … and showed courage today … but ye would do well to leave matters of war to yer menfolk."


Draco watched the interaction between the Lady of Dunnottar and William Wallace with interest.

His leader's last words had angered her. She raised her chin, her heart-shaped face tensing, while those blue eyes turned hard.

Mithras strike him down. She was a sight to behold.

Few men would have the guts to hold the Wallace's eye so boldly—the man wore a belt, scabbard, and baldrick made of another man's skin for pity's sake. Even Draco minded him when he was in a temper.

Yet the lady stared back at the freedom fighter with ire smoldering in her gaze.

Long moments passed before Gavina finally spoke. "Ye are right, William ... I know little of war." Her tone was clipped, and a nerve flickered under one eye. The fingers wrapped around her goblet clenched. "But nonetheless, I *do* know of its consequences, and I will do all I can to prevent a massacre here."

Wallace stared back at her, his heavy features softening a little. "Sometimes bloodshed is the only way forward, My Lady," he rumbled. "Please let me do what I'm best at. Captain Gaius and I are ready to the lead the defense of Dunnottar. If Longshanks wants a fight, let's give him one."

Gavina's pale throat bobbed, before she gave a slight, barely-perceptible nod. She turned her attention to Cassian then, their gazes meeting. "Very well," she said, her voice strained now. "I can see it is no use. I hand the defense over to ye then, Captain."

*Curse men and their bull-headed ways. If women ruled this land, there would be far fewer wars and feuds.*

Gavina crossed to the sideboard and poured herself a cup of sloe wine. She noted that her hands were shaking and muttered a curse under her breath. Her parley with Edward and debate with the Wallace had unnerved her more than she'd realized.

She wasn't much of a drinker—not like her late husband, who'd imbibed a jug of wine most evenings. But this evening was different.

Gavina crossed to the window seat and sat down. The wooden shutters were closed, for it was a cool evening outdoors. The wind had died with the dusk, and a dank sea mist had crept in. Not only that, but with the shutters open, she could hear the shouts of men and the rumble of activity throughout the keep as it readied itself for the coming battle.

Tomorrow, Longshanks would attack—and there was nothing she could do to prevent it.

Taking a large gulp of wine, Gavina's thoughts returned to the words she'd exchanged with Edward beneath the keep. He was ruthless and stubborn. Her only hope had been that William Wallace would agree to leave. But she should have known he wouldn't. The man was a proud Scot, the bravest freedom fighter this land had ever known. He'd never run from a fight.

All the same, his refusal had frustrated her.

He was of the opinion that Edward of England was devoid of mercy, but Gavina disagreed. The English king was a man of keen intelligence. If she'd been able to prove that the Wallace didn't shelter within Dunnottar, he might have spared them all.

*But now we'll never know.*

Gavina had just taken another gulp of wine, and was mulling over her exchange with Wallace and the others, when a soft knock sounded on the door to her solar.

Gavina sighed; she'd hoped for a little more time alone. However, it was clearly not to be—not on the eve before battle. Drawing in a deep breath, she called out, "Who is it?"

"It's me ... My Lady," Aila called back. "Are ye ready to be undressed for bed?"

Of course, Aila always attended her at this hour. With everything that had happened, she'd lost track of time.

"Not yet," Gavina replied. "But come in anyway."

The door creaked open, and an elegant woman clad in dove-grey, her thick brown hair pulled back from her face, entered. Aila had changed so much since she and Cassian had wed, Gavina reflected. She'd always been a pretty lass before, but now she possessed a serene beauty that Gavina envied.

Ever since their marriage, Aila usually wore a wide smile. She was blissfully happy with Cassian, Gavina knew it. But this evening, her winsome face was tense, her grey eyes troubled.

"Pour yerself a cup of wine, Aila," Gavina greeted her, motioning to the sideboard. "I think we could both do with something to calm our nerves."

Aila paused a moment, before nodding. She helped herself to a cup and crossed to where Gavina sat at the window, perching upon a stool.

"I hear Longshanks will indeed attack tomorrow?" Aila murmured, raising the cup to her lips and taking a sip.

"Aye ... unless I deliver him the Wallace."

"Which ye would never do."

The certainty in her maid's voice made Gavina huff a bitter laugh. Of course she was never actually going to hand Wallace over to Longshanks—but helping him escape would be a different matter.

She met Aila's eye then, favoring her with a tired smile. "I apologize, Aila ... I haven't been myself of late."

It was true. She'd barely spoken to her maid since her return, and hadn't spent afternoons with Heather either as she usually did.

*Guilt weighs too heavily upon me.*

Aila offered her a wan smile in return. "I know what happened ... Cassian told me all."

"I imagined he did."

"Ye don't have to look so worried, My Lady. I don't judge ye ... I too wouldn't want to wed a man I didn't love."

Gavina stiffened, surprised by Aila's response. "But the curse—"

"Ye forget ... I was with ye all those years while ye were wed to David. I saw how unhappy ye were. Why would I wish ye to enter a loveless union again?"

A lump rose in Gavina's throat at these words. Aila's selflessness made tears prickle the back of her eyes. "But I know how much it means to ye all ... that the curse is broken," she said huskily. "Maximus, Cassian, and Draco may never get another chance. I feel as if I'm robbing ye all of a normal life ... of a family."

Aila stared back, her own eyes glittering as tears rose. "Nonsense, My Lady … the curse is stronger than all of us," she murmured. "Please don't take such responsibility upon yer shoulders."

# XIV

## WITH THE DAWN

ALL HE COULD hear was the roar of his own breathing, the thunder of his own heart. All he could see was pitch-black, smothering darkness.

He clawed at his stone tomb. He tried to kick it, to elbow his way out. But the stone wouldn't give an inch. It bruised and bloodied his fingers and toes, and all the while, the ragged sound of his breathing mocked him. Sweat coursed down his face. Hunger gnawed at his belly. His throat was so dry that he could barely swallow, barely breathe.

Panic assailed him then, mounting in sickly waves till it couldn't be borne. Sometimes the darkness and stone walls surrounding him on every side felt as if they were closing in.

Alone in the dark, he began to scream.

Draco sat up, heart pounding. He was panting as if he'd just sprinted up ten flights of stairs.

For a few instants, he was disoriented. The horror of the nightmare still clung to him. He was still interred in the stone tomb: forgotten, alone, and silenced.

Sweat bathed his naked body, and despite that it was warm inside the barracks, a shiver went through him.

Draco dragged a hand down his face. He needed to get hold of himself.

*It is only a bad dream.*

He hadn't had a nightmare like that in a long while. In the years following his escape from that tomb, he'd awoken often in the night, dripping with sweat, heart pounding like a battle drum. But as time drew out and the years passed, the dreams gradually grew less vivid.

Only, some things could never be forgotten.

He might be occupied with other matters, but sometimes he felt as if there were still a part of him that was locked underground, screaming to be freed.

*Enough of this nonsense.*

The barracks, and the snoring of the other men in the cots around him, suddenly felt oppressive. It was an effort to drag in each breath. Draco needed fresh air; he had to get outside. He wouldn't be able to sleep now anyway.

He reached for his clothing in the darkness, pulling on his braies and a leather vest. He then scooped up his boots and carried them with him out of the barracks, stopping to pull them on once he reached the steps outdoors.

Mist wreathed into the lower ward, snaking fingers drifting across the sea of glistening cobblestones. The air was damp and cool out here, and Draco sucked in deep, steadying lungfuls of it.

*That's better*. The horror of that dream was drawing back now. His heartbeat was slowing down.

But Draco didn't go back inside the barracks once his pulse had calmed. Instead, he crossed to the postern door that lead up to the top of the guard tower—to the Watch. With Edward's army at the gate, Wallace's men were also taking turns guarding the walls, aiding the Dunnottar Guard. Draco had done a shift earlier that evening. But since he had no wish to return to that suffocating barracks, and the possibility of more bad dreams, he decided he might as well resume his station.

Torches and braziers glowed upon the wall, casting a lambent light over the rough grey stone and the snaking fog that surrounded the fortress now. From this height, it was a surreal sight. Tonight, Dunnottar was an island floating on a milky sea. Walking to the wall, and acknowledging the man to his right with a nod, Draco stared out at the view to the west.

The mist had crept in there, obscuring the cliff-top and the spreading hills beyond. It hid the camp, yet the glow of the vast English army still penetrated the mist.

"Couldn't sleep either?"

Draco turned to see Cassian standing behind him.

Draco's mouth twisted. "Yes, but I don't have a beautiful woman warming my bed ... if I did, I wouldn't be out here."

Cassian raised an eyebrow. "But you could have a 'lady' in your bed, if you wished it."

Draco snorted. He'd walked straight into that one. "I thought we agreed to let that subject lie?"

"What subject?" Cassian's tone feigned innocence as he moved closer, so that the two of them stood shoulder to shoulder looking out over the misty night.

Draco sucked in another deep breath. Since his return from the meeting with Irvine, he'd had some tense 'talks' with both Maximus and Cassian. The worst of them had been yesterday afternoon. Draco had been so intractable that Cassian had actually lost his temper with him. Maximus had stepped between the two of them before they came to blows.

"I'm sorry about yesterday," Cassian murmured after a pause. "I was an arse."

Draco cut his friend a look. "You're never an arse, Cass," he admitted. "We both know that's my role. Your anger was deserved."

Draco shifted his attention back to the fog-shrouded cliff-face before them. The mist seemed to have a life of its own tonight, shifting and wreathing like the tentacles of some great sea beast. It was an eerie sight, and one that put him on edge.

Things weren't looking rosy for Dunnottar and its inhabitants. Even with the Wallace and his men's assistance, and the reinforcements they'd brought in, the stronghold wouldn't stand long-term against such a force. They all knew it, although the Wallace was stubbornly refusing to admit the truth.

Draco stared off into the fog, his gaze becoming unfocused. Sometimes he wondered why he was fighting Maximus and Cassian over this. After all, they all wanted the same thing.

*This is your chance to finally break the curse*, a voice whispered to him then. *You've chased death for so long. Why are you throwing away this opportunity?*

The question brought Draco up short. The voice was cruel and cold, yet it spoke the truth. Why was he resisting a union with Gavina?

He didn't wish to wed anyone, let alone the proud Lady of Dunnottar. But if the others were right, this was indeed the opportunity he'd long yearned for. Otherwise, he'd continue living forever.

Draco's throat tightened. That chilling dream had been a reminder of the burden he carried. He'd lived through too much, seen too much, and done too much.

Draco turned to Cassian then, meeting his eye squarely. "Actually, I've thought on what you said," he replied softly. "You were right. I've completely ignored the fact that all three of us are in this mess together. You and Maximus need this from me."

Cassian's gaze widened. "Does this mean—"

"Yes, it does," Draco cut him off, impatient now. "But the battle isn't won yet, Cass. Lady Gavina has a say in this too ... in case you forget." He paused there. "I will talk to her once more ... and see if she is willing to overlook her objections to wedding me ... but I can't make you any promises."

Cassian cocked an eyebrow. "She doesn't dislike you that much, does she?"

Draco snorted. "I think I'm a little too rough around the edges for the lady."

Cassian laughed. "You are for most of us, but we love you nonetheless." His gaze searched Draco's face then, as if he was seeking the answer to a question he didn't want to ask. Draco knew what it was. He had never spoken of those lost years under Saint Margaret's Chapel to Maximus or Cassian. Draco had let them believe that losing Magda in the raid a few years before that incident had turned him cruel and bitter.

Cassian knew he was hiding something—but now, as in the past, his friend didn't press him. Draco had always appreciated that about him. He knew when to let things be.

"Discovering Gavina and I are part of the riddle came as a bit of a shock," Draco admitted after a pause, deliberately moving the subject of conversation on. "One I'm still struggling with to be honest. I've always known what my name means, but I thought the answer to the last line would be more complex than that."

"We all did ... but sometimes the easy answers are the hardest ones to accept." Cassian flashed him a rueful smile then. "Plus ... do you think I really want to put my fate in your hands?"

Draco snorted. His friend had turned into a bit of philosopher of late. In the past, Draco might have mocked him for it, yet tonight he held his tongue. He didn't always need to be right, to always prove a point. Sometimes he could just let a comment pass.

Despite that he'd never openly admitted it, Maximus and Cassian meant more to him than anyone else. It was time he focused on breaking the curse that held them all captive. However, their success now hinged on the cooperation of a woman who didn't like him, a woman who'd only been recently widowed.

*Let's see if I can get the Lady of Dunnottar to warm to me ... just a little.*

Gavina rose well before dawn. Wrapped in a fur mantle, she climbed the steps to the guard tower and joined the Wallace and Cassian as they stood waiting for the sun to rise. Draco and Maximus were present as well, shadowy figures in the murk.

"How far off is dawn?" Gavina asked. Her voice, although soft, sounded unnaturally loud in the eerie silence that had settled upon the castle. She stepped up next to the Wallace, lifting her chin so that she could meet his gaze.

"It will break soon," he rumbled. "Longshanks is down there waiting."

Gavina's lips thinned. Indeed, the English king would be hoping she'd turn the freedom fighter over to him.

Her gaze shifted then to Cassian. The captain acknowledged her with a nod.

Not for the first time, guilt arrowed through Gavina, and her chest tightened. Her conversation with Aila the night before had discomforted her. Afterward, she'd lain in bed, staring up at the darkness, unable to get to sleep. Maybe if her maid had shown anger or frustration, it might have been easier to bear. But Aila believed in her, trusted her. She didn't want her mistress to suffer another unhappy marriage.

Her kindness had humbled Gavina.

Friendship had always been something that had eluded her over the years. She'd lost her mother early, and hadn't had any sisters to share things with. Her relationship with her sister-by-marriage, Elizabeth, was still oddly formal, and Gavina's position here at Dunnottar had always isolated her.

But in Aila and Heather she'd found acceptance and companionship.

The pressure in Gavina's chest deepened, making her catch her breath. It was hard to focus when guilt plagued her like this. At least she didn't have the defense of Dunnottar to worry over too—she didn't like admitting defeat, but she'd done all she could to prevent bloodshed. It was in the hands of the men now.

Maybe she should seek out Heather today? Aila's elder sister was more plainspoken and had a fiery temperament. She likely wouldn't be as understanding as Aila—and if she gave Gavina the sharp edge of her tongue, some of this gnawing guilt might ease a little.

The trouble was that Gavina liked Cassian and Maximus too. They were both good, honest men who'd fallen in love with wonderful women. They all deserved a future. Once again, Gavina swallowed down self-reproach at the thought that she and Draco appeared to hold the key.

The group of them waited on the walls, unspeaking, while the surrounding braziers died down and the torches started to gutter. And with the rising of the sun, a faint glow at first in the east, the fog started to shift. It rolled away, revealing the line of mounted soldiers that bristled along the length of the cliff-face.

The English were awake and ready for them.

Gavina shifted uncomfortably, her pulse accelerating at the sight. The warmth of the rising sun upon her cheeks chased away the night's lingering chill, but it couldn't warm the cold knot of fear tightening in her belly.

She had already lived through a siege, and it had been terrifying. But this attack was going to be infinitely worse.

The mist continued to roll back, and Gavina glanced around, taking in their defenses. Rows of men in mail shirts and gleaming black helms now lined the walls. Archers wielding both cross and longbows stood at the ready. Much bigger crossbows had been erected upon the defenses as well, big enough to hurl projectiles at the enemy from above.

An acrid odor filled her nostrils then—the burning stench of quicklime and pine resin. Pails of Greek fire lined the walls. A useful weapon indeed, for when mixed with water, it burst into flames. Unfortunately, the English would have plenty of it too.

Once Edward's men tried scaling the walls, they would have arrows and rocks cast down on them, but that wasn't likely to happen today.

First, according to the Wallace, the English would do some damage to the curtain walls. After that, they would turn their attention to the gates.

Gavina's jaw tightened. Dunnottar was fortunate in its position, perched high upon the headland with only one side landward. The Wallace's men had dug a deep ditch around the base on that side, and filled it with iron spikes. That would make it harder for the enemy to put up ladders.

To reach the castle gates, the army had to pick its way down a steep slope and then climb through a defile—a narrow path that would slow them further.

As if reading Gavina's thoughts, the Wallace spoke up. "There are many of them, My Lady," he rumbled. "But it wouldn't matter if twice that number were to lay siege to the castle. Only a handful at a time can get close to us."

Gavina nodded. He was right, yet his words didn't make her feel any better.

The sky lightened further, shifting from rose-pink to a fiery red.

The sight made Divina's already nervous belly tighten. It looked as if blood stained the morning sky—an ill omen for the first day of battle.

Then, as they waited, a long, drawn-out wail echoed over the cliff-top—a horn.

Gavina had been waiting for the signal, but even so, it startled her. Her breathing caught, and her heart started to race.

A heartbeat passed, and then another, and Gavina continued to hold her breath.

Then on the cliff-edge opposite, the English army gave a great roar. It had begun.

# XV

## TO WHATEVER END

THE MOMENT GAVINA ventured out into the walled garden and the castle's upper ward, she regretted it.

Indoors, the shouts of soldiers and the whooshing sound of trebuchets launching was muffled. Every so often, the keep would shudder from the impact of rocks and Greek fire hitting the curtain walls, but for the most part those indoors could keep their heads down and ignore the siege.

Outdoors was a different matter.

Gavina inhaled a lungful of acrid smoke, which caught in her lungs and made her cough. Out here, the clash of iron on stone and the thunder of stones and debris hitting the walls rang in her ears.

The roar of men's voices had screams blended with them.

Scots were dying.

Whomp. Whomp.

Two more projectiles hit the curtain wall, sending a deep shudder through the entire fortress.

Sucking in a deep breath, and then regretting it as another fit of coughing seized her, Gavina wiped her stinging eyes and walked over to the rose bed. In an effort to distract herself, her gaze traveled over the magnificent blooms of red and pink. Bees were buzzing there, and a butterfly had just landed on the wall, oblivious to the turmoil going on around it.

As he promised, Edward had begun his siege at daybreak. And he hadn't paused since. The bastard had set up a line of trebuchets—big iron and oak machines of war from which he hurled chunks of lead and slate, and Greek fire—along the cliff-edge opposite.

At noon, when Gavina had dared peek out the window of the solar to see how their defenses were holding up, she was frustrated to realize that she couldn't see much from her vantage point. After the siege began, she'd retreated from the top of the wall. It had been too dangerous for her to remain there.

Now, as the afternoon drew out, she found that she dreaded discovering what damage the English had already wrought.

"You really shouldn't be out here, My Lady. It's not safe."

A male voice drew her from her brooding. Tearing her gaze from the roses, Gavina swiveled to see a tall man with tightly-curled, short dark hair, clad in leather armor, emerge through the stone arch leading into the garden and stride toward her.

Draco Vulcan, battle-ready, was an intimidating sight. A sword hung at his side, and he carried a domed metal helmet under one arm. Dust and ash from the siege covered his lean body.

For a moment, Gavina merely stared at him. What was he doing in her garden?

"I had to get outside for a few moments," she replied, irritated that she felt the need to defend herself. "The walls were closing in on me."

"Well, you'd better hope that Longshanks's Greek fire has a short reach," he replied. "Or you might get an unwelcome guest in your pretty garden."

Gavina tensed. She hadn't invited this man in here. And yet here he was telling her how to behave. "Did ye want something, Vulcan?" Her tone was unwelcoming, yet she didn't care.

He stopped a few feet back from her. His gaze then roved over her face, as if he was trying to judge her mood. "I wish to speak to you, My Lady … if I may?"

She frowned. The man had poor timing indeed. "What about?"

"About that riddle you and I are part of."

Gavina's pulse fluttered at the base of her throat. Despite that it was a mild day, she drew the light cloak about her shoulders close. "Now really isn't a good time."

"*Time* grows short, My Lady," Draco countered, his tone polite. He didn't appear remotely affected by her chilly response. "Perhaps it's time for you and me to do our part."

Gavina stilled. *Our part?* "Ye told me to forget about the riddle," she reminded him. "Why are ye bringing it up again?"

He huffed a heavy sigh, before he dragged a hand down his face. "There's nothing like a siege to get you thinking." The warrior's expression was suddenly weary. "I'm not asking for myself, but for Cassian and Maximus. If Edward reduces this castle to rubble, my friends aren't going to want to live through it … only to see the women they love die. If we all go down … we go down together."

Gavina drew in a shocked breath. His words were a slap across the face. The bleakness of such a proclamation made her queasy. As such, her voice was strained when she finally replied, "That is a dire prediction … maybe ye are wrong … maybe Cassian and Maximus value their lives more than ye think."

Draco shook his head. "Not if they lose their wives." He paused then, his eyes shadowing. "It might take Longshanks a while, but eventually he'll take Dunnottar … and when he does, few of you are going to survive his wrath, My Lady. You might, perhaps … and Lady Elizabeth. You're high-born ladies, so Edward might decide to take you hostage. But he'll put every other soul in this keep to the sword or burn them alive once he breaches the gates. Aila and Heather will die, and I know that my friends would prefer to go with them ... if it comes to that.”

Gavina fell silent. She didn't know how to answer him. Like when he'd approached her the morning after their discovery that Gavina was the 'White Hawk', she was struck by how much he cared for Maximus and Cassian. It was incongruous in someone who usually appeared so hard and cold.

What a bitter irony though, to care for his friends, and wish them dead at the same time. But Gavina understood.

She'd been there in that clearing when Cassian had stabbed himself in the heart to prove who he was to Aila. She'd seen the pain in his eyes that had nothing to do with the injury he'd inflicted upon himself. It had dawned on her then that immortality was far crueler than she could possibly comprehend.

“So, we are all doomed?” she asked, her voice barely above a whisper.

Draco stepped closer to her, his dark gaze pinning her to the spot. “I'm not a man given to optimism, and I wish I could say different,” he murmured. “But if this were a game of Ard-ri, your king would now be surrounded, My Lady. It may not be for a few days ... but this castle *will* fall.” A harsh smile split his face then. “So, you can rest assured that you and I won't be wed for long. Assuming our union breaks the curse, you'll be widowed a second time very soon.”

Gavina's body drew taut. How could he make fun of such a situation? There were some things that one shouldn't joke about. “Is this a game to ye?” she rasped. “Don't ye want to live?”

Draco held her gaze fast, and in the depths of his obsidian eyes, she saw nothing but bleakness.

The castle shuddered then, the impact so sudden that Gavina staggered. An instant later, something hit the wall behind her.

Gavina gasped, her gaze swiveling to where a massive hunk of lead had torn a hole in the garden wall.

"Come." Draco took hold of her arm and firmly led her toward the archway. "I told you it wasn't safe out here."

Heart pounding, Gavina meekly went with him, shock rendering her biddable. However, the moment they were inside the keep, and had entered a long colonnaded gallery, she wrenched her arm free and turned to him. "It can't really be that simple, can it?" she demanded. "How can ye and I marrying change anything?"

He stared down at her, his look so intense that Gavina suddenly forgot to breathe. She'd never met a man who looked at her like he did. She felt laid bare under that stare. "Over one thousand years ago, a witch woman cursed three centurions she'd taken captive," he replied, his gaze never leaving hers. "And from that moment onward, things were set in stone. All that remains is for us to do our part."

Gavina stood at the open window of the solar, looking out across the lower ward and the walls, which now smoked in places. Heaviness pressed down upon her; it had been a long, nerve-wracking day.

The attacks had ceased with the setting of the sun. The silence that followed sounded unnatural, hollow. The quietness unsettled Gavina more than the siege had. For with the quiet, Longshanks would be plotting his next move.

Hearing the door whisper open behind her, Gavina turned from the grim view.

A comely woman with a curvaceous figure and a thick mane of walnut hair entered. Heather had visited her, as Gavina requested.

Her friend's grey-green eyes were wary, even as she favored Gavina with a smile. Ever since Heather had returned to Dunnottar a couple of months previously,

the two of them had become close. Gavina had employed
Heather as her companion, and they'd spent nearly every
afternoon together in this solar weaving and sewing, and
chatting. Heather had proved to be lively and interesting
company—the sort of woman who drew Gavina out of
herself and made her forget her worries.

But there was a reserve between them now.

A reserve that Gavina completely understood.

"How are yer parents faring?" Gavina asked. She
hadn't seen the steward and his wife all day, for they had
kept to their quarters high in the tower.

"On edge," Heather reported, her smile turning
rueful. "Da keeps pacing the floor, demanding to be let
out on the walls to fight, while Ma tells him he's too old
for such things."

Gavina managed a tight smile of her own. She
appreciated Donnan's courage. There may come a time
when the steward would be forced to join the fight; once
the English breached the gates, he'd have no choice.

Her belly cramped then, and she hurriedly pushed
the worry away.

"Thank ye for coming, Heather," she said, moving
over to one of the high-backed chairs near the hearth.
"I've missed our chats."

"As have I," Heather replied softly. Did Gavina
imagine it, or was her voice tinged with hurt. She moved
over to join Gavina, seating herself in a chair opposite.
Gavina studied her face. Heather's expression was
usually so open and frank, yet the lines of her softly
rounded face were strained this evening. "I was
beginning to think ye were deliberately avoiding me ...
have I offended ye in some way, My Lady?"

Gavina shook her head. "Ye have done nothing
wrong, Heather." The words gusted out of her. "My
distance has more to do with my own conscience
needling me." She met her friend's eye then. "Ye must
resent my choice?"

She braced herself to receive the blunt edge of
Heather's tongue. This was what she needed, rather than

Aila's kindness and acceptance. Heather would be refreshingly frank, harsh even.

However, Heather merely swallowed, her gaze widening. "Of course I don't."

"I know how much this means to ye," Gavina pressed. "If I don't help ye … the curse won't be broken."

Heather's full lips pressed together. "Aye," she murmured, "but no one would force ye into a marriage against yer will. I would hate to be cornered so."

Gavina dropped her gaze to her lap, to where she'd clasped her hands. *Lord, why do they have to be so kind?* She now twisted her fingers together, as a pain rose in the back of her throat and her belly churned. Her gaze lowered then, her eyes fluttering shut.

"Lady Gavina?" Heather's voice intruded, this time laced with worry. "Ye have gone as pale as a wraith … are ye unwell?"

Gavina shook her head. She opened her eyes, although her attention remained upon her clasped hands. She literally couldn't meet Heather's eye. "I'm not worthy of the consideration ye bestow upon me," she whispered.

"Of course ye are," Heather countered. "Why would ye say such a thing, My Lady?"

"Ye and Aila are being so selfless. I'm not sure that I would be, in the same situation."

Heather gave a soft laugh. "We are women of different ranks … born to fulfil different roles … but there should be a sisterhood between us. Ye have been good to me … I would never throw ye to the wolves."

Gavina's chin snapped up. *A sisterhood.* "I never had a sister," she whispered, her eyes stinging.

Her gaze met Heather's, and she saw that the woman's eyes also gleamed with unshed tears. "Well, ye have two now," Heather replied huskily. "Please know that Aila and I love ye … and we will stand by ye … to whatever end."

*To whatever end.*
The words mocked Gavina long after Heather left.

Returning to the window, Gavina watched the last of the light drain from the heavens.

They both knew what the end meant—even if neither woman had spelled it out.

Draco had done a fine job of making things clear to Gavina earlier in the day. If the curse wasn't broken, Heather and Aila would likely die during the siege, while their husbands would live on, consumed by grief.

The prospect of another loveless marriage, however short, was bleak indeed—but she could at least give the centurions their mortality back, so that they could finally find peace.

Tears escaped then, running silently down Gavina's cheeks.

She knew how much Heather loved Maximus, and yet she hadn't said a word to try and convince Gavina to help him.

Eyes fluttering shut, Gavina swallowed the sob that rose in her chest.

Love was what truly mattered. And not just that which existed between lovers, but also the bond between friends, between kin. When the world turned to dust and only the stars and the moon remained, love would live on, woven into eternity. Power, pride, revenge, gold—all of it was meaningless in comparison to the invisible threads that bound them.

A pain rose in her chest. Gavina lifted her hand, her knuckles pressing against her breast bone in an attempt to ease the ache.

She didn't love Draco Vulcan, and he didn't love her. But she'd seen the brotherhood between the three centurions, and she knew how much she cared for Heather and Aila.

She couldn't abandon them—she just couldn't.

"Very well," she whispered to the darkening sky. "I will wed him."

# XVI

## DESPERATE MEASURES

"A WIDOW IN mourning cannot wed." The chaplain's outraged voice rang through the chapel. "Surely, ye realize that, My Lady?"

"I do, Father … but during times like these, surely rules can be broken?"

Father Finlay drew in a sharp breath, his dark eyes widening. He stared at Gavina as if a stranger stood before him. She wasn't surprised by his reaction. The words she'd just uttered didn't sound as if they came from her at all.

However, she'd been right about one thing. Desperate times called for desperate measures.

It was shortly after dawn on the second day of the siege, and already Longshanks had resumed his attack. Debris pounded the fortress. Gavina could hear the impact, even through the thick walls of the chapel.

This needed to be done—before the situation grew dire. If Dunnottar fell, Maximus and Cassian deserved the mercy of dying alongside the women they loved.

Draco Vulcan stood at her side, silent and brooding. He'd wisely let Gavina take the lead. A few feet away stood Maximus, Cassian, Heather, and Aila. All of them needed to be elsewhere—the men should have been fighting on the walls—but this meeting had to take place first.

And while the chaplain resisted them, time was wasting.

Gavina hadn't told Elizabeth about what she'd planned this morning. She was close to her sister-by-marriage, but Liz would have been furious at her decision.

Better to get this done in stealth.

"Ye can't just bend and break things to suit yer own whims, My Lady," Father Finlay finally managed. "Ye and David made vows before God."

"Aye, but he is dead now, and I *must* wed Draco."

Outrage rippled through the chaplain's tall, lanky frame. Her lack of propriety shocked him. She was standing before him like a harlot, demanding he wed her to her lover.

Humiliation prickled over Gavina. For that was what she'd told him—she'd professed that she'd fallen madly in love with the Wallace's right-hand, had lain with him, and now carried his bairn. Dunnottar balanced upon a knife-edge, and she had to wed her lover before the end came.

The lies had slipped off her tongue with surprising ease, although she'd been unable to look Draco's way as she'd said them.

The disappointment on the good Father's face, and the indignation that swiftly followed, had cowed her a little. She liked Father Finlay and knew him to be a fair and kind man.

And her behavior *was* outrageous—worrying about her love life while Edward of England catapulted Greek fire over the walls.

It made her look self-centered and grasping.

The urge to laugh bubbled up within Gavina then. If only Father Finlay knew the truth behind this all.

"I love the lady." Draco spoke up there. His voice was cool and clipped, at odds with the words he'd just spoken. "And wish to make our union right before God."

The chaplain's mouth twisted. "Ye should have stayed away from her," he snarled. "What kind of man takes advantage of a widow?" He swiveled back to Gavina then, his cheeks reddening. "Yer husband has been barely dead a month! It is an offense to the Lord that ye wed so soon."

Gavina clenched her hands at her sides and cast Draco a warning look. He wasn't helping. It *was* an offense, she knew it. Here she stood in a house of God, clad in a sea-blue kirtle instead of her widow's black, flouting her lover.

The chaplain wasn't moving; she would have to humiliate herself further if this wedding was going to take place.

"My marriage with David was in name only," she replied, holding Father Finlay's eye with a boldness she didn't feel. "We hadn't shared a bed in years ... and ye know as well as I about all the lovers he took. He's rumored to have at least three bastards running about the streets of Stonehaven."

It took all her will not to wince at these words. She sounded so bitter—and she was, for this wasn't a lie at least.

Her union with the De Keith laird had been empty from its first days.

Even so, to admit such a thing—especially with an audience—made her flush hot with shame.

What a failure of a wife she was.

Gavina felt Draco watching her. Shoulders set, she refused to look his way. This was all too humiliating as it was; she didn't need to see the scorn in her husband-to-be's eyes.

The chaplain's gaze shadowed. He knew she spoke the truth.

"Ye and David weren't happy together, My Lady," he said after a long pause. "But that's nothing unusual. It is a cross ye must bear."

Panic surged within Gavina, a deep chill that doused her burning embarrassment. He wasn't going to soften. She had to do something.

"Please, Father." She took a step forward and sank to her knees at his feet, grasping his hands. "I implore ye … grant an unhappy woman but a short reprieve. I fear we are all doomed here. Let me die as Draco Vulcan's wife."

Tears sprang to her eyes as she spoke. They weren't feigned. She really was this desperate. She couldn't save everyone in this keep—but she could give the three centurions of a lost legion the end to a terrible curse. She could grant Maximus, Cassian, and Draco freedom to live or die as they pleased.

Staring up at the chaplain, she saw him waver. He was a pious, righteous man, but a soft-hearted one. He hated to see a woman suffer.

Guilt returned, causing Gavina to swallow. Damn this mantle of remorse that she carried around—how she wished to be rid of it. Unfortunately though, in helping her friends, she would hurt others.

"I don't understand ye, My Lady," Father Finlay eventually rasped. "If ye wed him, ye will lose yer position here."

*It doesn't matter.* Nothing mattered right now except helping her friends. Aila and Heather had both been shocked by her decision when she sought them out the evening before. But she'd managed to persuade them that this was her choice—a decision she'd made of her own free will.

"I care not about that," she murmured. "I wish only to be with the man I love."

The chaplain shook his head, his face sagging. "Very well, My Lady. I shall perform the ceremony," he muttered. "Even if I think ye are making a terrible mistake."

Gavina squeezed his hands and dropped her gaze to the flagstone floor. "Thank ye, Father."


Father Finlay wed Gavina and Draco in the doorway to the chapel, while the party of four silently looked on.

It was a brief ceremony. Gavina continued to play the role of besotted woman though. She gazed up at Draco, a smile frozen upon her lips, as the chaplain wound a length of De Keith plaid around their joined hands and muttered the words that would bind them.

Draco stared down at her, his expression shuttered. However, his hand clasped around hers was warm and strong, providing a steadying influence.

"I now pronounce ye man and wife," Father Finlay finally intoned. He then unwound the plaid ribbon.

Draco released Gavina's hand, and she thought he'd step away, now that the ceremony was done. But instead he moved closer, his hands cupping Gavina's burning cheeks.

And then, surprisingly, he leaned down and kissed her.

# XVII

## MAN AND WIFE

GAVINA'S BREATHING HITCHED, her body going rigid. She hadn't expected him to kiss her. However, it was part of the ceremony, and since they were both playing a role, he might as well take it to the limit.

Draco was a striking man with hawkish good looks. As such, she hadn't thought that anything about him would be soft.

But his lips were.

They brushed hers, as light as a moth's wings, before pressing gently.

And despite her churning belly and jangled nerves, Gavina leaned into him.

Around them, oily, choking smoke drifted across the lower bailey, but Draco smelled clean, a mixture of leather and lye soap. And as their lips pressed together, the boom and thuds of missiles hitting the curtain walls, the whoosh of catapults releasing, and the shouts and cries of men all faded. The heat of Draco's body enveloped her, even though they weren't touching. His palms, cupping her cheeks, felt oddly comforting.

A heartbeat later, he pulled back, breaking the spell.

Whoosh.

A bolus of flame flew over the walls and landed on the roof of the smithy behind them. The thatch roof exploded.

Father Finlay cried out, raising his arm to shield his eyes from the blaze, while on the steps below, Maximus and Cassian hauled their wives to safety. Draco took hold of Gavina's arm as he did the same, drawing her toward the postern door and the stairs that would take them to the upper ward.

The ceremony had come to an abrupt conclusion.

Reaching the door, Gavina turned, her gaze going to where Aila and Heather now sheltered a few feet away. It was the first time she'd looked at them properly since entering the chapel to convince Father Finlay to perform the wedding.

Both women were watching Gavina. Tears streaked Aila's face, while Heather's chin trembled.

Despite her assurances, they both worried for her.

Casting them a wobbly smile, Gavina called out to them, "Get to safety ... it's done now."

Draco drew her through the postern door then, and they hurried up the stairs. The keep shuddered, throwing Gavina against Draco. He caught her, his arm going around her waist before they continued on their way.

Gavina's heart started to race then, not just from the fire ball that had set alight the smith's forge, but from the knowledge of what lay ahead.

Of course, it wasn't all done.

Gavina and Draco's union wasn't complete until he bedded her. And despite the siege that howled around them, the bedding was going to have to take place now. There was little point in delaying it; the sooner the curse was broken, the better.

Wordlessly, they emerged from the postern stairs and crossed the upper ward. Debris littered the cobbled bailey, and chunks of burning matter still fell from the sky. It was dangerous to be outdoors.

Draco had taken her hand, holding it in a firm grip as they negotiated the bailey. But once they were inside the gallery beyond, he continued to hold her hand. Still not speaking, they made their way to Gavina's quarters: three large chambers that flanked the southern side of the keep, consisting of a dressing room, bed-chamber, and solar.

They entered the women's solar together to find it dimly lit by a glowing lump in the hearth and a single lantern on the mantelpiece. Usually at this hour, the shutters would be thrown open to let in the morning sun, but today they were bolted shut to keep out the smoke and din of battle.

But Gavina could still hear the roar of the attack, even through the thick wood and stone. The keep shuddered then, a reminder of what raged beyond these walls.

Slowing her pace as nerves danced in her belly, Gavina led Draco across the floor toward a closed door. "My bed-chamber is through here," she murmured, deliberately avoiding his gaze.

This felt all wrong, as if she were watching the scene unfold from a distance.

This wasn't happening to her, was it?

Draco continued to say nothing, which only added to her discomfort. His silence had a weight to it.

Like the women's solar, her bed-chamber was dimly lit. The room was spacious—or it had seemed so before Draco Vulcan stepped into it. He was still holding her hand, and Gavina wanted to pull away, to take a few much-needed steps back from him. Although to extricate herself from him would seem rude. Especially in light of what they were about to do.

"Gavina," he murmured finally, his voice a deep rumble in the silent chamber. "You're going to have to look at me ... sooner or later." There was a note of male amusement in his tone, rather than chastisement.

Sucking in a deep breath for courage, Gavina lifted her chin and met his eye.

"I'm sorry to put you through this," he said, his mouth lifting at the corners. "I'm not in the habit of coercing women into lying with me." Gavina found herself staring at his lips then, remembering that tender kiss before the chapel. It had been brief, and yet her reaction had been startling. On the few occasions David had kissed her, she'd never leaned into his embrace. However, Draco's next words made her raise her gaze to his. "But we won't be man and wife without it."

Gavina tried to steady her breathing. She was so nervous now she felt queasy.

*He's yer husband.*

Draco unbalanced her. The man was rude and arrogant, his manner grating, and yet he was making an attempt to go softly. His assurance, as well as his directness, steadied her. After the performance she'd put on for the chaplain, she wanted to keep this scene real. There was no need for mummery now. They both knew why they were here, and what needed to be done.

Nonetheless, it didn't stop her belly from pitching as if she were trying to row a rickety boat across a storm-swept sea.

Could she actually go through with this?

*I must ... for my friends.*

Draco released her hand then, but didn't step away. Instead, he reached up and stroked her cheek with the back of his hand. "I'm not a good man, Gavina ... but even *I* find this situation ... difficult." His voice had roughened slightly, and Gavina wondered at the cause. Could it be that he was actually nervous too?

Gavina gave a brittle laugh. "Ye mean I'm the first woman ye've been forced to wed?"

He flashed her an unexpected smile then, the expression transforming his face. "You are the first woman I've *ever* wed."

The admission made her suck in a surprised breath. "Really?"

"I've made an art of avoiding such entanglements ... until now." He paused then, his smile fading. "And I prefer my women ... willing."

Gavina tensed. She remembered then her wedding night with David. They'd been virtual strangers, but nevertheless, she'd looked forward to becoming his wife. She'd had notions of a tender scene between them in the bed-chamber. Instead, the encounter had been brief and passionless. Afterward, David had sneered at Gavina and said that bedding her was like swiving a dead flounder.

She'd never forgiven him for that.

"Can I ask what made you change your mind?" he asked, still holding her gaze. "When I spoke to you yesterday, you seemed set against wedding me."

"I thought on what ye said," she replied, "and on the fact that I'd be helping those who matter most to me." Gavina attempted a brittle smile then. "In the end, it's just marriage, isn't it?"

He inclined his head slightly, his gaze narrowing. "Just marriage?"

"Well," she said, uncomfortable now under the directness of his gaze. "I suppose we should get this over with."

He snorted. "I'm afraid you aren't helping. You sound as if you're preparing to have a boil lanced rather than be bedded."

Gavina's eyes widened. A moment later, mirth bubbled up inside her, and she laughed. The look of wounded male pride on his face settled her nerves a little. "I'm sorry," she replied. "I'm nervous. I don't know what to do, or what to say … and now I'm babbling. I really think I should pour myself some wine or something, otherwise I'll never relax."

"You don't need wine," he assured her, a lazy smile curving his lips as he stroked her cheek once more. "You just need to trust me."

Another nervous laugh escaped her. Trust him? A few days ago, she'd have snarled at him for saying such a thing. But everything was different now. "Very well … but I apologize in advance if this whole thing is … awkward."

"It doesn't need to be," he replied, his mouth lifting at the corners once more. His gaze was bright as he stared down at her. Outdoors, the boom and rumble of battle continued, but all of a sudden, Gavina's world had shrunk.

Draco Vulcan filled her senses, and the feel of his skin against hers, the tenderness of his caress, made it difficult to focus. She felt as if she were in the presence of a warlock, and he'd somehow woven a spell about her.

The man was cold and callous, and yet he was suddenly difficult to resist.

Silence stretched out between them, and Gavina was readying herself to reply to him when Draco leaned in, his mouth covering hers for another kiss.

And like the first, it was gentle, beguiling.

His lips moved across hers in light brushes, teasing her own, while his hand slid to her neck. Gently, he pulled her toward him.

Gavina went meekly. She had no choice really; this had to be done, and she'd only make a fool of herself if she resisted him.

The kiss was tender, and it made something that had been tightly coiled within her slowly unfurl.

The tension that had pulsed off her since the evening before—when she'd made the decision to go ahead with this folly—sloughed away. Her eyelids fluttered closed and, like in the chapel's doorway, she leaned into him.

Draco's lips moved across hers, a little firmer now. One hand rested on her cheek, while the other stroked her neck.

Heat flickered in the cradle of Gavina's belly. The gentleness, the reverence, of his touch surprised her. Honestly, she'd expected him to be rough. She sighed then. The tip of Draco's tongue swept along the seam of her lips, teasing her further. The heat expanded, and Gavina's pulse quickened.

She liked this.

And then, Draco swept her lips open with his tongue and kissed her deeply.

Gavina gasped at the intrusion, her body going rigid for an instant before she melted against him.

*God's teeth, this man can kiss.*

And he tasted good, both sweet and spicy. She found herself wanting more of it.

He drew her close to him then, stepping up so that their bodies lay flush for the first time. And then, as he continued to kiss her, his tongue entwining with hers, he reached up and unpinned her hair.

Aila hadn't braided it that morning. Instead, she'd coiled her mistress's pale mane up and pinned it high on her crown, with strands falling softly about her face. As such, it came free easily, cascading gently over her shoulders.

And to her surprise, Draco gave a soft groan in the back of his throat. He tossed the hair pins aside. They thudded to the rug at their feet, ignored. He then ran his hands through her hair, letting the strands slide through his fingers.

He pulled back from the kiss, and when he spoke, his voice had a strained note to it. "Hades … your hair is like spun silk."

Warmth started to pulse in Gavina's chest. His words, his voice, did something to her—something she didn't understand. She melted as she watched his face and the surprised look upon it.

"It's annoying sometimes," she breathed. "So fine that it tangles when there's the slightest breeze. That's why I wear it braided."

"You should wear it unbound all the time," he murmured. The sensual way he touched it was making her breathing quicken, yet he appeared too entranced by her hair to notice. "It's lovely."

# XVIII

## NOT A GOOD MAN

GAVINA'S EYES FLUTTERED shut. Things were getting too intense now. She felt like a field-mouse trapped in a hawk's sights. His words wrapped around her, drawing her in against her will.

And then, as her eyes remained closed, she felt a tug at the laces of her bodice. He was undressing her.

*Mother Mary give me strength.* How was she going to get through this without embarrassing herself?

He undressed her in silence. Gavina's jaw clenched as she felt the garments slip away and heard them drop to the flagstone floor. Although it wasn't cold in the bed-chamber, her naked skin prickled under his stare.

Eventually, the silence between them grew too much. He'd undressed her, but he hadn't yet touched her.

Gavina reluctantly opened her eyes.

Draco had stepped back a pace and was stripping off his vest, even as he watched her.

The heat of his gaze made her breathing hitch. The chill across her skin ebbed, and warmth bathed her. The man was, indeed, a warlock.

Draco shrugged off his vest, revealing a lean, muscular torso. A faded tattoo had been inked above his right nipple: the sign of the Eagle. Knowing who this man was, Gavina realized it was likely a mark from his old life—from when he'd been a soldier of Rome.

And then, as Gavina's gaze slid down to his leggings, her breathing hitched.

The hard length of his erection strained against the tight leather.

Gavina's knees weakened, and she slowly exhaled. She was truly out of her depth now.

Draco unlaced his leggings and pushed them down, and his shaft sprang free.

A small gasp escaped Gavina. *Holy Saint Margaret preserve me ... what am I supposed to do with that?*

Draco's beautiful mouth curved, his dark eyes gleaming. He advanced upon her then, and without realizing what she was doing, Gavina took a few steps backward.

She really wasn't ready for this.

But Draco followed her, and when Gavina's back hit cold stone, she realized there was nowhere to go.

He stopped close to her, yet still not touching. The heat of his body was like a furnace, contrasting against the ice-cold wall she leaned against.

His mouth softened then, before he raised his hand, tracing her jaw with his fingertips. "I said I wasn't a good man," he murmured. "But ... I promise I won't hurt or humiliate you."

Gavina's heart thudded against her ribs at these words. He was lying; the few times David had bedded her, she'd burned with shame afterward. How could this man be any better?

And yet, the touch of his fingers as they traced a lazy path down her jaw and neck to her collarbone sent a shiver of need through her.

*A need for what, exactly?*

He cupped a breast then, running the pad of his thumb over her nipple. Gavina's breathing caught once more, and she glanced down to see the bud had hardened at his touch.

"See," he murmured. "Your *body* trusts me."

It was betraying her, but she couldn't stop it. And when he lowered himself before her, his mouth fastening upon her traitorous nipple, a soft whimper escaped her.

His mouth was so hot.

He suckled gently at first, allowing her to lean into him, before increasing the pressure.

Gavina started to tremble. Draco really did have a druid's touch. A dull ache had started between her thighs. She couldn't believe it; she actually wanted this.

After bestowing the same treatment upon both breasts, he rose to his feet and leaned in, placing his hands either side of Gavina's shoulders, boxing her in against the wall.

His mouth slanted once more over hers. This kiss was different to the earlier one—hungrier and more demanding.

And Gavina found herself responding to it. Without even realizing what she was doing, her tongue slid against his and her teeth grazed his lower lip.

In response, Draco made a soft growl in the back of his throat. A strange thrill went through Gavina. Had she the power to elicit such a response from a man?

Boom.

A deep shudder went through the wall, rattling the jug and bowl by the bed. The impact made Gavina cling to Draco. One of Longshanks's trebuchets had found its mark upon the keep's walls this time.

Ignoring it, Draco kissed Gavina again, with an urgency that made hunger coil up within her.

The devil take her—she wanted this. She wanted him.

He slid his leg between her legs, gently parting them. And then his hand stroked a lazy path down her belly.

Gavina's breathing quickened, excitement heating her blood.

When he stroked the sensitive flesh between her thighs, she gave a soft cry. The sound was muffled by their joined mouths, but Draco responded to it nonetheless. His kiss grew sensual, his tongue sliding into her mouth as he slid a finger deep inside her.

Gavina arched back against him, her legs parting wantonly.

He stroked his finger in and out, drawing back from the kiss to gaze into her eyes as he did so. Gavina stared back at him, her breathing coming in needy gasps now.

And then, gazes locked, he withdrew his hand, lifted her against the wall, and entered her.

He slid into her with aching slowness, all the while staring deep into her eyes. Draco was a sight to behold, his face all tight, hawkish lines, his black eyes hooded with lust.

And the way he watched her as he took her unraveled the last of Gavina's restraint. Panting, she arched her hips against him, taking him deeper with each thrust.

Aching pleasure started to throb in the cradle of her hips. She felt as if she was reaching for something—although she didn't know what.

She had no idea coupling could be like this. Her body sang for him.

Boom.

The walls shook, and the shuttered window rattled from the impact. However, this time, neither of them paid it any notice. Lost in pleasure, they moved against the wall together, dancing in a rhythm of their own making.

Draco's fingers bit into the soft flesh of her hips and buttocks now as he drove her over the edge.

With a ragged cry that chorused with the roar of the assault upon Dunnottar, Gavina shattered.

Breathing hard, she came down to earth.

Still entwined against the wall, she and Draco clung together for a few moments as they recovered from the storm that had just engulfed them both.

Neither of them spoke, and Gavina pressed her face against the sweat-damp hollow of his shoulder. Her heart was galloping, and she felt as if she were floating ten feet above the ground.

No wonder Heather and Aila both wore contented looks these days.

If this was how they spent their time alone with their husbands, she was surprised they didn't have smug grins plastered permanently over their faces.

What had Draco done to her? The pleasure that had just rocked her left her gasping in the aftermath. How would she ever meet his eye again without her cheeks glowing like twin embers?

Long moments passed, and then she became aware of the chill of the stone against her back, of the cries and shouts beyond the walls and the rolling boom and thunder of the siege.

"I need to get back to the wall," Draco said finally, his breath feathering against the shell of her ear. "It sounds as if Longshanks is hitting us hard."

Gavina nodded, not trusting herself to speak.

However, when he pulled away from her, she felt an odd pang of loss. In his arms, for just a brief spell, she'd been able to forget the dire mess they were all in.

Draco's words brought it all back.

He stepped away from her then and went to retrieve his clothing.

Gavina remained there, leaning against the wall, watching him.

Draco Vulcan was a joy to gaze upon—all lean, sinewy muscle and smooth, dusky skin. Her mouth went dry as the desire to go to him, to trace those carven muscles with her fingertips, to taste his skin with her tongue swept over her.

Gavina swallowed, pushing down the carnal urge.

*Enough. It's over.* They'd consummated their union.

"Does this mean the curse is broken?" she asked finally.

Draco paused from lacing up his leggings and glanced up, his expression serious, his gaze veiled. "It should be."

"But ... can ye tell? Do ye feel any different?"

He shrugged. "Not yet ... although I'm sure I can put it to the test soon enough."

Gavina tensed. Was he going to throw himself in the path of a volley of Greek fire and see if he survived? Surveying the suddenly hard lines of his face, she wouldn't have been surprised if he planned just such a thing.

She said no more then, for his comment had cowed her. Surely, he wasn't keen to die? It was hard to believe he'd just made love to her, had just played her body like a harp.

Pulling on his boots, Draco then scooped up his vest and deftly laced it.

Still, Gavina said nothing. A chill stole over her then, goose-bumps rising on her skin. She should really reach for her own clothes, but instead she was frozen in place.

When he was dressed, Draco's gaze returned to her. "You're cold," he murmured, the harsh lines of his face softening just a little. Scooping up a blanket from the bed, he approached her before wrapping it around her shoulders.

Their gazes met fully then, for an instant, and his mouth curved. "You're a surprise, Gavina," he said softly. "An unforgettable combination of fire and ice."

Gavina stared back at him, not sure whether to be flattered or insulted by this assessment.

Draco's eyes gleamed. "David De Keith was a great fool indeed not to value you."

And with these last words, he stepped back from her, turned, and left the chamber.

# XIX

## DESPAIR

DRACO FOUND IT difficult not to break into a run as he left the keep. After what had just transpired in Gavina's bed-chamber, he felt as tightly wound as a crossbow. Coupling usually provided a release of tension, but this hadn't.

He needed to fight, to kill. He had to do something to ward off the unwelcome feelings of tenderness and protectiveness that had swept over him inside that room.

He hadn't wanted to leave her. When he'd wrapped the blanket around her shoulders and looked down into those luminous cornflower-blue eyes, an ache had risen deep his chest.

She looked so small, so fragile standing there. So alone.

He'd wanted to gather her up in his arms and kiss away her loneliness. He'd wanted to pick her up, carry her over to the bed, and spend the rest of the day making love to her.

Draco's jaw clenched.

This wouldn't do at all. He'd wed Gavina De Keith in order to break the curse, and for no other reason.

And now, he and his friends would find out if the riddle was true after all—or just a cruel game set in motion by a long dead bandruì.

Draco's belly twisted.

It had always been his fear over the years. The woman who'd cursed them had been cruel, and to make this whole thing a farce would be her final revenge upon them all.

The lower ward bailey was in chaos. Warriors and guards rushed by, carrying armloads of longbow arrows, crossbow quarrels, and stones to hurl at the attackers. And all the while, debris rained down upon them.

Just a few yards from Draco, a flying shard of slate felled one of the Wallace's men. The man sprawled, his skull cracking upon the cobbles, the quivers of arrows he'd been carrying scattering.

Draco rushed to him, but one look at the back of his head, caved in where the slate had hit him, told him the man was dead. Scooping up the quivers, Draco turned and made for the postern door that would take him up onto the walls.

He stepped out of the stairwell to see one of the guards aflame. Blood-curdling wails rang out across the wall, as the men around him dried to douse the flames with their cloaks. Water didn't work with Greek fire—it only made the inferno burn hotter. But the fire had taken hold now.

Screaming, the guard stumbled to the walls and threw himself off it.

His cries echoed through the smoky air before abruptly cutting off.

Jaw set, Draco strode along the walls to where Cassian was bellowing orders. Maximus was at his side, firing a crossbow. Despite that the weapon was heavy and cumbersome, Maximus made it look easy. As Draco looked on, his friend placed his foot in the stirrup at the front of the bow, pulling the string back to cock it. He then set a bolt in the barrel, nocked it securely into place, sighted his target on the ranks of soldiers now flooding up the defile below the castle, and fired.

Not even pausing for breath, his face set in hard lines, Maximus repeated the action. Cock, load, aim, and shoot. Cock, load, aim, and shoot.

Draco drew near to Cassian and Maximus, his attention shifting behind them to where the Wallace was overseeing a line of catapults. Wooden trebuchets had been set up along the wall, and they were firing chunks of lead, slate, iron, and stones—anything they could get their hands on to use as missiles.

A hail of arrows hit their defenses then, clattering against stone and wood shields.

Draco's gaze shifted to the cliff-top opposite, settling upon the rows of men wielding longbows there. He then spat a curse.

Edward was famous for his archers, fierce Welshmen who wielded elm longbows. They let forth further volleys, bringing down two men loading the catapults.

The English had reached the gates now, although their spears were useless against the heavy iron and oak. Instead, they had carried a large oaken battering ram up the slope, and were starting to drive it into the gates.

Even at a glance, Draco could see the battering ram wasn't heavy enough to break down the gates, especially since they'd been reinforced with iron bars.

An arrow whistled past Draco's right ear, and he ducked. It wasn't wise to be peering over the walls at present. Moving past Cassian, Draco handed out the quivers to their own archers before returning to his friends.

Cassian gave him a quick look. A shard of something had cut him across the forehead earlier in the battle, and blood streaked his face. However, the injury was no longer bleeding. "Is it done?"

Draco clenched his jaw once more. He understood Cassian's urgency, for the same desire boiled within him. But after seeing the vulnerability in Gavina's eyes when he'd left her, he wished Cassian didn't have to state things so baldly.

Gavina was his wife after all.

*Wife.* How strange it felt to be wedded, almost as if this had all happened to someone else.

Draco nodded. "If we are right about the last pieces of the riddle, then the curse should be broken."

Cassian glanced at him once more, his hazel eyes narrowing. "Let me put it to the test then."

Next to him, Maximus had just fired his crossbow. However, instead of reloading it, he swiveled to Cassian and Draco, his peat-brown gaze intense.

Draco's throat tightened. The three of them had waited so long for this. He couldn't believe the moment was finally upon them.

Without another word, Cassian drew his pugio, held out his hand, and cut himself deeply across the pad of his thumb.

Blood welled, and all three men waited.

Since they'd been cursed, none of them bled long. When they made the blood sacrifice at the Bull-slayer's altar, the wound would staunch within moments. If it didn't do that now, then they could finally leave the curse behind them.

They stood in the midst of chaos, but in that moment, a calm settled over the trio. The siege could wait. This couldn't.

Draco watched blood drip down Cassian's thumb and splatter onto the stone ledge. And then, the bleeding abruptly stopped.

Draco glanced up at Cassian's face, to see his friend was scowling. "What?"

"The wound is itching," Cassian ground out the words. "I can feel it knitting ... healing."

Next to him, Maximus cursed.

Draco sucked in a disbelieving breath. "Already?" the word gusted out of him, disappointment crushing his ribs in a vise.

Cassian nodded. "Damn that bandruì to the pits of Hades ... the curse hasn't broken."

*The curse hasn't broken.*

Draco left the keep as night cast its dark veil over the world, making his way down the narrow steps outside the curtain walls to the dungeons. Few folk within Dunnottar knew about the rope ladder, and the rowboat that waited far below.

When things worsened—and they surely would, for the *Scottorum malleus*, the Hammer of the Scots, was only warming up—two people at most would be able to flee this fortress.

Who would it be?

*Not me,* Draco thought grimly. *I intend to die here.*

However, circumstance now appeared to be working against him.

He entered the dungeons, which were empty at present. Since David De Keith's death, what few prisoners remained had been given their freedom in return for joining the ranks defending this fortress.

As such, no guards greeted Draco as he passed through the archway and entered a wide, dark tunnel. His boots whispered on damp stone, and he heard the pattering of rodents scurrying away at his approach.

He ignored the rats, heading straight for the mithraeum Cassian had created at the back of the dungeons.

The torches inside guttered, on the verge of going out. Cassian hadn't been down here all day, as he'd been busy on the walls until the English ceased their attack at dusk. Draco fetched two fresh torches from their brackets and lit them. Warm light flooded the shrine once more, illuminating the wooden effigy of Mithras himself that stood next to the stone altar.

Draco's gaze lingered on the statue a moment. He'd carved that for Cassian, many years earlier.

Approaching the altar, Draco knelt and lit a wand of incense. The pungent scent tickled his nose and caught in his throat, as it always did, yet the perfume comforted him.

Along with Cassian and Maximus, the Bull-slayer had been one constant in his life over the centuries. Heaving in a weary sigh, for his body ached from an afternoon of defending the walls, Draco drew his dagger and cut his thumb.

Blood welled, and he smeared it over the stone altar before him.

He held his breath as he did so, hoping that Cassian had been mistaken. Maybe, the curse just needed a little time to break. However, after a few moments, he felt that tell-tale itch and the bleeding stopped.

No, the curse held him in its grip as steadily as ever.

Draco's vision blurred, despair overtaking him. He was pulled back then to those years trapped under the floor of Saint Margaret's chapel. Despair had ripped him to shreds over and over again during his imprisonment, splintering his mind—but it didn't matter how greatly he suffered, he couldn't die.

"Great God Mithras," Draco finally managed to choke out the words, his voice rough. "Slayer of the Bull. Lord of the Ages. The wheel turns, and the Broom-star is again in the sky. Draw back the mists and grant three men of the lost legion peace ... at last."

# XX

# UPON THE WALL

GAVINA LOOKED DOWN at the bowl of mutton stew in front of her, before reluctantly reaching for her wooden spoon. It was a late supper. Darkness had long since fallen, but after the events of the day, her belly had closed. However, since she'd been too nervous that morning to break her fast with porridge, as she usually did, she knew she should eat.

Seated alone at the large table in the laird's solar, she felt on edge, brittle.

The day's drama hadn't ended with Draco's departure from her bed-chamber. Shortly after, Elizabeth had stormed into her solar and demanded to know if the rumors flying about the keep were indeed true.

Had she wed Draco Vulcan?

Gavina stared down at the rapidly cooling bowl of stew. Indeed, she had.

As she'd expected, Elizabeth had been livid. "I know ye want to help Heather and Aila, but this is too much!" she'd railed. "Ye can't remain laird now."

"Aye, and maybe that's for the best," Gavina had replied, too emotionally drained by events to even argue with her sister-by-marriage. "Ye'd make a better laird than me anyway."

Elizabeth's face had gone white and pinched at that proclamation. For a moment, Gavina thought she might even slap her. But, instead, the woman had muttered a curse, turned, and stormed from the solar.

They both knew the truth of it; this fortress would eventually fall. It wouldn't matter then who was laird of Dunnottar.

Gavina had spent the rest of the day alone. Mercifully, Heather and Aila hadn't sought her out. They would want to leave her be, let Gavina and Draco spend time together.

Only, he wasn't here. Gavina hadn't seen him since he'd stridden from her bed-chamber.

Of course, most newly wedded couples spent the evening together after their union. There was usually a banquet held to celebrate, and then husband and wife would retire to bed together.

Gavina pushed the spoon around the bowl of stew. But her and Draco's union had already been consummated.

They had no use for each other now.

Even so, a strange loneliness had settled over her as the day stretched on.

*This is what ye wanted,* she reminded herself, irritated by the turn of her thoughts. *Ye should be relieved he's left ye alone.*

She was, but all the same, her mind had traitorously turned to Draco all afternoon. Her breathing quickened whenever she recalled how he'd taken her against the wall.

Gavina squeezed her eyes closed. *Stop it.*

She had to stop thinking about it. Lust had taken her by surprise, yet it was a distraction, especially now with Longshanks poised to slaughter everyone in this keep.

Drawing in a ragged sigh, Gavina tightened her grip on the spoon. She wondered if the curse was now broken. If it was, wouldn't Aila come and tell her?

She hated not knowing. Draco could have returned here to give her the news at least. But none of them had.

Instead, she sat alone, in this stark, masculine space, with her supper. Despite the crackling hearth, it was oppressively silent in the laird's solar.

Gavina took a spoonful of stew and forced it down, and then another. She then cast the spoon aside, frustration exploding within her. Pushing back her chair, she rose to her feet.

Supper be damned, she wanted answers—and she was going to get them.


A misty rain was falling when Gavina stepped out of the keep and wrapped a cloak about her shoulders.

"My Lady?" A guard keeping watch at the keep doors cast her a wary look. "It's not a night to be outdoors."

"I'm looking for Draco Vulcan." she replied, brushing off his concern. "Do ye know where he is?"

The guard's wary expression deepened. Most likely, he had no idea of what had taken place in the chapel while he and the other men kept the English army at bay.

However, he'd discover it soon enough.

"Vulcan," Gavina repeated her husband's name, her gaze steady. "Where is he?"

The guard cleared his throat. "He's up on the western walls, My Lady."

With a nod of thanks, Gavina drew her cloak tighter still and set off across the lower ward bailey. Torches burned around her, hanging on chains from the walls, some of them smoking a little in the gentle rain. Their golden light reflected off the wet cobbles.

Gavina mounted the stairs to the walls and emerged to find the ramparts eerily still. The outlines of cloaked and helmeted men stood out against the glow of braziers.

Moving carefully, Gavina picked her way along the wall, stepping over chunks of rubble that littered it—the aftermath of the day's siege. Farther on, her gaze alighted on the silhouettes of trebuchets. At this hour, the wall seemed to be slumbering, ready to awake with the dawn.

Up ahead, she spied a tall figure.

Even though she couldn't see his face, Gavina knew it was Draco. There was something about the way he carried himself that made him stand apart from other men. As she approached him, her gaze settled upon his profile.

Draco stared out into the night, his expression grim. He looked like a man holding court with the grim reaper.

"Draco," she said softly, jolting him out of his reverie.

Draco turned swiftly and moved forward, looming over her. "Gavina? What are you doing up here?"

The soft light of the brazier behind them cast deep shadows over his sharp features. It made him look even more intimidating than usual. Gavina stared up at him and reminded herself that this was the man she'd wed that morning—the man she'd given her body to.

Otherwise, the fierce expression upon his face would have terrified her.

"I was looking for ye," she replied. Her voice was barely above a whisper, but it seemed to carry nonetheless. There was a brooding atmosphere upon the walls tonight. Darkness shrouded the castle, but Longshanks was ever watchful, camped on the cliffs opposite ready to strike with the rising sun.

"It's dangerous up here," he growled back. "You shouldn't come up on the walls."

Gavina's spine stiffened. Her time as Lady of Dunnottar was drawing to a close. However, tonight she still ruled this keep, and she wouldn't be spoken to like an errant child. She wasn't goose-witted—she would never have come up here in daylight while the walls were being pelted with missiles.

"I haven't seen ye since this morning," she replied, ignoring his comment. "And I wondered how things have gone." She stepped closer, lowering her voice further. "Is it broken?"

He stared down at her. This close, Draco smelled of smoke. Fatigue etched the sharply handsome lines of his face, and his eyes were hollowed. It didn't look like the face of a man who'd spent the afternoon celebrating his freedom. As such, it came as little surprise to Gavina when he shook his head.

Nonetheless, her belly clenched, disappointment arrowing through her. It wasn't for herself, but for him—and for her friends.

She'd done all she could to help them. But it hadn't been enough.

"Why?" she whispered.

"I don't know."

"But I thought—"

"We all did," he cut her off tersely. "Go back inside, Gavina … it's getting late."

Mouth flattening, Gavina took a step back from him. Aye, they were wed, but he wasn't her master.

She wouldn't be ordered around like a hound.

Instead, she turned to the west and approached the edge of the walls, her gaze sweeping over what lay beyond.

The glow of the English encampment lit up the sky, turning it a deep shade of indigo, rather than black.

Like Dunnottar, it was quiet. There were no sounds of revelry or drunken voices drifting across the steep gully that lay between the castle and the cliff-top.

Edward Longshanks wasn't celebrating his victory just yet. His men had taken Dunnottar once, but all those who lay siege to this fortress ended up cursing its defensive position, perched upon a rocky outcrop, at the top of a steep defile.

Edward would take the castle in the end, but his army would be depleted and exhausted when he did.

And so, the camp before her slumbered.

As she stood there, looking west, Gavina was aware of Draco stepping up to her shoulder. Even before this morning, she'd always been conscious of his presence. But now that they'd lain together, the awareness of him made her breathing quicken and her skin prickle.

"Maybe it's too soon," she whispered after a long pause. "Perhaps ye and I need to spend some time together before the curse will break?"

Her cheeks warmed as she said these words. She hoped he didn't think she was keen to pass days in his company—she wasn't. However, they'd taken things this far. They might as well do the whole thing properly.

"A ceremony and a bedding isn't enough?" he asked, bitterness lacing his voice.

Gavina's cheeks warmed further. She was glad the darkness hid it. "Evidently not." She turned to him then, raising her chin so that their gazes met. "When ye finish here, please come to my quarters ... I will have a bath drawn for ye."

# XXI

# A CANDLE IN THE DARKNESS

IT WAS LATE when Draco finally dragged himself from the walls. Fatigue pulled down at him, and his eyes stung. He longed to return to the barracks and sprawl out onto his narrow cot amongst his snoring chamber companions. But he'd told Gavina he'd go to her after his shift ended.

The hallways and stairwells of the keep were deserted at this hour, apart from the odd sleepy guard. Bleary-eyed, they greeted Draco with a nod as he walked by. Reaching Lady Gavina's quarters, Draco knocked on the door.

Surely, the woman would be fast asleep by now. If she didn't respond, he'd return to the barracks.

"Come in." A soft voice from within greeted him.

With a sinking heart, Draco pushed the door open and stepped inside.

Surprise filtered over him then—when he saw that an iron tub stood in the center of the solar, steam rising from the water. The lady herself sat a few feet away, wrapped up in a blanket upon a chaise longue.

Rubbing her eyes, Gavina pushed herself upright and favored him with a sleepy smile.

Draco's breathing hitched. The Great Bull-slayer strike him down—the woman was full of contradictions. One moment haughty and cold, the next soft and vulnerable. Her pale hair was unbound and tumbled messily over her shoulders. Draco's throat constricted at the sight of it, remembering how he'd tangled his fingers in those silken strands.

A strange ache welled within his chest at the memory.

Ignoring it, he cocked an eyebrow at Gavina. "The bath's still hot?"

Gavina's sleepy smile widened. "Aye … the servants kindly just filled it. I thought ye'd be finishing up about now." She rose to her feet, pulling the woolen robe she wore over her night-rail about her. "I'll leave ye to bathe."

"Please … stay," Draco found himself saying. He then caught himself. What was he doing? Best to let Gavina go to bed. After his bath, he could stretch out on that chaise longue and sleep. It looked comfortable enough.

Gavina stilled, her smile fading. "Really?"

He crossed to the tub and started to unfasten his vest. His skin itched, and smoke and dust felt ingrained in his hair and eyes. He needed this bath. As he undressed, he caught Gavina's eye once more. "You've already seen me naked, after all."

A pretty blush rose to her cheeks then, and Draco found himself smiling. Despite that she'd been a widow, and previously wed for years, the lady was charmingly innocent.

"Aye … but that was … different," she murmured, keeping her gaze firmly fixed upon his face as he stripped off the rest of his clothes.

"How so?" He stepped into the steaming water and sank into it with a sigh. Hades, how he needed this.

"I don't know … it just was," she replied weakly.

Draco huffed a laugh. "What kind of answer is that … could you pass me the soap?"

Gavina's throat bobbed, her gaze narrowing slightly. She then moved stiffly over to where the servants had left a stack of cloths and a cake of lye soap upon a nearby table. She picked up the soap and a wash cloth and moved over to the tub, holding the objects out to him.

"How did the watch go?" she asked.

"Uneventful ... the English are all sleeping tonight it seems." His mouth quirked. "Wrecking Dunnottar tires a man out."

Gavina gave an unladylike snort, settling down upon the chaise longue while Draco began to wash. He'd barely started when she spoke up once more. "Aila told me that Cassian used to have another name ... before he enlisted in the Roman army," she began, curiosity lacing her voice. "Did ye?"

Draco glanced up, surprised by the question. He then nodded. "I was born Amestan, the youngest son of a wealthy merchant in Valentia."

Gavina considered his words, a groove appearing between her finely arched brows. "It must have felt odd ... to be given a new name."

Draco shrugged. "Not really ... I've always thought Draco Vulcan had quite a ring to it."

"How old were ye when ye enlisted?"

"Twenty ... they didn't take men younger than that."

"So, ye liked being a soldier of Rome?"

He met her gaze. It felt odd to be questioned like this; Draco rarely spoke of his past. In truth, most of his old life was little more than a hazy memory. "I loved it," he admitted softly. "I wasn't interested in becoming a spice merchant like my father." He paused then, deciding that it was time they turned the conversation away from him. "Yours is a strong name. Gavina ... *White Hawk*."

Gavina's lovely mouth lifted at the corners. "It's a common enough one among the Scots. It was my grandmother's name."

"The Romans believed hawks were a bringer of both war and victory," he replied. "Birds of sharp intelligence and wisdom."

His comment roused a proper smile. "Are ye trying to flatter me, Draco?"

Draco favored her with a wicked smile in response, before holding up the soap and cloth. "Guilty as charged

... I don't suppose my White Hawk could wash my back, could she?"

Gavina huffed. She knew he was teasing her.

Draco couldn't help himself. His thoughts snapped then to an image from that morning: Gavina naked and spread-eagled against the wall, gasping as he plowed her.

Heat spiked through his groin, and his rod grew rigid under the hot water.

Moments passed, but Gavina didn't refuse his request. Instead, she moved around to his back. The water splashed as she wet the cloth and lathered it up. She then started to wash Draco's back in long, firm strokes.

A deep sigh of pleasure escaped him.

Maybe spending the night here wasn't so bad after all?

His eyes fluttered shut, and the day's worries and disappointments sloughed away. She washed his back and shoulders, and when she halted, Draco felt an unexpected pang of loss.

"My chest could do with a scrub too," he said.

A long pause followed, and then Gavina moved around to do his bidding. He watched her lather up the cloth. The steam from the bath had made her hair curl prettily around her face. Her cheeks were still flushed.

Draco's breathing stilled for a few instants. He'd noted the Lady of Dunnottar's beauty from the first moment he'd seen her, but at the time, he'd told himself that it had left him cold.

She was a vision. He found it hard to believe this woman was actually his wife.

*In name only.* He caught himself—no, that wasn't true. They'd consummated it. They were wedded.

Gavina moved in closer and began to wash his chest. They were so near now that he could see the sharp rise and fall of her breast. Her soft lips were parted slightly, and Draco inhaled the scent of roses.

His rod started to ache, a deep throb that made it difficult to concentrate. He'd found her ministrations

relaxing earlier, but now that she faced him, his whole
body tensed.

*I should be too tired for this.*

After Cassian had revealed that the curse still held
them in its sway, rage had descended upon Draco. He'd
felt duped. Many hours later, anger still simmered within
him. A trip down to the mithraeum at dusk had helped
calm him, but it wasn't until he sat in this bathtub,
watching his beautiful wife sponge down his chest, that
the day's trials finally left him.

At that moment, there was only one thing he wanted.

Raising a hand, he reached out, caught Gavina
around the neck, and gently drew her down to him. Their
mouths met, and an instant later, her lips parted for him.

The kiss was slow and deep, and by the time Draco
pulled back from her, his breathing was ragged, his pulse
beating like a hammer in his chest.

Without a word, he hauled himself up in the bath,
water streaming off him.

Gavina rose to her feet and stepped back, her blue
eyes widening as they roamed over him. He saw the way
her breathing hitched when she dropped her gaze to his
groin—when she spied the rock-hard column of his shaft
straining against his belly.

Draco stepped out of the bath, heedless of the fact
that he was still wet, and pulled Gavina hard against
him. His kiss this time was hungry, demanding. And she
responded in kind. Her body melted against him, her
arms entwining around his neck.

Frustrated by the clothing that separated them, Draco
deftly undid the tie to her robe and stripped it off. The
night-rail she wore underneath it was made of a sheer
material that appeared almost transparent in the glow of
the hearth behind her. But it was still too much.

Draco wanted her naked.

Tearing his mouth from Gavina's, he reached down,
grabbed the hem, and pulled the night-rail up over her
head. Drawing back, he let his gaze devour her, while
Gavina stared back at him. She was an achingly lovely
sight: her lips swollen from his kisses, her hair a tangled

mess. There was no timidity to her now. Her eyes had turned dark with desire, and she was breathing fast.

Firelight bathed her body. Gavina was a small woman, and before he'd seen her naked, Draco had thought her body would be as slender as a reed. Yet the woman had breathtaking curves: high plump breasts and womanly hips. He pulled her against him again, his mouth claiming hers once more, before he slid his hands down the curve of her back and cupped her buttocks.

Then, he lifted Gavina up, allowing her to wrap her legs around his waist. He carried her out of the solar, dripping water over the flagstone floor as he went, into the adjoining bed-chamber.

This time, he was going to take his wife upon a bed.

Gavina arched back against the coverlet, her eyes fluttering shut.

*God's bones ... what's he doing to me?* Draco's tongue ... his lips ... were making her melt. He was weaving that same enchantment around her as he had that morning, and she was powerless in its thrall.

And strangely, the loss of control thrilled her.

With a ragged gasp, she let go, let the pleasure he was giving her build and crest.

Trembling, she opened her eyes to see Draco rise from between her thighs. He then moved up, holding himself over her, his mouth claiming hers once more.

He kissed her with an abandon that made the same wildness explode within Gavina. She'd never felt like this—utterly unfettered.

Dunnottar was besieged. She was on the brink of losing everything, and yet at this moment, she couldn't care less if the whole world burned to cinders around her.

She just wanted this man inside her.

Draco entered her in one smooth, gliding thrust. Gavina arched her hips up to meet him. Aching pleasure rippled through her loins as he stretched her, filled her. She gasped his name, clutching at his shoulders. It was almost too much.

But Draco continued to drive into her, in deep, punishing strokes that pushed all coherent thought from her mind.

Heart pounding, Draco lay upon his back, staring up at the rafters.

The Bull-slayer be praised ... this woman turned him feral. He hadn't thought this morning's wild coupling against the wall could be bested, but the pleasure that had just consumed him had turned the world black for a moment.

Buried deep inside Gavina's tight heat, he'd lost himself.

For the first time since the cursing, he'd been completely present. No regrets. No disappointments. No bitterness. No hope.

Nothing but this bed. This woman.

And as Draco lay there, trying to recover his breath and wits, a chill stole over him.

Letting go like this was dangerous.

Gavina affected him too strongly. He needed to get a leash on himself.

He turned his head, focusing upon the beautiful woman who lay sprawled on her back next to him. Gavina's eyes were closed, her long lashes dark blonde smudges upon her cheeks. Her lips were parted, and as his attention rested upon her mouth, Draco felt hunger rise once more.

He didn't understand it. He didn't even *like* this woman.

*Liar,* a cold voice whispered to him. *You've wanted Gavina De Keith from the first moment you set eyes on her.* Indeed, it was *because* of her confident, proud manner that he found her attractive. He'd just told himself otherwise.

Draco's breathing hitched, the chill that had enveloped his body deepening. Had he really deceived himself so fully? Running a hand over his face, he attempted to net his racing thoughts.

*Enough.* He'd bedded his wife once more, in order to end the curse upon him, Maximus, and Cassian. Not because he had feelings for her. Not because this woman lit up his world like a candle in the darkness.

If she couldn't help him break the curse, he had to distance himself from her.


Gavina stretched slowly and languorously like a cat basking in the noon sun. Her body had never felt so relaxed, her limbs so loose. Twice since their wedding, Draco Vulcan had taken her—and twice he'd made her forget herself.

This time, she'd literally been rendered speechless in the aftermath. They'd lain, side-by-side upon the bed, reeling in the aftermath. The ragged rasp of their breathing had filled the bedchamber.

Shortly after, Gavina had fallen asleep.

Her exhaustion wasn't surprising. This had turned out to be the most dramatic day of her life—more of an upheaval than even her wedding to David had been.

That day had literally been the opposite to this one.

On the dawn of her first marriage, she'd been excited. Her handsome husband hadn't been particularly warm during the ceremony or the banquet that followed. However, Gavina had been unable to take her eyes off him. Unfortunately, the bedding that had ended the day destroyed her hopes for a happy marriage. In contrast, she'd dreaded lying with Draco. She'd expected the experience to be humiliating at best and traumatizing at worst.

Instead, this man had shown her what true passion was.

Eyes flickering open, Gavina stretched once more and rolled onto her side. She'd slept a while, for her senses still felt heavy as she awoke. It wasn't dawn yet though, for there was no noise outside the walls and no tell-tale light filtering through the gaps in the shutters. The last embers of fire in the hearth a few yards away still glowed, casting a faint light over the bed.

Her gaze rested upon Draco then. He'd rolled over, with his back to her. They had slept apart.

Disappointment flickered to life within Gavina. He was sleeping at the farthest edge of the bed as if to deliberately avoid touching her. She imagined that most lovers curled up together after coupling. Obviously, David never had. Whenever he'd visited the bedchamber, he'd done the deed swiftly and coldly before rising, dressing, and leaving the room as quickly as he entered.

But after the passion she and Draco had shared, Gavina was surprised, and a little hurt, that he hadn't reached for her all night.

Nonetheless, she couldn't keep her eyes off him. Her gaze traveled from his broad shoulders, down the columns of muscle either side of his spine, to his tight buttocks.

Her breathing quickened.

He really was a beautiful man—and despite that he had lived so long, his body wasn't a patchwork of scars either. There were one or two blemishes, silvered with age, but Gavina guessed these were old wounds from before his cursing. His body was that of the man he'd been on that fateful day. A moment forever frozen in time.

Tentatively, she reached out a hand and trailed her fingertips gently down his spine.

With a rumble deep in his chest, Draco stretched and slowly awoke.

A smile curved Gavina's lips. A dragon indeed.

Draco rolled over onto his back and scrubbed at his eyes with his fists. "What time is it?" he asked, his voice husky with sleep.

"It's still early," she murmured. Her fingertips itched to reach for him again. She wanted to explore the carven muscles of his chest and belly. She wanted to take his shaft in her hands and explore that too. Yet she suddenly felt oddly shy. She wasn't used to taking the initiative with men.

"I should get up," Draco murmured. "I'll be wanted on the walls."

Disappointment arrowed through Gavina. Selfishly, she'd hoped he'd stay in bed with her just a little longer.

She craved his touch. But the moments drew out, and she didn't voice her desire.

Draco rolled off the bed and padded naked through to the solar to retrieve his clothing. Lying upon the bed, Gavina heard him moving around, heard the jingle of his belt buckling as he dressed.

Presently, Draco appeared in the doorway. For a moment, he leaned against the door frame, just watching her. His expression was veiled.

Meeting his eye, Gavina screwed up the courage to speak. "Surely, we must have broken the curse by now?"

His mouth twisted. "You'd think so, wouldn't you?"

The coldness in his voice made Gavina tense. She reached for a sheet and drew it around her, shrouding her nakedness. She suddenly felt used. His words were a sharp reminder that he'd only lain with her because he was desperate to break the curse.

Lust had addled her brains. She'd nearly forgotten.

"I have to go now," he said when the silence between them lengthened. "I'd advise you to stay within the keep today, Gavina. Don't come up to the walls."

She stared back at him, treacherous tears stinging the back of her eyes, her throat too tight to speak. Silently, she nodded.

A heartbeat later, Draco turned and left.

# XXII

## AN UNLIKELY ALLY

"THE DEVIL CURSE this blasted land ... how difficult can one castle be to take?" Edward of England's rage was blistering, sweeping through the surrounding crowd of soldiers. "Are its walls unbreakable? Are its gates made of granite?"

Many of Edward's men looked down at their feet in the face of his wrath, while Hugh De Burgh, his second-in-command stood stoically before him. Nonetheless, the big man's face was pale and tense as he weathered his king's anger. "Dunnottar's never been an easy fortress to take, sire," he ventured finally. "But we'll get there in the end."

"I don't have the time or patience for this," Edward snarled, turning on his commander. "Our battering ram should have breached the gates by now—like it did last time—why hasn't it?"

"They've reinforced the gates somehow," Hugh admitted. "The steep approach makes it impossible to raise siege towers ... and so far, they've repelled all our ladders. Their archers have taken every one down."

"Then put up more," Edward bit the words out. He was trying hard to keep a leash on the fury that roared in his veins. He'd always been cursed with a terrible temper, one that had gotten him into trouble in the past. As such, he preferred to let intellect rule him.

However, after five days of laying siege to Dunnottar, he'd had enough.

They'd torn chunks off the castle's massive curtain walls and blackened its towers with fire, yet the heavy gates remained intact.

Impatience seethed within Edward, and he started to pace before the entrance to his tent. Age hadn't granted him forbearance it seemed—if anything, his advancing years made him even more restless. His chainmail clinked, his longsword's scabbard banging against his thigh with every stride. He longed to draw the blade and sink it into Wallace's neck. The outlaw had evaded him for too long, had whipped the Scots up into a patriotic frenzy.

He had to be dealt with.

Dusk was settling around them, painting the sky with ribbons of purple and gold. It was a warm evening, following a hot day. The air reeked of smoke and death. He'd seen a number of men fall on the walls, and one or two topple off it. But Dunnottar still wasn't his.

"This is taking too long," he snarled. "Stirling can't remain with just a garrison to defend it … I need to get back there."

It was true. While his focus was on Dunnottar, Lord knew what the likes of Comyn would get up to. The baron had pledged fealty to Edward, but he didn't trust him. He didn't trust any of them.

Foolishly, he'd thought they'd have breached the gates of Dunnottar by now. The castle *would* fall eventually, but he didn't have the patience to wait the bastards out.

He wanted William Wallace *now*.

"Your Highness … men approach from the north!"

The shout made Edward cease his pacing. Swiveling on his heel, he fixed Hugh De Burgh with a gimlet stare. "Scots coming to Dunnottar's aid?"

The knight's lantern jaw tensed. "We'll deal with this, sire."

Edward glared back at him, his temper still simmering. "See that you do."

"They're carrying a white banner, sire." The man who'd shouted the news now elbowed his way through the crowd toward the king. "They're here for a parley."

Edward went still at this, his frustration momentarily forgotten as he considered what it might mean. His allies were few this far north, and his son was busy keeping hold of the south-west—he wouldn't be riding to his aid.

"Well then," he said, motioning for Hugh to follow him as he turned and cut north through the crowd, his long legs eating up the ground. "Let's see what they have to say."

A heavyset man with a bald head and a short white-blond beard came forward to talk to Edward. He led a force of around one hundred men. Many of them, including their leader, wore sashes of bright green and blue.

The plaids of the clans of Scotland were many, and Edward only knew the most prominent of them—these colors and the design were new to him.

Swinging down from his horse, the leader swaggered toward Edward, chainmail jangling and leather creaking. He had a pugnacious face and bright-blue eyes that gleamed as they met Edward's gaze.

Edward watched the man approach, impressed by his arrogance. Even surrounded by his warriors, the Scot was greatly outnumbered. But either the fact had escaped him, or he didn't seem to care.

"Edward of England, I take it?" the man greeted him in French.

Edward inclined his head. He stood before this Scot in a glittering hauberk, wearing a blood-red surcoat, and with a crown atop his coifed head. He was hardly a squire and wasn't about to dignify this cur with an answer.

"And you are?" he asked after a pause.

The Scot grinned. "Shaw Irvine, clan-chief and laird of Drum Castle ... at your service."

"*My* service?" The Irvines were a neighboring clan, Edward knew that much. "You aren't here to aid your neighbors?"

Shaw Irvine's grin slipped, his gaze narrowing. "The De Keiths are no friends of mine," he replied. "Long have I waited for a chance to strike them where it hurts."

Edward cocked an eyebrow. "Are you offering to fight alongside us ... the hated English?"

Irvine snorted. "If it gets me what I want, aye."

"And what is it you want?"

Shaw Irvine gave him a sly look. "I have watched this siege unfold from a distance. Despite your numbers, you are having trouble taking Dunnottar."

Edward scowled, his temper rising. If this fool didn't answer him directly, he was going to lose his head.

"The De Keith stronghold is a challenge to take," Irvine continued, his gaze never leaving Edward's, "but I have a weapon that will smash down the gates."

"Do you?" Edward drew in a steadying breath in an attempt to manage his quickening temper. "Even if the gates have been strengthened with iron bars?"

A smirk twisted Shaw Irvine's face. Then, he nodded.

Edward clenched his jaw. These Scots really were a traitorous lot. Although Irvine hadn't yet admitted it, Edward could plainly see that this greedy laird was aching to get his hands on Dunnottar Castle. "And what is this weapon?"

Irvine flashed him another grin, before motioning to the men behind him to draw aside. A deep rumble filled the dusk air. Edward squinted in the gloaming, and then his gaze settled upon a great battering ram that slowly moved toward him. Built of wood and iron, it rolled in on a massive wagon that groaned and creaked under the sheer weight of the siege weapon.

Edward's breathing quickened at the sight of it. This battering ram dwarfed all others he'd ever seen. The ram itself—a great oaken trunk tipped in iron—swung by ropes from a wooden scaffold. Tarred hide and planks of wood created a sturdy roof that would protect the weapon and the men operating it from being bombarded from above during an attack.

Irvine was now grinning like a loon, his chest swelling with obvious pride. "This is my 'Battle Hammer' … a weapon I designed myself. It took three months to build."

"Impressive," Edward replied, careful to keep his expression neutral. "But why should I care?"

The laird's grin slipped. "Without my help, it could be another two weeks before you take Dunnottar." His voice rose as he continued. "You need my Battle Hammer."

"But I repeat, what do you get out of this?" Edward folded his arms across his chest then, staring the Scot down. Indeed, he required this siege weapon. But at the same time, he didn't trust this weasel. He wanted Shaw Irvine to spell out his terms.

"I wish to rule Dunnottar and De Keith lands," Shaw Irvine eventually admitted. His throat bobbed then, as Edward frowned. "As your steward … of course."

"*Of course,*" Edward murmured. He stared at Irvine a few moments longer, letting the man sweat. Meanwhile, he pondered what the laird had just said.

Eventually, Shaw Irvine's face grew tense, a muscle working in his bearded jaw. Perhaps it was dawning on him that he'd led his men straight into the wolf's den. The Battle Hammer wouldn't save him from Edward's wrath if he decided Irvine was no use to him.

But luckily for the laird, Edward did require his assistance. In other circumstances, he wouldn't have bothered allying himself with such a venal individual—but he was impatient for this siege to end. Scotland was wearing upon him. He just wanted Wallace dead; with the Scottish spirit crushed, he could return to London and his lovely young wife.

"I take it you know the reason I'm laying siege to Dunnottar?" Edward asked after a pause.

"Aye," Irvine replied warily, as if suspecting he was walking into a trap. "David De Keith tried to slit your throat. You are taking vengeance upon his clan ... as is your right."

"Yes," Edward answered with a harsh smile. "But I'm also here for William Wallace."

Irvine's blue eyes drew wide. His surprise was unfeigned; this really was news to him. "The Wallace is here?" His gaze cut left at where Dunnottar's bulk rose against the darkening sky.

"He is ... the De Keiths have been sheltering him for the past couple of months, it seems." Edward stepped forward then, towering over the shorter, broader Scot. "Very well, Irvine," he murmured. "Help me take Dunnottar, and you will rule as my steward. All *I* want is Wallace's head."

"Do you want to take bets on how many more days it'll be before Edward manages to take Dunnottar?" Draco broke the heavy silence at the table. "Although, at his current pace, summer will be over before he manages."

Cassian and Maximus glanced up from their cups of wine. Neither man smiled at his joke. The pair usually enjoyed a bit of dark banter, but not tonight.

The three of them sat alone at the captain's table in the guard's mess. Supper had come and gone. The men of this keep, exhausted from five days of fighting, were elsewhere—sleeping, drinking, or taking their watch on the walls. The Wallace was heading the watch tonight. Not for the first time, Draco was impressed by the man's fortitude. William Wallace wasn't immortal, but he had the strength and resilience of ten men. None of the warriors he led dared flag under his command.

"I'd rather not," Cassian mumbled, before raising the cup to his lips and taking a deep draft.

Next to him, Maximus scowled. "Neither would I," he growled. "And I don't know why you're looking so cheerful. Even if it takes Longshanks a while to scale the walls ... once he does, it's the beginning of the end." He paused there, a deep groove etching between his eyebrows. "The end for everyone inside this keep ... except us."

Draco put down the piece of wood he'd been whittling and reached for his own cup of wine. It had been another exhausting day. Abandoning the battering ram, Edward's men had tried to put up ladders against the walls. The defenders had managed to repel them—but they'd lost over a dozen men doing so.

"You could send Heather and Aila away," Draco pointed out. "There's De Keith's boat. It only takes two ... but that would be enough. You could meet up with your wives later ... after all this is over."

Cassian muttered a curse under his breath. "Don't you think we have already thought of that?" he ground out. "They both refused."

"Heather slapped me when I suggested it," Maximus added, his fingers tightening around the cup of wine he held. "Our wives are loyal, Draco. They won't abandon their parents ... or their people." His mouth twisted then. "And I wouldn't either in their place."

Draco returned to his whittling. It was the same piece of rosewood he'd started a couple of weeks ago. He'd thought the figurine was going to be a siren, a beguiling mermaid. But instead, a woman's figure with legs emerged. She had a neat, yet lush body, with long hair tumbling down her back.

Draco's throat tightened. The woman reminded him of someone.

His wife.

He'd kept his distance from Gavina over the past days. He hadn't returned to her bed since their first night together—their *only* night together. That morning, after leaving her bed as the first glimmers of dawn sparkled over the sea, he'd tested the curse once more by cutting his thumb. And as always, it healed swiftly.

Bitterness had flooded his mouth then. He'd done as the riddle commanded. If he was the Dragon and Gavina was the White Hawk, the two of them had done their part by wedding. He'd bedded her twice—that should have been enough.

But it wasn't.

"I don't understand it," Cassian growled out, reaching for the jug to refill his cup. "Why hasn't the curse broken?"

"The riddle was a ruse," Maximus replied. His voice was weary, almost as if he could barely bring himself to speak. Draco watched the Roman, his chest constricting at the despair he saw there. He'd really hoped that by wedding Gavina he'd spare both Cassian and Maximus this pain.

Cassian's features tightened. "So, the bandruì was just playing with us?"

Maximus stared back at him. "I think so."

"But I don't understand. Everything fell into place. Why tell us about the Broom-star, the fort upon the Shelving Slope, and the Hammer of the Scots ... if it's all a lie?"

Maximus didn't reply.

Draco drew in a deep breath and shrugged. The gesture belied the ache in his chest. "She was a vindictive bitch ... We should have never trusted her word. We were fools ... hopeful ones, but fools nonetheless."

His friends stared back at him, their gazes desolate. And suddenly, for the first time in a long while, Draco wished he'd tempered his words.

# XXIII

## SEEKING ANSWERS

THE WOMEN WORKED in silence. It had been a number of days since they'd gathered together like this to weave, spin, and sew. But as night had fallen and the siege had halted once more—if only for a few short hours—they'd all sought solace in familiar activities.

Gavina sat at her loom, using a wooden beater to push down weft threads she'd just woven. She was weaving the De Keith pennant now, a splash of turquoise and blue fluttering from the top of the keep.

A sense of doom settled over her as she worked. When Longshanks took this fortress, the De Keith flag would be torn down and the Plantagenet banner raised in its place.

A few feet away, Elizabeth wound wool for the tapestry onto a wooden spindle. And seated opposite each other near the gently flickering hearth, Heather and Aila both hunched over clothing they were mending: their husbands' lèines and braies that had gotten a severe beating during the siege so far.

Gavina passed the shuttle through the loom once more. She worked mindlessly, without thinking or caring, for her thoughts were elsewhere this evening.

She'd met with Cassian and the Wallace earlier in the evening, and they'd given her a full report on the day's siege. The attack grew evermore furious. Edward's archers were relentless, as were his catapults. The English were determined to get men up over the curtain wall, although the defenders had managed to repel their ladders thus far.

Dunnottar was feeling the strain. Around three hundred warriors and guards had defended the fortress when the siege began nearly a week earlier, and now just one hundred and eighty remained. The dead had been laid out in the chapel, where Father Finlay shrouded the corpses ready for burial.

Gavina's throat tightened further. The men defending Dunnottar were doing an admirable job, but they could not hold out forever.

Her attention settled upon the sisters. "Will ye both not reconsider taking the boat?" she spoke up, shattering the silence.

Heather's shoulders tensed, her narrowed gaze snapping to Gavina. "I've already made it clear to Maximus," she replied, her voice clipped, "but I thought ye understood My Lady. We will not abandon our kin. *Ever.*"

Gavina sighed. She understood that—on a rational level. But she was desperate now. She needed to be able to save at least two souls in this fortress.

Her attention swiveled to Elizabeth. Relations between the two women had been strained ever since her union with Draco. However, there had been no more talk of Gavina stepping down as laird for the moment. The situation here was too dire for politics. Gavina and Elizabeth needed to be united right now. Even so, there was reserve in Elizabeth's midnight-blue eyes as she met Gavina's gaze.

"Liz ... ye and Robbie could take the boat, Gavina tried once more. "That way, when Robert is eventually released, ye can go to him. Ye can start anew. Ye can even take back Dunnottar together."

Elizabeth stared at her. A nerve flickered on her cheek, a sign of the severe strain her sister-by-marriage was under at present. "I can't do that, Gavina," she whispered, the slight tremor in her voice betraying her. It was rare to see Elizabeth, whom Gavina had always looked up to as being the stronger of the two of them, look so broken. But she knew the reason why. The offer tempted Elizabeth, but she couldn't accept it. "I could never live with myself if I betrayed my people," she whispered. "And if Robert still lives, he wouldn't want that either."

Anger twisted Gavina's belly then, taking her by surprise. She was sick of everyone being so noble, so proud—so brave. Couldn't just one person here save themselves? If David had been alive, he'd have been the first person into that boat. "So, ye shall die by the English sword?" she demanded. "We'll all martyr ourselves?"

"*Ye* could go, My Lady," Aila said softly, speaking up for the first time. The young woman's face was pale, her smoke-grey eyes red-rimmed.

Gavina's mouth thinned. "The Lady of Dunnottar does not abandon her people, Aila," she replied. "*Or those she loves.*"

Aila stared back at her, eyes glittering with unshed tears. Her throat bobbed then. "Well then," she replied huskily. "It looks as if we'll all face the end together."

"Have ye seen Draco?" Heather spoke up then, splintering the tension.

The sound of the warrior's name fell heavily in the women's solar, and Gavina sucked in a sharp breath. "No," she replied flatly. "Not for days."

Since their wedding night, he'd stayed away. Clearly, once it became evident that the curse hadn't broken, he had no use for her. And despite that Gavina told herself she didn't care, it was difficult not to feel hurt by his behavior.

"The riddle can't be wrong," Aila spoke up once more, her voice as brittle as her face. "Everything else has been true ... this must be too."

"Not if the Dragon and the White Hawk refer to other people … or something else entirely," Heather reminded her sister. "I'd say we made a mistake. Draco and Gavina aren't part of the curse like we thought."

Another silence fell in the solar. Gavina turned once more to the tapestry, her fingers tightening around the beater she still held. The urge to throw open the window and cast the tapestry and all her weaving tools out of it surged within her.

*Useless woman's work. What does it matter now?*

"Ye don't think ye have all given up hope too soon?" Elizabeth's soft voice intruded then.

Gavina turned to her. "Too soon? Ye never wanted me to take part in all of this. Ye never believed it."

Elizabeth snorted. "Ye forget I was there in the clearing that dawn … I saw Cassian stab himself in the heart and live. I might not want to believe it, but I know my own eyes didn't lie to me." Her gaze swept around the solar, taking in the strained faces of her companions. "Ye are all letting despair get the better of ye. At this rate, gloom will take us all before Longshanks gets his hands on us."

"I don't know what ye expect us to do?" Gavina replied wearily. "None of us can work miracles, Liz."

Elizabeth drew herself up, her gaze narrowing. "I don't think ye have explored all possibilities. For one thing, ye haven't consulted anybody who knows about curses and witchcraft."

Gavina didn't answer. She merely stared at her sister-by-marriage, taken aback. When she didn't reply, Elizabeth let out a huff of frustration. "There's a wise woman, a seer, who lives in Stonehaven." She set aside her spindle, placing it on top of the basket of wool beside her. "Locals say she practices old magic. Some say she's even a witch. Ye and Draco should pay her a visit. Maybe, she has the answers ye seek."

"Ye want them to consult a *witch*?" Heather asked, her voice incredulous. Both sisters were staring at Elizabeth as if she'd lost her wits.

Elizabeth's full mouth curved into a smile. "Aye," she murmured. "After all, a witch made this curse ... maybe another can end it."

"What are those cunning bastards doing?"

Draco leaned over the walls and watched the men below the keep. They were laying down long wooden planks. They'd started at the base of the defile and were slowly making their way up the incline toward the gates. All the while, the defenders pelted them with crossbow bolts, arrows, and chunks of rock. But clad in chainmail and iron helms, protected by men shielding them from the blows with shields, the soldiers worked tirelessly.

"They're bringing in a weapon," William Wallace announced.

Draco cut a glance at their leader. The big man stood at his shoulder, a fierce scowl creasing his face. Like all of them, the Wallace was tired and dirty, although his gaze was as determined as ever. He didn't even appear to notice the weeping cut on his forehead, where an arrow had grazed him that morning. "Not a siege tower?"

"No, he'd never get something that big up the defile ... something else I'd say."

"Look." A few feet farther down the wall, Cassian pointed to the cliff-top. And as they watched, a bulky outline pushed its way through the ranks of soldiers. From this distance, it looked like a huge covered wagon. But as the object was slowly lowered down the steep slope beneath the cliff-top, Draco's breathing stilled.

It was an enormous battering ram.

The day was grey, but even so, the weapon's iron tip glinted. It was at least thrice the size of the one the English had been using previously.

"I don't believe it," Cassian hissed a moment later. "Is that Irvine plaid I see?"

Draco frowned. "Where?" His gaze scanned the crowd of soldiers upon the cliff-top, bypassing the English banners: the red and white Saint George's Cross flag and the gold and red Plantagenet lions. And there he saw them, fluttering pennants of bright green and blue.

Irvine plaid was actually quite similar to that of their neighbors, the De Keiths.

An irony really.

"Hades take us all," Maximus cursed, stepping up at Draco's shoulder. His own gaze was trained upon the bulky siege weapon, which the soldiers were having trouble keeping in check as they descended the rough slope. "Irvine's 'Battle Hammer' is actually real," he breathed.

Wallace cast him a dark look. "So, we have two 'Hammers' to deal with, do we?" he growled. "It matters not … we'll defeat them both."

Draco cast his leader a wary look. Wallace was the bravest man he'd ever met, but he was beginning to think he was also one of the most foolhardy. The arrival of the 'Battle Hammer' was ill news indeed. "Irvine has betrayed us," Draco muttered, his attention shifting back to the battering ram.

He thought then of Gavina. Although he'd been avoiding her, she often crept into his mind. How would she react when she discovered her brother wasn't just a man who broke peace agreements with his neighbors, but was also a traitor to his own people?

As if reading Draco's thoughts, Wallace growled a filthy curse and spat on the ground at his feet. "When I get my hands on Irvine, I'll rip out his guts and strangle him with them."

Draco believed him—Wallace was quite capable of it.

The arrival of the battering ram had caused a pause in the attack for the moment. However, the reprieve was a double-edged one. For it heralded the arrival of a weapon that would be their downfall.

On the walls, the men defending Dunnottar watched as the soldiers struggled with the cumbersome siege weapon. If the situation hadn't been so dire, it might have been a comical scene. The bulky wagon and the weapon it contained hadn't been designed to travel such steep, rough ground. It nearly got away from the men twice on the way down the slope, and by the time the wagon reached the bottom of the cliff, angry voices echoed up the defile.

They were arguing about what to do next.

Meanwhile, the long planks—runners that would allow the wagon to roll up to the gate—slowly inched up the slope. Soon the siege would restart.

Muttering another curse, the Wallace turned then to Draco, fixing him with a penetrating look. "Yer wife needs to see this," he growled. "Bring her up here."

# XXIV

## NOTHING AT ALL

GAVINA STARED DOWN at the battering ram that slowly rumbled up the incline. It was so big and bulky, so heavy, that a huge crowd of men had gathered behind it to push. Their grunts and curses echoed through the humid air.

Breathing fast, Gavina attempted to keep her reaction under control. She could feel the gazes of the surrounding men boring into her, challenging her. Overhead, the overcast day was oppressive, adding to the tension that rippled through her.

*Traitorous dung rat ... what have ye done?*

She already had a low opinion of her brother, but she hadn't thought he'd be the type to betray Scotland.

"What has Longshanks promised him, I wonder?" Wallace's voice intruded. Gavina tore her gaze from the siege weapon and met his eye.

"Who knows ... with my brother anything is possible."

"During yer meeting ... he didn't say anything of uniting with the English?"

Gavina raised her chin a little, aware that the nearby guards were all glaring at her.

*They think I'm part of this?*

"If he had, I'd have told ye, William," she replied.

"The lady speaks the truth," Draco's low voice intruded.

He stood a few feet away now, his handsome face as unreadable as ever. He'd found her in the infirmary earlier, helping to bandage the lacerated or burned limbs of injured warriors.

Gavina cut him a glance, her jaw tightening. The devil take him—the sight of Draco in the doorway to the infirmary had made her breathing hitch and heat ripple through the pit of her belly. Yet he'd appeared utterly unmoved, before he'd spoken, "The Wallace wants a word, Gavina."

*Gavina.* He was the only one here, besides Elizabeth, who addressed her so informally. He was her husband after all. Even so, the intimacy of it had caused Gavina's pulse to accelerate. He'd groaned her name once, on their wedding night. Just for a moment, he'd lost control—and it had thrilled her.

But, a few days later, upon the walls of Dunnottar, all sign of that man was gone. A cold stranger stood in his place.

"Maximus and I were with Lady Gavina when she met with her brother," Draco added, holding his leader's eye. "We heard all words that passed between them. He said nothing of allying himself with Longshanks."

Wallace gave a non-committal grunt and swung his gaze away from his second-in-command. He moved forward then, to the wall's edge, tracking the 'Battle Hammer's' slow progress up the slope.

"Yer brother will suffer for this," he said, his voice a low, threatening rumble. "In this life or the next ... he will pay."

A chill slithered down Gavina's spine. Wallace was intimidating at the best of times—and terrifying when riled. She wasn't about to cross him, yet she'd caught a glimpse of what it was like to be the man's enemy.

"If ye wish to be the one to take vengeance upon him, so be it," she answered honestly. Shaw had ruined things between them when she'd tried to make peace with him—this last insult burned the final bridge between them. "I no longer have a brother."

Behind them, Cassian cleared his throat. "We need to ready ourselves for the next assault, My Lady ... it's best if you get to safety."

Gavina turned, her gaze meeting Cassian's. "Thank ye, captain ... I shall." She shifted her attention to her husband then, discovering that he was watching her under lowered brows. "Draco ... can I have a word ... alone?"

Gavina led the way into the guard's mess—the nearest covered space once they'd exited from the wall.

As she'd expected, the hall was empty at this hour. Everyone was on the walls, watching her brother's siege weapon creep up the defile toward them.

*I can't believe he'd side with the English.* Gavina's belly twisted, as the full impact of her brother's betrayal hit.

Edward likely would have promised him Dunnottar, once the fortress fell. Longshanks wanted the Wallace. He didn't care what happened to the castle or the lands on which it stood.

And even though she'd been born an Irvine, fury pulsed through Gavina at the thought of this castle falling to her brother.

"What is it?" Draco asked as she stopped and turned to him. His tone was terse. "I'm needed on the wall."

"The wall can wait," Gavina replied, folding her arms across her chest. "But this conversation can't."

He stared back at her, his mouth thinning.

Undeterred, Gavina continued. "Elizabeth has come up with an idea ... one that might help us—*ye.*" When he didn't answer, she pressed on. "There's a wise woman in Stonehaven ... a woman who practices 'old magic'. Ye and I should pay her a visit."

"You want us to visit a witch?" Draco's face screwed up. Her suggestion was clearly distasteful to him.

"Aye. Today."

His mouth twisted. "And how do you suggest we do that … with Longshanks baying at our gates?"

She held his eye, even if his derision stung. "Ye forget … there's another way out of Dunnottar. David's wee boat."

His brows knitted together. "You're serious about this?"

"I am."

"This is pointless, Gavina. Don't you think we've consulted witches over the years?" A shudder rippled through him as he spoke. "None were ever able to help us."

His attitude rankled, yet Gavina persisted. She wouldn't let him get to her. "But ye probably never visited *this* witch," she pointed out. "Heather and Aila both agree it's worth a try. What have ye got to lose, Draco?"

They stared at each other for a long moment, time drawing out. And then he shrugged, his face turning to stone. "Nothing at all." His voice was flat, emotionless.

Gavina stiffened. It was hard to believe that the man before her had made love so passionately, had touched her with such tenderness.

But the tenderness had been a ruse. This was who he really was.

"I'll have to speak to Maximus and Cassian first," he said after another pause, turning away from her. "Although they're so desperate at this point, they'll try anything."


The day drew out, the shadows lengthening, when a small party ventured beyond the curtain walls and made their way down the snaking steps to the dungeons.

Maximus, Cassian, and Draco led the way, followed by Heather, Aila, and Gavina. The thunder of battle, the boom of the 'Battle Hammer' hitting the gates, shook the damp air. The sun hadn't shown its face all day—almost as if it didn't dare. An oppressive atmosphere of doom hung over Dunnottar.

Even out here, on the eastern edge of the cliffs, an ominous air held Gavina in its grip.

Reaching the entrance to the dungeons, where the stairs widened out to a ledge, the party halted.

Maximus peered over the edge, his brow furrowing. "De Keith clearly thought himself an acrobat … that's quite a climb."

Gavina's belly clenched, although next to her, Heather gave a snort. "Aye … but ye don't have a head for heights, my love."

Maximus cocked an eyebrow at his wife, yet didn't contradict her. He took a hasty step back from the edge then, and Gavina realized that Heather wasn't lying. The strained look on Maximus's face told it all. The man was so formidable—Gavina had always found the Roman a little intimidating—that this knowledge made her feel better.

She wasn't fond of heights either.

Draco stepped up beside her then, cutting her a look. "Are you sure you want to do this?" he asked. "I can go on my own."

Gavina frowned, aware that all of her companions were now watching her. She was terrified of climbing down from here, especially as the crash of the surf seemed even louder than the roar of battle at present. Would that little boat even still be intact or tied to its moorings?

"Draco's right, My Lady," Aila murmured, casting a worried look toward the edge. The rope ladder hung just below it, although Gavina wouldn't see it until she hung herself over the side. She broke into a cold sweat at the thought. "Ye don't need to go."

Gavina straightened her spine and gathered her failing courage. "I do," she replied with a shake of her head. "If Draco and I haven't broken the curse, we must find out why. The wise woman will need to see both of us."

"Dusk is around an hour away," Cassian interrupted then. "If you're going to make your move, it must be now."

"I'm ready," Draco grunted, moving toward the edge.

"Once you've concluded your business in Stonehaven, don't try returning in the dark," Cassian warned. "The surf is rough down there in all weathers ... and the rocks are perilous. Wait till dawn ... we'll be waiting for you."

Gavina swallowed, grateful for his practical advice. She then nodded, for she didn't trust her voice not to betray her. On shaky legs, she moved closer to the edge, watching as Draco lowered himself over. He paused there while his feet scrabbled for purchase.

And then he disappeared from sight.

Gavina's heart began to pound so fast she started to feel lightheaded.

*Merciful Lord, am I capable of this?*

"Your turn, My Lady." Cassian was at her side then, guiding her by the elbow. "Take hold of my hands, and I'll lower you over. Draco will be waiting on the ladder below."

# XXV

## TO THE ROCKS

THE CLIMB DOWN to the rocks was terrifying. Gavina resolutely didn't look down, concentrating instead on the rope ladder she clung to and the rock wall of the cliff-face.

If she let her gaze drop to the foaming water and the jagged rocks below, her heart would surely fail her.

As Cassian had promised, Draco was waiting for her below the ledge. Clinging to the rope with one hand, he'd taken hold of her right leg with the other, guiding her foot onto the ladder.

"Climb down slowly," he'd warned her. "The rope's slippery ... and it's a long way to fall."

*Indeed.*

Rung by rung, she made her way down the ladder, the blood roaring in her ears. The boom of the waves against the rocks below grew louder, and the damp spindrift surrounded her, rising up from the crashing surf.

They were almost there.

"Can ye see the boat?" she finally called, still not daring to look down.

"Yes ... and it appears intact."

Relief flooded through Gavina at this news.

Her feet hit stone then, and her knees almost buckled in relief.

An instant later, Draco was at her side, supporting her. "You did well." His breath feathered against her ear. "That was quite a climb."

She glanced up at him, expecting to see mockery in his gaze. However, to her surprise, she saw none.

Taking her hand, he led her over the slippery, seaweed-covered rocks to where the tiny rowboat had been wedged in, just above the tideline.

Relief filtered through Gavina when she spied two oars sitting in it. However, although made of sturdy oak, the craft was tiny—big enough to take two, and no more.

"Help me drag it out to the water," Draco instructed, grabbing hold of the prow.

Gavina hurried over to him, grateful that under her woolen cloak she'd dressed in men's braies and a lèine belted at the waist. There was no way she'd have attempted the climb down the cliff-face in her usual attire.

She too gripped the prow, her fingers digging into the wood, and together they dragged the craft down to where waves pounded the rocks.

"Getting this boat out beyond the breakwater will be … interesting," Draco observed. "You'd better get in … and hold on tight."

His words didn't reassure Gavina. She too had been wondering how such a small craft would handle the rough waves, yet she did as bid, climbing into the boat and clinging to the sides as if her life now depended upon it.

Draco shoved the boat into the waves and leaped in.

Icy water showered Gavina, soaking through her cloak immediately. She gasped, her grip tightening till her fingers ached.

Draco moved swiftly, gripping the oars and maneuvering the tiny craft through the breakwater.

She didn't speak, preferring instead to let him concentrate on keeping the rowboat upright.

Another wave of frigid seawater doused them. Gavina swallowed a cry of fear, squeezing her eyes shut. When she'd insisted on them taking this journey, she hadn't thought the boat trip would be so dangerous.

There was a reason why no laird before David had put a boat down here for escaping in.

The boat lurched and rolled, bobbing in the surf like an apple.

Gavina murmured a prayer under her breath. At this rate, they were going to capsize any moment now.

And then, all of a sudden, they were through the breakwater.

Gavina opened her eyes and twisted around to see the line of foaming waves crashing against the rocks behind them. She then turned back to Draco. Water dripped down his face, glistening despite the dull day, as he rowed them north.

Seeing her looking in his direction, he flashed her a grin. "That was exhilarating."

Choking a laugh, as hysteria bubbled up inside her, Gavina relaxed her hold on the sides of the boat. The man looked the most cheerful she'd seen him. It was rare to receive a spontaneous smile from Draco Vulcan. "For ye maybe … I was sure we were going to end up dashed against the rocks."

His mouth quirked once more, his dark gaze gleaming. "What … you didn't trust I'd get you to safety?"

"No." Gavina looked away from him, glancing behind her again at where Dunnottar loomed above, perched on the cliff-top like an eagle's eyrie. Had they really climbed down from so high? She wasn't looking forward to the return journey.

*Don't think about that,* she counseled herself. *Focus on one step at a time. Just like ye did with the ladder.*

She then turned her attention back to Draco. His lean face was taut with effort now, as he rowed with long, even strokes, taking them away from the perilous rocks and farther north.

Stonehaven didn't lie far from Dunnottar. It was a relatively short ride on horseback and so wouldn't take them long by boat either. The port village had a harbor, with a long beach stretching north of it.

They traveled north, and soon the line of low-slung, white-washed houses with thatched roofs that huddled along the seafront of Stonehaven hove into view.

"Where will ye land the boat?" Gavina asked, breaking the silence between them.

"On the beach," Draco replied, struggling to catch his breath now. "It'll attract less attention … and should be easier to launch from there later."

The light was fading—a grey day merging into an equally murky dusk. As they neared the village, Gavina inhaled the scent of smoke from cook fires, blending with the salty tang of the sea air. Most folk would likely be preparing their supper now; it was a good time to land in the village and go to the wise woman.

Farther on, the beach hove into sight, a wide pebbly crescent.

Gavina peered into the gloaming, scanning to see if anyone was about. The area appeared deserted.

Draco rowed them into the shallows, before he put down the oars, leaped overboard, and dragged the rowboat the rest of the way.

The hull of the boat hit the shingly shore with a crunch, and climbing to her feet, Gavina scrambled out onto the pebbles. She then helped Draco drag the craft properly out of the water.

Another crunch echoed through the damp air, this one louder than the last, as the pair of them pulled the boat up above the tideline.

Breathing hard, Draco straightened up, his brow furrowing. "That didn't sound good," he muttered. He circled the boat, peering at it. "Let's hope it gets us back to Dunnottar without foundering."

"I can't *see* anything wrong with it," Gavina replied, making an inspection of her own.

"Well … we'll find out soon enough," Draco replied. He stepped back from the boat, his gaze traveling south to where the smoke from chimney stacks stained the darkening sky. "Do you know where this wise woman lives?"

"In a hovel just north of the village," Gavina replied, glad that she had an answer ready for him. Elizabeth had explained how to reach the woman's house. Her sister-by-marriage had surprised her then, by revealing that she'd visited the woman when her womb failed to quicken after her marriage to Robert. Shortly after, she'd gotten with bairn.

"Let's pay her a visit then."

Leaving their boat upon the wide strand, amongst clumps of seaweed and kelp, Gavina and Draco crunched over the pebbles and rocks and headed for the green hills beyond, and the pathway leading into Stonehaven. Around them, the light faded further and the first stars twinkled above.

The wise woman's hovel was easy to find. As Elizabeth had explained, it sat apart from the other houses, ringed by a high fence made of planks of wood. Pushing open the gate, Draco led the way into an overgrown garden and up a narrow dirt path to the door.

The woman's dwelling was indeed a hovel. Unlike many of the homes of the port itself, this one wasn't made out of stone, but wattle and daub. It had a shabby sod roof. Smoke drifted lazily from the smoke-hole at the top.

"Stay a few feet behind me," Draco warned, lowering his voice. "Till we know it's safe."

Gavina complied, although she thought he was being a trifle over-cautious. She didn't think the woman they'd come to see posed any threat.

Halting before the wattle door to the cottage, Draco raised a hand and knocked on the lintel.

Tension filtered through Draco as he waited for someone to come to the door.

Just the sight of this hovel put him on edge. It reminded him of another hut, many years previous, where he'd been trussed up like a hog ready to be slaughtered. He, Maximus, and Cassian had sat in a corner, watching while a woman—coldly beautiful with pitiless eyes—cursed them.

It was ridiculous really. It was so long ago. But even so, his pulse quickened and every sense went on alert when he heard the scuff of footfalls approaching the door.

The door creaked open, and a face peeked out. The wise woman was younger than Draco had expected—no older than thirty—with a pretty face and shrewd pine-green eyes. "Aye?" she greeted them.

"Are you, Nessa?" Draco asked. "The wise woman of Stonehaven?"

The woman nodded, as her gaze raked up and down the length of him, taking in his measure. "Aye … some folk call me that." She opened the door farther, revealing a tall, curvaceous form encased in a deep-blue kirtle. Thick red-blonde hair tumbled around her shoulders. "And who might ye be?"

"Good evening, Nessa." Despite that Draco had told Gavina to stay back till he was happy with the situation, Gavina moved up to his side now. "My name is Lady Gavina … and this is my husband."

Nessa stared at her, momentarily poleaxed. "The Lady of Dunnottar?" she asked, finally finding her tongue.

"Aye."

"But ye are just recently widowed." The wise woman's gaze snapped back to Draco, curiosity suffusing her face.

"May I present Draco Vulcan. We wed just a few days ago."

Nessa's eyes went wide, her gaze flicking between the faces of the two individuals before her. A moment passed, and then she stepped back, throwing the door open to reveal a messy space and a smoking fire pit. "Ye had better come in," she murmured.

# XXVI

## SHADOW AND STARLIGHT

"OUT WITH IT then," Nessa said as she bustled across to the fire pit and lifted a cast iron pot from the fire. Draco wrinkled his nose. Turnip and onion pottage from the smell of it—they'd interrupted her supper. "What brings ye both to my door?"

She wasn't a woman to bandy words. Draco liked that. Even so, he wasn't looking forward to revealing his secret.

In general, folk didn't respond well to the story.

"I must have yer word ... nothing of what we are about to tell ye will ever be told to another living soul." Gavina spoke then, her voice surprisingly firm and calm. If she was nervous about the meeting, she wasn't showing it.

Nessa turned, a frown creasing her brow. "Ye have my word, My Lady. Nothing folk say to me ever leaves this cottage. I know how to keep secrets."

Draco drew in a deep breath. *Just as well.* Nonetheless, her assurance didn't make him dread this any less.

Gavina's gaze cut to him. "Do ye want to tell her about the curse, Draco?"

No, he didn't. Yet it was his story, and he'd known he'd have to be the one to recount it.

Nessa's pine-green eyes grew wide once more at the word 'curse'. "Please … take a seat." She motioned to two stools behind the fire pit. The wise woman then took another stool opposite, her gaze settling upon Draco. "Go on … I'm listening."

Draco began the tale. He told her how he hailed from southern Spain, how he'd been born over a millennium earlier, and how a Pictish bandruì had cursed him and two others to immortal life.

And to her credit, Nessa didn't interrupt him, didn't order him out of her hovel for spouting lies.

Instead, she continued to watch him, her face growing tauter with each passing moment. Those sharp green eyes narrowed, and a muscle worked upon her jaw, but she continued to hold her tongue.

Draco told her of the curse—of how he, Maximus, and Cassian had spent each coming of the Broom-star hoping that the curse would finally be broken. He then revealed that they'd believed he was the 'Dragon' and Gavina the 'White Hawk'.

He didn't look at Gavina while he spoke. She already knew the story, and it was hard enough to recount it. He hated reliving the memories. The words left a bitter taste upon his tongue.

And when he finally concluded his explanation, silence fell in the hovel.

Eventually, Nessa broke it. "Well." She cleared her throat then, wiping her palms upon the skirt of her kirtle. "That's quite a tale."

"It's all true," Draco growled, tensing.

Nessa met his eye, boldly and without a trace of fear. "I don't doubt ye, Draco Vulcan. Few folk would have the wits to come up with such a lie."

Draco inclined his head, respect rising within him. He'd expected her to call him the 'devil' or a 'demon'. The fact that she believed him outright shocked him.

As he'd told Gavina, he and his friends had seen a number of 'witches' over the years. Most of them had been foolish, superstitious women. A few had reacted badly to the story—and none had provided any useful advice.

This woman had responded with such a calm, intense focus that it took him aback.

"Few folk would take my words at face value," he replied softly. "Who are you, Nessa?"

Her mouth curved, even as her gaze shuttered. "That doesn't matter," she replied, her attention shifting to where Gavina sat silently next to him. "Ye aren't here for that ... instead, the pair of ye are in a right mess. Ye need answers."

"Can ye help us?" The hope in Gavina's voice made Draco glance her way. "Can ye help Draco break the curse upon him and his friends? It has been a terrible weight for them all to bear over the years." She was staring at Nessa, the veiled expression she'd worn until now lowered. She looked achingly vulnerable sitting there.

Draco's chest constricted. Why did she have to be so kind, so gracious? He'd given her nothing of himself; he certainly didn't deserve her compassion.

The wise woman's gaze flicked from Gavina to Draco, her expression softening. "I will do what I can," she murmured. "Although the curse upon ye is an ancient one ... and cast by one far more powerful than me."

Disappointment closed Draco's throat at these words, and his lips flattened. They weren't off to a promising start. Maybe he'd been right about coming here after all. Despite his initial impression, this woman wouldn't be any cleverer than the others who'd wasted their time.

Only barely holding his tongue, he watched as Nessa rose to her feet, dusted off her skirts, and picked her way across the messy, rush-strewn floor toward a bench that lay along one wall of the hovel.

The woman started murmuring to herself, bustling about, as she sorted through piles of drying herbs, clay jars, and baskets of objects. And as she worked, Draco cast a sidelong look in Gavina's direction.

She wasn't watching Nessa, but him.

In the flickering firelight, her face looked pale, her gaze worried. She didn't need to say a word; he could see the regret writ upon her face. Like him, she now feared that Nessa couldn't help them.

The wise woman spent a while collecting objects from the bench, before she placed them into a small basket and carried it back to the hearth. "I was concerned I'd lack some of the ingredients for this," she explained, her brow furrowed. "But lucky for ye, I found them. There's a Mead Moon out tonight too ... the timing for this divination is good."

Draco stared back at her, biting back a snort. Why did he have the feeling she was about to make a fool of him?

"There is one more ingredient I need," the woman continued, holding his gaze. "Fresh blood."

Draco tensed, and his alarm must have shown, for Nessa smiled. "Not yers. I've a fowl coop behind this cottage ... the birds will all be roosting. Can ye fetch me one?"

Draco let out the breath he'd been holding and glanced over at Gavina. The hopeful look on her face now pained him, and so he gave a reluctant nod, rose to his feet, and went to do the wise woman's bidding.

Returning shortly after, a brown hen in his arms, he found Nessa adding items to a small iron pot, murmuring words under her breath as she did so.

A chill feathered down Draco's spine. Once again, he was reminded of his cursing. The urge to throw the fowl at her and then sprint from this hovel surged within him. However, he'd not abandon Gavina to the witch. So, instead, he crossed the floor and handed the sleepy hen to her.

The bird died swiftly, from a deft twist of the neck, before Nessa drew a knife and cut open its breast, letting blood gush out into the pot. Then, once its feathered body had stopped twitching, Nessa put it aside. She glanced up at where Draco still stood before her and winked at him. "That's for the pot tomorrow."

Draco didn't answer. Instead, his attention went to the disgusting-looking concoction the woman was mixing.

"I need a lock of hair from ye both now," Nessa continued, wiping the fowl's blood off her hands with a cloth. "And the potion will be done."

Misgiving feathered within Draco, and he started to sweat. This really had been an ill-advised idea. He hated the thought of giving this witch power over him; he'd already spent centuries in one's thrall.

As such, he didn't move, his jaw clenching as he opened his mouth to refuse her.

"Draw yer knife, Draco … here." Gavina spoke then, lifting the end of her braid up. Their gazes fused, and the moment drew out. Gavina sensed his struggle and knew the reason for it—he could see understanding in her eyes. "All will be well," she said finally.

*Will it?*

Reluctantly, Draco choked down the refusal and drew his pugio. Moving to Gavina, he took hold of her braid, cutting off a lock of silver-blonde hair. He then reached up and sheared off a tightly cropped curl from his own head, before handing both to Nessa.

The wise woman held them upon her outstretched palm, another smile curving her full lips. "Look at that," she murmured. "Shadow and starlight."

And then she leaned forward and dropped their hair into the pot.

Nessa removed the pot from the heat, took a wooden spoon, and began to stir the mix, first to the left and then the right—and all the while, she murmured more enigmatic words under her breath, her eyes fluttering shut.

Draco dragged in a breath. It suddenly felt overly stuffy and airless inside this hovel. He was sweating heavily now, and every instinct screamed for him to run. He'd had enough of witchcraft to last a thousand lifetimes.

But he remained where he was, rooted to the spot.

Gavina wanted them to try this, and he wouldn't let her down.

Eventually, Nessa's eyes flickered open. "The potion will have cooled a little now," she announced. "It is time."

Moving from her stool, she knelt beside the fire pit and cleared away the soiled rushes, revealing the packed dirt floor beneath. And then, to Draco's disgust, she plunged her hand into the pot of blood, hair, and Hades knew what else, scooping the dark liquid into her hand. Leaning forward, she splattered it over the ground.

Draco's bile rose as he watched Nessa decorate the floor with dark swirls and splatters. He didn't look at Gavina while the wise woman worked; she'd likely be horrified by now, would likely regret ever suggesting this visit.

But it was too late. They'd given Nessa locks of their hair, and she would give them answers in return.

Sitting back on her heels, Nessa cast a sharp eye over the patterns and splashes before her. To Draco, they appeared meaningless, but to the witch they clearly held significance, for her gaze narrowed, her jaw firming while she studied the blood stains.

Time drew out. The woman was taking an age in her observations, and Draco suppressed the need to fidget. He was on edge as it was; the urge to start pacing rose within him, but he quashed it.

For once in his long life, he needed to counsel patience.

Eventually, Nessa looked up, her gaze fixing upon Draco. Her eyes were luminous, and she wore a look of sympathy upon her face. "Ye are a man with secrets, Draco" she murmured. "One who has known the depths of despair. Ye have stared into the abyss ... and barely survived."

Draco's heart started pounding.

*She knows*, he thought, panic grasping him around the throat. He hadn't told a soul about those lost years trapped in stone, but somehow this woman knew. He read it in her eyes.

He stared at the wise woman. Indeed, she was far more than she seemed. The woman had an insight and sharpness that belied her youthful appearance and carefree manner.

"Ye need to let it go, Draco," Nessa continued, her voice sharpening. "While ye carry darkness in yer heart, ye can't give yerself to a woman." Her attention flicked to Gavina before returning to Draco's face. "A marriage isn't just a promise before yer God," she said, her mouth lifting at the corners. "It's not two people living under the same roof, or sharing the same bed." She paused then, ensnaring Draco's gaze with her own. "The curse knows lies from truth. If ye want to break it, then ye must truly love yer wife."

# XXVII

## A MAN WITH SECRETS

THEY LEFT NESSA'S hovel and walked in silence back toward the beach.

Gavina glanced up and saw that a full moon now rode high in the sky—a bright disc against the pitch-black curtain of night. She noted that the moon had a slight golden hue this eve.

*A Mead Moon indeed.*

They'd been with the wise woman for longer than she realized.

A breeze feathered her cheeks as she followed Draco down the path, away from Stonehaven. It was a mild night out, but they still couldn't risk returning to Dunnottar. Approaching the cliffs was something one wanted only to do in daylight— and even then, it was perilous.

Draco and Gavina walked in silence. Ever since Nessa's proclamation, her husband hadn't uttered a word.

Gavina's thoughts turned to their last moments in the wise woman's hovel.

Draco's face had turned to stone, his dark eyes guttering. Danger had crackled in the smoky interior of that hut then. They'd all felt it, and Nessa had said no more.

But when Draco had stalked outside, Gavina turned to the wise woman. "Thank ye, Nessa."

The woman had favored Gavina with a tight smile in response, meeting her eye. "Ye have an answer to yer problem, My Lady," she'd said softly. "But it may not be an easy one to resolve … and remember that it takes two to make a marriage. I suggest ye examine yer own feelings as well."

Pondering the wise woman's words a short while later, Gavina's attention swiveled to Draco's back. Dressed in black leather, he blended in with the night: a tall, dark shape outlined by the moonlight. A man from another time.

Gavina drew in a steadying breath, in an attempt to settle the brownies that danced in her belly. She wasn't looking forward to the conversation looming on the horizon. It was clear Draco didn't want to speak to her about what Nessa had said.

But if they didn't discuss it, the curse would never be broken.

Still, she bided her time, letting him burn off some energy as he stalked over the last hill toward the beach.

*Examine yer own feelings.*

Nessa's words mocked her as she walked. How did she really feel about Draco Vulcan?

Gavina's thoughts whirled. Right now, she wasn't sure.

Reaching the wide strand, they crunched across pebbles, to where the boat awaited them on the shore, nestled into the shingle.

There wasn't anywhere else to sit, so Gavina climbed into the boat, drawing her knees up to her chest as she leaned her back against the side. It wasn't the most comfortable of seats, but it would have to do.

Draco climbed in after her, lowering himself at the opposite end of the tiny craft.

Silence drew out between them, and then Gavina cleared her throat, shattering the tense quiet. It was time to be brave. She couldn't let this lie.

"Are ye going to tell me what Nessa meant back there?" she asked softly.

"No," came his flat reply.

"Some of it I understood," she continued, ignoring the steely note in his voice. "We're not in love ... and unless we are, the curse can't be broken."

The moonlight accentuated the brutal beauty of his face, as he twisted his mouth. "So she says."

"Ye don't believe her?"

"No."

Silence fell between them once more. Once again, Gavina eventually broke it. "Well ... I do."

He gave a snort, making it clear he didn't care what she thought.

Anger quickened in Gavina's belly. She'd had about enough of his rudeness. She'd weathered too much scorn at the hands of her first husband. This union with Draco wasn't likely to last much longer—not with Longshanks and her brother battering at their gates—but while it endured, she'd continue to speak up for herself.

"She said ye are a man 'with secrets'," she pressed on. "What happened to ye, Draco? What made ye this way?"

"I don't want to talk about it," he growled. "Let this subject lie, Gavina ... it can't lead anywhere good."

"I wish I could leave it," Gavina countered, her temper fraying, "but my fate is entwined with yers now. This isn't just about ye, Maximus, and Cassian anymore. Heather, Aila, and I are all part of this too. Tell me what happened to ye!"

Draco snarled a curse, lunged to his feet, leaped from the boat—and stormed away.

Gavina watched him go, but made no move to follow.

He'd be back. And when he did return, she'd resume her questioning. Gavina's heart pounded as she waited, her belly clenching with nerves. Damn Nessa—she'd known this task would fall upon her.

And it was no easy one, for the walls that Draco Vulcan had built around him were as tough as five feet of granite. Nonetheless, she would try to break through them.

Dawn was still a few hours off, and she wasn't going to be able to sleep tonight anyway.

He did return—sooner than she'd anticipated.

Gavina knew why.

For all his arrogance and careless attitude, Draco was protective of women. She'd seen that when she'd met with her brother. He'd defended her from Shaw as he'd raised his hand to strike her.

Draco didn't like leaving her out here alone in the dark, even if the look upon his face told her he'd rather spend the night with a rabid dog for company.

He didn't climb back into the boat though; instead, he perched upon a log of driftwood a few yards back—a dark, silent presence.

The hiss of waves lapping upon the shingle and the whisper of the breeze encircled them, and Gavina gathered her courage once more. It was time for her to change tack. She needed to tackle the subject from a different angle.

"Was it a woman?" she eventually asked. Her belly tightened when she asked the question, as unexpected jealousy stirred within her. "Cassian told Aila that ye had a lover once ... who was killed in a raid. He said ye were never the same afterward."

A beat of silence followed, before Draco replied. "Cassian's got a big mouth."

"Cassian loves ye like a brother," she countered, her voice hardening. "He worries about ye ... although I sometimes wonder why he bothers, for ye are a mulish bastard."

Gavina's voice died off there, and she cursed herself. She was supposed to get answers out of the man, not insult him. He'd never open up to her now.

*Is this how lovers speak to each other?* The pair of them were supposed to be besotted with each other for the curse to break.

Gavina's throat constricted, tears prickling her eyes. *Examine yer own feelings.*

She felt knotted up inside, queasy with misery. What a mess this was. She'd done her best to help of late, but all she'd done is make things worse.

Silence drew out, and Gavina was about to apologize for insulting him when Draco spoke up. "My lover did die in a raid," he admitted, his voice rough as if he was literally forcing himself to speak. "Many years ago. Her name was Magda … and I helped slaughter the men who killed her and her kin." He paused then, letting the rumble of the surf intrude. "But that didn't make me this way. I let Max and Cass think that … because it's an easy explanation."

Gavina's breathing quickened. She leaned forward, her gaze dragging over him. Sitting there, bathed in moonlight, he appeared carved of ice. Yet the pain in his voice betrayed him.

"So, what's the real reason, Draco?" Suddenly, she wanted to go to him, wanted to sit by him on the log and take his hand in hers. Yet she sensed that wasn't the right thing to do; he needed this physical distance from her at present.

He let out a heavy sigh. "One hundred and sixty-six years ago, I fell foul of the King of Scotland's son." Draco's voice was odd, brittle, as if the wrong word would shatter him. "His name was Henry, son of King David."

Gavina didn't respond. Instead, she slowed her breathing, her fingers clasping the sides of the boat while she waited for him to continue.

"I was a guest at Edinburgh castle … and I came upon Henry forcing himself upon a lady. I intervened and made sure I humiliated him at the same time." Draco heaved in a deep breath then, as if steeling himself, before he continued. "The story should have ended there, but I worsened the situation when I became the woman's—his betrothed's—lover. I soon discovered that Henry wasn't a forgiving man … and when he tried to kill me thrice, and I survived … he discovered my secret."

Dread closed Gavina's throat. The edge to his voice now warned her she wasn't going to enjoy the story that would follow. Yet she didn't dare interrupt, didn't dare prevent the words that now flowed out of him.

"I've always enjoyed cheating death, Gavina." How bleak his voice sounded. "It doesn't matter how many times I die, I never fail to rise with the next dawn. I've been thrown off cliffs, burned at the stake, hanged, and chopped into pieces at various times over the centuries. I don't enjoy the pain of being 'killed' … but during my long life, I've experienced agony in all its facets."

Gavina winced at the brutality of his words, but Draco continued, relentless now.

"I should have stayed away from Edinburgh, but I'd grown reckless after losing Magda … and Henry and his bruised pride amused me." Draco sucked in a deep breath then before slowly releasing it. "One afternoon, he and his men finally caught me again."

The wind whistled across the beach, catching at the strands of Gavina's hair that had come free from the braid. Pushing them aside, she waited, her gaze riveted upon the man who sat a few yards distant.

"They dragged me up to the castle and took me to the chapel of Saint Margaret … which had recently been built in honor of the king's mother. There, Henry revealed a stone tomb under the floor. He buried me alive."

Gavina's breathing caught. "How long were ye there?" she asked, dreading the answer.

Draco's gaze glinted in the moonlight. "One hundred and five years."

Gavina gasped. "No?"

Draco dragged a hand down his face. "I screamed, begged, and shouted, but to no avail. I clawed and kicked at the stone till my fingers were bloody, till my bones cracked, but no one heard me … no one came to my aid."

Gavina's hand went to her throat, horror cloaking her. She couldn't even begin to imagine how awful it had been. Mother Mary, what had the poor man suffered?

And yet, he kept it all in. He'd never told a soul.

"I suffered in that tomb, Gavina," he said after a pause, his voice cracking. "Thirst takes a man before hunger does ... it was slow agony ... and I weathered it again and again."

# XXVIII

## JUST FOR ONE NIGHT

GAVINA BREATHED AN oath. Her heart thudded painfully against her ribs now. She really didn't want to hear any more of this, and yet she couldn't stop him. This memory had been poisoning him for too long.

However, Draco now fell silent anyway.

"Why haven't ye said anything to yer friends?" she asked finally. "Maximus and Cassian would never have judged ye."

He barked a harsh laugh. "They always wondered why I missed the last coming of the Broom-star, but I told them later I was too busy fighting in a clan-war to join them that year." His features tensed. "I couldn't bear to speak of it ... to relive it ... as I am doing right now."

Gavina moved then. Rising from the boat, she climbed out and crossed to him, sinking to her knees upon the pebbles before Draco and reaching for his hands. Whenever he'd touched her before, his hands had been warm—yet they were ice-cold now.

"Tell me more, Draco," she whispered. "Free yerself of it."

And so he did. Nausea churned in Gavina's belly as he spoke of the smothering darkness, his tears and despair.

"I went mad," he whispered, his voice a low rasp. "The tomb broke me … but the curse held me together … and forced me to suffer through it."

Gazing up at him, Gavina saw that his cheeks now gleamed. He was silently weeping.

Her own vision blurred then. It was a terrible thing to see such a strong man cry. She was sorry to make him relive this—but instinct told her it had to be done.

He would never be able to cast off the terrible memories otherwise.

"How did ye get free in the end?" Her voice was husky as she struggled to keep her composure.

"A priest discovered me," Draco replied, his fingers closing around hers. "He'd been swiving a maid in the castle, and was lying prostrate on the floor, begging for forgiveness from Saint Margaret. With his ear to the pavers, he heard something—the faint whisper of my screams—underneath him." Draco paused there, his mouth twisting. "Father Macum fetched himself an iron bar and pried up the flagstones, freeing me from my prison."

"He must have been shocked to find ye?"

"He was … I would've been quite a sight to behold." Draco's gaze ensnared Gavina's then. "And there you have it … my 'secret'. Nessa was right. I have stared into the abyss."

He released her and closed one of his hands into a fist, which he then pressed against his heart. "Ever since, I've been numb here … empty. The only time I feel alive is when I'm killing, or when my opponent's blade finds it mark and agony takes me."

Gavina swallowed. "What about when we lay together?" It embarrassed her to ask the question—yet she'd seen the passion on his face, felt the need in his body as he'd taken her. "Did ye feel dead inside then too?"

He stilled, his head inclining as he studied her. "I've lain with many women over the years. My body knows how to seek pleasure, even if my soul is arid."

Heat flushed across Gavina's cheeks, and she dropped her gaze. So, it hadn't meant anything to him. An ache rose in her throat.

"Gavina?" He caught her gently under her chin and raised it so that she met his eye once more. "What is it?"

"Nothing," she murmured, bitterness spiraling up within her. "I'm a fool … that's all."

"How so?"

Gavina drew in a deep breath. "I only wed ye to help my friends, Draco Vulcan … but those two times we lay together were …" She broke off there, embarrassed and wishing she were anywhere but here. He'd been open with her, had revealed his deepest, darkest secret, yet she struggled to admit this. Tensing, she forced herself to finish the sentence. "They were … special."

She lapsed into silence then, feeling foolish.

"They were," he agreed softly. Draco let go of her chin then, the back of his hand tenderly brushing her cheek. "You've been lonely, haven't you?"

A lump rose in her throat, and she nodded.

"Why?"

She tried to raise a smile, but failed. "I was brought up to do my duty … and I did my best. But in the end, I failed. My husband scorned me, and my own brother has now betrayed me. I wanted to build peace between the Irvines and the De Keiths, but from the first night of my union with David De Keith, I realized that I never would."

Draco's mouth twisted, even as his hand continued to gently stroke her cheek. His touch made Gavina tremble, as it always had. "De Keith was a prize idiot," he murmured. "Few men are fortunate enough to find a wife like you."

Gavina huffed a brittle laugh. "There's no need to try and save my feelings, Draco. Ye don't even *like* me."

He stilled at that, his gaze searching hers. "*Like* is too bland a word to describe how I feel about you," he murmured. "When we first met, you fascinated me … but I told myself that you were proud and disdainful." His mouth twisted. "A bitter man will do anything to protect himself."

His words made Gavina pause before answering. The pair of them had clashed from the beginning, but their relationship reached a low point when she'd watched Draco slay that young English soldier. Draco and his band had saved her, Elizabeth, and Aila's lives, yet the memory of how the soldier had begged for his life still haunted her. "That morning … on the hills south of Dunnottar," she began hesitantly. "Ye were unnecessarily brutal."

"I did that lad a mercy by killing him," Draco replied. He'd known exactly what she was referring to. "How do you think he'd have fared as a Scottish prisoner? Strung up by his neck on the walls … or left to rot in the dungeon until time or disease took him."

Gavina stiffened. "But ye were so cold."

His gaze seized hers, gleaming in the moonlight. "And now you know why."

Gavina stared up at him. Aye, she did.

Sighing, she sat back on her heels, her gaze sweeping around the deserted beach. It was lovely out here, surrounded by the rhythmic rumble of surf and the whispering wind.

And as the moments drew out, longing rose within Gavina. She shifted her attention back to Draco, to find him watching her. Wordlessly, she reached out, her fingers tracing his stubbled cheek. "Dawn is many hours away," she whispered, gathering her strength yet again. "We have time."

He inclined his head, his gaze boring into her.

Gavina swallowed and pressed on before her courage failed her. "Lie with me again, Draco," she whispered. "Just for one night … cast the world and all yer worries aside."

He stared at her, his breathing catching. Clearly, he hadn't expected such bold words. When he spoke, his voice was husky. "This doesn't change anything, Gavina," he murmured. "One night won't shatter the curse."

"I know," she replied, moving closer to him, her fingers exploring the chiseled line of his jaw. "But it will keep reality at bay … if only for a little while."

Gavina's pulse quickened. Nessa's words earlier had unlocked something within her. It dawned upon her then, as she stared into Draco's shadowed eyes, that she indeed felt something for him.

Something that frightened her just a little.

Draco didn't answer her. He merely held Gavina's gaze, letting her explore the hawkish lines of his face with her fingertips. She could feel the tension vibrating off him.

Emotion boiled within her—a strange kind of possession, a tenderness, that robbed her of breath. It made her want to protect him, made her want to shelter in his arms. It made her want to remain at his side no matter what fate dealt them.

Gavina's breathing caught. Was this what love felt like? Had she actually fallen for him?

Or maybe, all she wanted was to chase his demons away?

And so, slowly, acting on instinct now, Gavina leaned in, tilting her chin up so that their faces were level.

Gently, she brushed her lips against his. Leaning in once more, she kissed him again, and then she boldly touched his lips with the tip of her tongue.

With a groan low in his throat, Draco's eyes fluttered shut. And then his lips parted. The kiss deepened, and he reached out and pulled her up so that she sat astride him upon his lap. The position was intimate, although layers of cloth separated them, for Gavina was clad in men's braies.

Even so, when he grasped hold of her bottom and pulled her hard against him, she felt his hard shaft pressing against her core—evident even through their clothing.

Excitement, dark and wild, beat like a Beltaine drum in her breast. Kissing Draco, touching him, unleashed something inside her. It was hard to form a coherent

thought when they did this, hard to remember all the
things that plagued them.

The kiss deepened further, growing hungry and
demanding. Gavina curled her arms around his neck.
She loved the feeling of being seated astride him like
this, of the thunder of his heart pressed against her
chest.

Eventually though, Draco broke off their embrace.

Breathing hard, he rose to his feet and gently let
Gavina down. Her knees wobbled when her feet hit the
shingles. Her breathing came in short, needy pants.

Was this it? Would he end things here?

She couldn't bear it if he did.

But he didn't. Instead, Draco removed his cloak and
spread it down upon the pebbles beside the boat. Then,
he did the same with hers. Unspeaking, they both heeled
off their boots.

Returning to Gavina, he slowly started to peel off her
clothing.

She stood there, her fingertips aching to touch him,
but letting him undress her nonetheless. And then, when
the breeze caressed her naked skin, she reached out and
started to unlace his vest. Gavina tried to steady her
breathing, for she was starting to feel dizzy with desire,
with a need that set her blood aflame.

Moments later, he too was naked.

Then they shifted onto the makeshift bed Draco had
made upon the shingle. He drew her to him there, his
mouth slanting over hers, and kissed Gavina long and
slow, with an aching tenderness.

Gavina melted into him, her hands sliding up the
sculpted planes of his chest.

He lowered her to the ground.

The shingle—even covered by cloaks—wasn't much of
a bed, but Gavina barely noticed the pebbles digging into
her back. Her only focus was upon the man who
stretched himself out over her, who covered her body
with his.

Skin slid against skin, and the warmth of him
enveloped her.

Draco whispered something to her in a tongue she didn't understand, his hands cupping her face. He then resumed kissing her, with such leashed passion that Gavina's pulse started to thunder in her breast. Tenderness rose within her, entwining with a fierce need to possess this man, and to be possessed by him.

Their limbs tangled as they rolled together on the cloaks, the kiss drawing out. There was no need to hurry this. They had the whole night before them.

And Draco had no intention of rushing.

When Gavina was breathless from his kisses, her lips swollen, he slowly moved down her body, worshipping every curve, every hollow—with his lips, his tongue, and fingertips.

Gavina's eyelids fluttered shut, and she gave herself up to it. This was exquisite torture, and yet she didn't want him to ever stop.

Draco moved farther down her body and spread her legs so that she was fully exposed to him. Sitting back on his heels, he stared down at her, his hot gaze devouring her.

Gavina watched him under hooded lids. She ached for him. And despite the cool night air feathering across her skin, sweat now beaded across her body.

"You are so lovely," he said, his voice a rasp. "Indeed … I could forget who I am when I'm with you, Gavina."

His words made her breathing hitch, hope flickering deep in her breast. "Then make it so, Draco," she whispered. "Make us both forget."

# XXIX

## HEART AND SOUL

HE MADE LOVE to her with a tenderness that caused Gavina to weep.

Her groans filtered across the deserted beach when he slid deep into her. He then began to take her in long, slow strokes. Achingly slow. Gavina wasn't sure she could bear it.

And all the while, Draco cupped her face and trailed kisses down over her cheeks, her eyelids, her jaw—before he captured her mouth once more, his tongue mimicking the slick slide of his shaft inside her.

Gavina started to tremble, pleasure flowering across her lower belly, wet heat pulsing deep in her core. She cried out, arching up against him.

Draco drove into her now, relentless.

Gavina peaked again, pleasure thrumming through her with each thrust. She couldn't bear it, and yet she felt as if she'd die if he stopped.

She gasped things to him, heated, sultry things she'd never dare say in other circumstances. She told him how much she ached for him, how he brought her alive.

Tears streaked her face once more as she shattered around his shaft again.

Above her, Draco's face was a study in feral lust, his skin drawn tight over high cheek bones. He continued to take her in thrusts that were becoming increasingly desperate. He bucked and rocked against her, and Gavina's body turned molten. She clung to him, as if they lay in the midst of a tempest and only he could shelter her.

And when he climaxed, both their cries echoed down the empty shore.

It took Gavina a long while to come back to earth afterward. At first, neither of them spoke, the ragged sound of their breathing mingling with the rumble of the waves and the murmur of the wind.

For a while, all Gavina could do was cling to him, as she attempted to recover from the madness that had swept them both up in its clutches. With him in her arms, she could believe that this man was truly hers.

Letting out a deep sigh, Draco heaved himself up off her, onto his elbows. "Am I crushing you?" he asked, his voice husky.

"No," Gavina replied truthfully. She loved the weight of his body upon hers. He was still buried inside her, and she never wanted him to leave. Never wanted this night to end.

Still propped up on his elbows, Draco's gaze sought hers. He then favored Gavina with a lopsided smile that made her chest ache. "You were right ... I did forget."

Gavina tried to smile, although the expression was wobbly. Even now, she could feel the magic they'd spun fading away, like morning mist burning off under the first rays of sunlight. "I wish it could have been more than that," she whispered. "If only passion could break the curse."

He stared down at her, his expression suddenly vulnerable. "I don't think I'm capable of love, Gavina ... but if I were, it would be you I'd give my heart to. Only you."

The ache in Gavina's chest increased. How she longed to reveal what lay in her own heart. And yet she was still reeling from the discovery herself.

When exactly had her feelings begun to change? She wasn't entirely sure. Perhaps when they'd actually conversed for the first time, rather than verbally sparring, and she'd discovered how loyal he was to his friends. With each interaction since then, she'd become increasingly 'aware' of him. And then when they'd been together in her bed-chamber, and he'd unbound her hair and run his hands through it, she'd realized things were about to get complicated between them.

Gavina hadn't lost her heart to anyone before. However, when she stared up into Draco's proud face, into dark eyes that a woman could drown in, she knew she was lost.

Now was her chance to tell him so—and yet she held her tongue.

He'd just told her that he didn't love her; admitting her own feelings would just make things awkward, would make him feel pressured.

Love couldn't be forced.

The curse would know the difference—and so would she.

When the first glow of dawn lightened the eastern sky, they rose from the cloaks and pulled on their clothing.

After their lovemaking, they'd fallen asleep awhile, drained by the night's events. But eventually, Draco had stirred.

"It's time to go back," he'd announced softly.

Pulling on her lèine, Gavina glanced around. The shingle beach was still deserted, although the fishermen in Stonehaven would already be up and about. Indeed, it was time to leave.

Her gaze shifted south, toward the rooftops of Stonehaven. Dunnottar was just out of sight, and Longshanks would be readying himself for the next assault.

*It would be so easy never to go back*, the thought arose unbidden, and Gavina clenched her jaw. Aye, it would be. She could turn and flee, run north, and leave Dunnottar to fall.

But she never would.

She hadn't been happy with David De Keith, but when she became his wife, she'd also become part of his clan. After a while, she'd grown to love Dunnottar and its people.

She'd not abandon them to their fate.

Slinging her cloak about her shoulders, she joined Draco, and together they pushed the boat down into the water.

Gavina climbed in first, and then Draco leaped on board. Grabbing the oars, he propelled the small craft out through the rolling surf. However, once they were beyond the waves, Gavina realized there was something amiss.

Cold seawater was soaking through her boots.

She tensed, remembering the sound the hull of the rowboat had made when they'd dragged it out of the water the evening before.

"We're taking on water," she announced.

Draco, who'd been occupied till now with rowing, glanced down to see an inch or two of water in the bottom. "Damn it," he muttered. "Let's hope she holds until we get back to Dunnottar. I don't fancy a swim. The North Sea is frigid … no matter the time of year."

A chill feathered across Gavina's skin, and she swallowed. "I can't swim," she murmured.

Draco's face tensed. "Well then … another reason why we can't sink."


Although he did his best not to let Gavina see his worry, Draco tensed when he saw the boat was taking on water. The approach through the breakwater to the cliffs was perilous enough at the best of times—navigating it with a sinking boat would likely spell disaster.

Clenching his jaw, he rowed on, sweat beading on his forehead from the effort.

He couldn't let Gavina come to any harm.

His gaze strayed to her then, despite that his focus needed to be on rowing. Perched at the stern of the rowboat, her hair newly braided, she'd never looked lovelier to him.

It was difficult not to stare, not to drink her in.

Draco yanked his attention away and glanced down at his feet. The ice-cold North Sea was now creeping over his boots. Soon it would reach his ankles.

This was the last journey the wee boat would ever make.

Draco rowed on, ignoring the protesting muscles in his shoulders and upper arms as he pushed himself.

The exertion felt good. It was a distraction from his own thoughts, and from the strange ache deep within his chest.

An ache he didn't understand.

Last night would be etched on his eternal soul. No matter what came now, he'd never forget it.

Edward of England was close to taking Dunnottar, and when the 'Battle Hammer' bashed down the gates, everything would change. Gavina would be taken from him—whether by death or incarceration, he'd lose her.

The thought made Draco's gut twist.

He clenched his fingers around the oars, forcing himself to concentrate. What was wrong with him? He'd actually wept last night—when he'd told Gavina his story. He hadn't cried since his entombment, since the smothering dark had finally ripped away the last of his defenses.

Last night had been strange, a moment out of time. He certainly hadn't felt like himself.

But now, as the first rays of dawn warmed his face, reality crashed back down upon him. With a jolt, he realized that he no longer felt numb. Instead, an odd sort of grief gripped his chest.

A loud rumbling sound filled Draco's ears then, distracting him.

"We're approaching Dunnottar," Gavina informed him, for she faced the direction of travel. "Edward's resumed his attack."

Draco nodded, his fingers tightening around the oars.

And as they inched closer to the fortress, the water in the bottom deepened, rising to their ankles now and making the boat sink low in the water.

"Take off your cloak," Draco shouted over the thunder of surf pounding against the rocks. He heard the edge to his voice, betraying his worry. "This will get rough … and if you go overboard, a cloak will only drag you down."

Face pale and taut, Gavina did as bid. She then gripped onto the edge of the boat as seawater sprayed over them both.

Taking his own advice, Draco shucked off his cloak too, and then he propelled the boat into shore, catching a wave.

The roar of the sea swallowed up Gavina's cry of fright. The wave lifted them high, and suddenly the cliff walls were racing toward them. They rode the wave in, and then Draco let go of the oars, lunging for Gavina instead.

His hand clasped hers. "Jump!" he yelled. "Now!"

The wave surged onto the rocks, bringing the small wooden craft with it.

The boat splintered, and its occupants flew forward, rolling over the wet, seaweed-strewn rocks.

Freezing water surged over them, dragging them back out to sea. Draco grabbed the edge of a rock, his boots digging against the lip of another boulder, while Gavina clung to his hand.

The strength of the retreating wave pulled at them both, but he managed to drag them to safety.

They were both gasping for breath, seawater dripping off them, when they climbed up the rocks. And there, a few feet away, the rope ladder hung, awaiting them.

"I never want to get in a boat again," Gavina managed through chattering teeth. "Never!"

Draco put an arm around her shoulders. "Come on." He gently pushed her toward the ladder. "The others will be waiting for us ... let's go."

# XXX

## NOT SIMPLE AT ALL

GAVINA FUMBLED A little when she attempted to climb the ladder. The chill of the water and fright of being ejected from the boat and nearly swept out to sea had made her shaky. Gritting her teeth, she forced herself upward, her gaze trained upon the cliff wall.

*Don't look down.*

Going up was just as frightening as the descent had been. Even more so, for she wasn't looking forward to clambering over the ledge at the top.

"That's it," Draco called up. "Not much farther ... just a few more yards."

His voice steadied her. Forcing herself on, Gavina continued to climb, and a short while later, she reached the ledge.

"What now?" she called down to Draco.

In answer, he gave a shrill whistle, the sound carrying above the rumble of the surf below, the cry of gulls, and the thunder of the assault on the castle.

Glancing up, she spied a strong male hand, which had just appeared over the ledge.

"Take it!" Cassian Gaius's voice echoed down to Gavina. "I'll pull you up."

Gavina hesitated. She was reluctant to let go of the rope and grab the captain's hand. What if she pulled him off the ledge and they both fell to their deaths?

"All's well, Gavina," Draco reassured her, his voice closer now. "Take his hand ... Cassian will look after you."

His words gave her the courage she needed. Taking a deep breath, Gavina let go of the ladder with her right hand and stretched it up. Cassian's hand clasped hers, the strength of it making her catch her breath.

A moment later, she was being pulled upward, as if she weighed nothing, up and over the ledge to safety.

"My Lady!" Aila was there at Cassian's side, her hands reaching for Gavina and pulling her away from the edge.

Gavina staggered away on wobbly legs, turning to see Cassian help Draco up over the stone shelf.

A few feet away, standing before the archway to the dungeons, Maximus and Heather looked on.

"Well?" Cassian asked, facing Draco as he climbed to his feet. "Was the wise woman any help?"

Draco's face shuttered. Watching him, Gavina's breathing quickened. So much had happened over the past night. How could they possibly explain things?

"Yes, we're fine, thank you. And yes and no ... in answer to your question," Draco replied, meeting his friend's eye.

Cassian frowned. "What kind of answer is that?" he asked.

"An honest one." Draco's voice was strangely subdued, his dark eyes still wary.

"What did she say?" Heather stepped forward, her gaze seeking Gavina's. Since Draco was speaking in riddles, she clearly hoped the lady would give a clearer answer.

Gavina tensed. Suddenly, she was loath to share what had happened in Stonehaven. It seemed too personal, too raw, to talk about just yet.

But Heather's gaze was imploring, hopeful. Gavina didn't have the heart to deny her.

"In order for the curse to be broken, Draco and I must be in love," Gavina said finally.

Silence followed these words.

Heather and Aila shared a long look, whereas both Cassian and Maximus wore bemused expressions, as if Gavina had just delivered her news in another tongue and they were struggling to comprehend her.

"It's that simple?" Maximus finally asked, his tone incredulous.

Draco barked a humorless laugh. "Simple?"

Maximus's brow furrowed. "Well, isn't it?"

"No," Draco replied. He pushed past Cassian and made for the stairs, making it clear he wasn't going to discuss the issue. "It's not simple at all."

And it wasn't.

Gavina watched him go, her belly twisting.

Feeling gazes upon her, she shifted her attention back to the four people who'd relied on receiving good news from them.

"I'm sorry," she murmured. "But some things aren't as easy as they seem. Ye can compel two people to wed, but ye can't force them to fall in love."

Aila's eyes glittered with tears, while beside her, Cassian's face turned stony. "Couldn't ye love him?" Aila asked, the tremble in her voice betraying her disappointment. They'd waited all night for news, and this was it.

Gavina swallowed. Damn this constant lump in her throat. "Aye," she whispered, the admission tearing from her. "But there are two of us in this union, Aila."

"How do ye really feel about Draco?"

Heather's voice made Gavina turn from the window of her solar.

Boom. Boom. Boom.

Below them, the 'Battle Hammer' was pounding at the door, demanding entrance.

From her window, although she couldn't see what was happening on the walls, Gavina had a direct view down into the lower ward bailey. She could see the formidable barricade the men defending this fortress had erected there: wagons filled with barrels, bales of straw and hay, and heavy wooden tables from the halls. They'd emptied the keep and surrounding outbuildings of anything that would keep the battering hammer from smashing through the gates.

However, it would only delay the inevitable.

The end was coming—they all knew it.

Gavina drew in a deep breath, but didn't answer Heather immediately. After her final words to the others before the dungeons, she'd known either Heather or Aila would come looking for her to continue the conversation.

Running her gaze over her friend, Gavina noted that she was dressed for a fight, in a plain woolen kirtle, a dirk buckled around her waist. Her thick brown hair, usually worn loose, was tied back into a long braid.

She looked like a woman who was readying herself for the worst.

Gavina had dressed in her oldest, plainest kirtle, for she'd spent the morning helping Elizabeth in the infirmary. The number of injured men was steadily increasing; soon they'd run out of beds for them all. Meanwhile, the chapel was now full of corpses.

Seemingly unbothered by Gavina's lack of response, Heather walked over to the window, and together, the pair of them looked down at the gates. It was dangerous to stand here while flaming projectiles sailed over the walls. Smoke wreathed inside, but the pair paid it no mind. Instead, they watched servants scurry around in the lower ward bailey below, putting out fires and gathering up chunks of lead and rock that could be used in the defense's catapults.

Gavina wasn't going to cower behind closed shutters. When the gates were breached, she wanted to see it.

"I love him," Gavina whispered finally, her gaze still focused on the flurry of activity below. A thrill went through her at making the admission aloud, even if her pulse now raced.

"I thought as much," Heather murmured back. "The moment I set eyes on ye again today, I knew something had changed."

Gavina sighed, before she glanced at her friend, taking in her proud profile "Aye ... but not for Draco. He doesn't feel the same way."

Heather's gaze swung around to meet hers. "Do ye know that for sure?"

"Aye," Gavina replied, her voice husky now.

Heather's eyes narrowed. "Maybe ye should tell him how ye feel."

Gavina shook her head. "What good would that do? Ye think I can 'guilt' Draco into loving me?"

"No ... but maybe if ye spoke plainly, it might break down his shields."

"He'd only think I was trying to manipulate him."

Heather held her gaze squarely, her jaw tightening. "Only if he senses ye are holding back. Sometimes love requires courage ... go find Draco and tell him exactly what lies in yer heart."

Gavina's breath gusted out of her, panic punching her in the belly. She really was a coward when it came to feelings. Truthfully, after what she'd weathered in her first marriage, she was terrified of being rejected. "What ... now?"

"Who knows how long it'll be till they breach the gates ... now is as good a time as any."

Gavina glanced away, looking for excuses. "He's up on the walls. I'm not supposed to go up there during the day ... not while the castle's under attack."

"Who rules Dunnottar?" Heather asked, a flinty note in her voice. "Ye can go wherever ye wish ... My Lady."

Gavina turned back to Heather. The glint in her friend's eye made determination quicken within her. Heather was right. Time was working against them. If she wanted to speak to him—it had to be now.

"Look at that thing." Draco peered over the ramparts at the smoking roof of the 'Battle Hammer'. "It's indestructible."

"It appears so," Maximus replied from next to him. "But we both know few things in this world are."

Draco's gaze narrowed. The structure that covered the battering ram had taken a beating. However, it still protected the siege weapon, despite that they'd lobbed numerous buckets of Greek fire upon its roof. A number of men operating the weapon had died over the past two days—Irvine's men. They'd brought some of them down with arrows and quarrels, while fire had sent others tumbling from the wagon, screaming as they beat at the flames that consumed their flesh.

But more men scrambled up the defile to replace them. And the siege continued.

"They're putting up more ladders!" Cassian shouted from behind Draco and Maximus.

Draco swiveled, focusing upon the southern edge of the landward curtain wall.

Tall ladders appeared, crashing against the stone, and men clad in chainmail and iron clambered up.

Maximus spat out a curse. "Not again."

The English seemed to have an endless supply of these ladders, which were easier to repel than siege engines, but also much easier to build and raise against the walls.

Both Draco and Maximus lunged for their crossbows, grabbed quivers of bolts, and rushed down the wall, taking up position to the right of the ladders.

The Wallace was there, at the top of a ladder. His huge hands were fastened around the top rung as he tried to push it away from the wall by sheer force. But even William Wallace wasn't strong enough to get rid of the attackers so easily. There were many of them on the ladder now, their weight pushing it firmly against the wall.

To his surprise, Draco spied Donnan De Keith up on the wall this afternoon. He jostled behind the Wallace, shield in one hand, sword in the other, his face set in grim lines. The steward had been wanting to join the fight for a while, and now he finally had his chance.

Draco loaded his crossbow, cocked it, sighted his target, and fired.

The bolt hit the head of the first soldier on the ladder. He wore an iron helmet, yet the force of the blow sent him reeling backward. The man's yells filled the warm morning air as he fell.

"Excellent shot," Maximus grunted, before he too loosed a bolt from his crossbow, hitting the next man in the shoulder. The soldier shouted out in agony, but clung on, despite the bolt now protruding from his hauberk.

"They're tough these English," Cassian observed. He drew his gladius, readying himself to fight those who managed to get up on the wall.

"Aye, but they still bleed, like all mortal men," Wallace snarled. He'd given up trying to repel the ladder, and now stepped back panting as he drew his own blade—a heavy claidheamh-mòr.

Draco shared a look with Cassian then. *All men bleed, even immortal ones.*

An instant later, something whooshed by Draco's shoulder. He whirled, even as he reached for his next quarrel. On the cliff-top opposite, Edward's Welsh archers were back. The bastards formed a dark line against the green hills beyond, their tall longbows bristling like winter thickets.

Draco scowled. Of course, they would pick off those on the walls who were trying to bring the ladders down.

A cry sounded behind him, as one of the Guard took an arrow to the chest. The arrows were peppering the wall now like enraged hornets.

Maximus dove for a shield, raising it just in time as three dark-fletched arrows embedded into the wood.

Draco ignored them all. Instead of reaching for his own shield, he reloaded his crossbow, cocked it, and sighted the next man on the ladder.

*Hades take the lot of them.* Not one English soldier was getting up on this wall. He'd make sure of it.

Thud. Thud.

The Welsh archers found their next target upon the wall—and this time it was Draco. Two arrows hit his chest, throwing him off his feet.

# XXXI

## ALL MEN BLEED

THE CROSSBOW FLEW from Draco's hands, crashing against the ramparts, and he hit the debris-strewn ground.

Dazed for an instant as he lay sprawled on his back, Draco lowered his chin to see two yew arrows sticking out of the lower left of his ribcage.

Pain barreled into him in a sickening wave, the sensation so intense that he nearly blacked out.

*Mithras.* All these years and pain still took him by surprise.

*All men bleed indeed. All men feel the bite of iron too.*

"Draco!" Cassian was at his side, dragging him away from the edge of the wall.

"It's alright," Draco tried to shrug him off. "Return to the fight!"

Cassian ignored him. Instead, jaw clenched, he hauled Draco toward the stairs.

"Draco!" A woman's cry shattered the roar of battle.

A chill swept through Draco, momentarily dousing the fire that ripped up his left side.

*Gavina.*

"Lady Gavina, get down off the walls!" The Wallace bellowed down the wall. "It's a shit-storm up here!"

Gavina didn't answer the outlaw, and a moment later, Draco felt a small, cold hand clasp his. "Lord, no," came her anguished whisper.

"No need to panic," Draco rasped. "You know I can't die."

"That doesn't mean you can't suffer, clod-head," Cassian growled. He'd knelt next to Draco and was inspecting the arrows. "Damn it ... these are buried deep."

"Good Welsh arrows," Draco wheezed, shutting his eyes as another wave of sickening pain washed over him.

"Shut your mouth, and save your energy." Maximus was there too, bending over him, his soot-smeared, sweat-streaked face taut. He then glanced over at Cassian. "We need to get him off the wall."

"Aaron ... Fergus!" Cassian bellowed, motioning to two of his men. "Over here!"


Gavina hurried down the steps from the wall, following the two guards who'd hauled Draco up under the armpits and were carrying him out of harm's way. Heather brought up the rear of the small group, hurrying close behind her.

Heart pounding, Gavina's gaze rested upon Draco's back. The tips of the arrows were both protruding—a good sign at least, for they would be easier to remove. The barbed end wasn't embedded in his flesh and could be snipped off.

*He's immortal, stop yer fretting.*

She knew Draco couldn't die—and she kept telling herself that—but the sight of his injuries made her queasy nonetheless.

She'd emerged from the top of the stairs to encounter a storm of arrows showering the air. Shrinking back into the relative safety of the stairwell, she'd told Heather to stay back. But when she'd turned to the wall once more, she'd seen Cassian raise a shield—and witnessed Draco step forward and sight his crossbow.

In full view of the archers.

*Idiot.*

Just because he couldn't die didn't mean he had to throw himself to the wolves. Once he healed from his wounds, she'd give him a piece of her mind.

Outside in the lower ward bailey, the boom of the 'Battle Hammer' hitting the gates was ear-splitting. The sheer force of the siege weapon was starting to buckle the gates—iron groaned with every impact, and the massive barricade behind it shuddered.

Fear stained the air inside the stronghold now; what few servants remained outdoors to help defend the keep had strained faces and wild gazes. The women, children, and elderly had taken refuge in Dunnottar's hall.

Gavina's breathing caught, desperation clawing at her throat. How long would it be until the battering ram finally broke through? Not today, surely?

The guards took Draco to the infirmary—the long, crowded chamber next to the guard's mess, where Aila and Elizabeth, and a handful of other women, tended injured men.

Many of those with relatively minor injuries sat propped up demanding to be let back on the walls, while other men lay groaning upon narrow pallets, their faces ashen with pain. However, one or two lay worryingly still.

Aila, who'd been bandaging a warrior's burned arm, glanced up. Spying Draco, her face went taut. She then motioned to the bed behind her, where a man lay. "Put him there."

Gavina frowned. "But there's—"

"He's dead, My Lady." Aila turned to the guards holding Draco upright. "Can ye take the body to the chapel?"

Aila's practicality both impressed and cowed Gavina. Her maid was a sweet lass, gentle and kind to a fault at times. Yet when times were tough, she showed a will of steel, as she had on their flight from Stirling.

The guards handed Draco over to Heather and Gavina, and went to do Aila's bidding.

Draco slumped against Gavina, groaning as his gaze fluttered shut.

Jaw clenched, Gavina put her arms around him, struggling to keep him upright. With Aila's help, the three of them lifted him onto the pallet, rolling him on his side so that the arrows didn't pain him any more than they were already. Meanwhile, the two guards carried the dead warrior from the infirmary.

"Don't waste a bed on me," Draco ground out. "Just sit me in the corner … I'll be right tomorrow."

The women ignored him. Immortal or not, they couldn't let him suffer like this.

"We need to remove those arrows," Heather said, glancing around. "But first, we must snip the tips off."

"Here." Elizabeth retrieved a pair of blacksmith pincers, presumably taken from the ruins of the forge. "These have already come in useful."

Gavina swallowed as nausea rose within her.

However, the other women here had stronger stomachs than her. Stepping forward, face set in a determined expression, Heather snipped off the arrow tips.

The jolt of it hurt Draco, waking him from the strange daze he'd fallen into.

He gave a pained grunt, his long body going rigid.

Heather's gaze met Gavina's then. "Ye are going to have to pull out the arrows, My Lady. Aila and I will hold him while ye do it."

Gavina started to sweat. She'd been helping on and off in the infirmary over the past days, dressing and tending wounds. But she'd left the harsher treatments to the other women.

"Don't mess around, Gavina," Draco instructed through gritted teeth. "Grab the arrow and yank it."

"He's right," Elizabeth added. "The slower ye go, the more it hurts."

"I'll try to remember that," Gavina replied, the tremble in her voice betraying her nervousness. Placing a knee upon the pallet to brace herself, she grabbed hold of the shaft. She then heaved in a deep breath and yanked.

Draco's hoarse shout of pain echoed through the infirmary.

Heart hammering in her ears, bile stinging in her throat, Gavina grabbed the second shaft and yanked it free.

Blood poured out of the wounds.

Elizabeth murmured an oath and rushed forward, placing a roll of cloth hard up against his back. "I need more bandages for the front of his chest," she called out.

Aila rushed to fetch additional strips of linen, handing them to Gavina, who shoved them against the twin arrow holes, staunching the heavy flow of blood.

Draco's eyelids fluttered as he struggled to remain conscious. His coppery skin had gained a worrying pallor.

Gavina tensed. For an immortal, he appeared in a bad state.

She glanced up, meeting Elizabeth's eye. From the look on her sister-by-marriage's face, Elizabeth was thinking the same thing.

"It looks bad," Heather spoke up then. "But if it's any consolation, I've seen Maximus in a worse condition."

Gavina wet her lips. Heather was right. She remembered Cassian leaning against that ancient oak, the knife blade embedded in his heart. Aye, she'd seen how these men could suffer and then be reborn. Even so, Draco was doing a convincing job of looking like a dying man.

"Come on," Elizabeth said, straightening up and reaching for the fresh bandages that Aila now passed her. "Help me wrap his wounds."

"We have to bring that 'Battle Hammer' down," Cassian announced, his expression grimmer than Maximus had ever seen it. "If we don't, it'll breach the gates before nightfall."

A chill settled in the pit of Maximus's gut at his friend's words. "You're right. We need to focus our attention on the battering ram," he replied, reloading his crossbow. "And if the bastards would just stop putting up ladders, we could."

"Let me deal with them!" William Wallace bellowed from farther down the wall. He and Donnan De Keith now wielded iron-tipped spears, which they were using to stab at the English soldiers who tried to scale the top of the wall. Just one ladder remained now, but it had so many men climbing it that it was proving difficult to budge.

Jaw clenched, Maximus favored his leader with a nod, fired his crossbow into the surging mass of helmeted heads below, and ducked as another volley of arrows whistled overhead.

He then turned to the two lads behind him. "How much pitch do we have left?"

"Just one pot," one of the youths panted. His face was red and sweaty, his eyes glassy with fear. He was one of the stable hands. By rights, the lad was too young to be up here—but they needed all the help they could get to bring missiles and weapons up to the wall.

"Is it still hot?"

"Aye." The lad motioned to where an iron cauldron smoked at the northern edge of the wall. The cauldron had been strategically positioned there, just in case the English tried to put up ladders at that end of the wall.

"We have to move it down, so that it's directly above the gates," Maximus instructed. "Come on!"

Ignoring Cassian's surprised glance, Maximus crouched down and followed the two lads to the cauldron. This part of the wall was exposed, and more than once he felt the draft of something flying past his head.

When he reached the cauldron, Maximus's eyes started to water. Acrid smoke wafted over him, catching in his throat. Choking down coughs, he joined the lads as they heaved the pot and its iron scaffold off its bed of glowing coals, and proceeded to push it over the rough stone.

It was hard work, harder than it looked, for the top of the wall was now littered with the bodies of the fallen and debris. The iron was too hot to touch with their hands—as such, they had to use their forearms and shoulders to move the cauldron. By the time they'd gone merely a couple of yards, sweat poured off Maximus.

"Need help?" Cassian appeared at his side then, and together, the four of them inched the cumbersome cauldron into position.

Boom. Boom. Boom.

The 'Battle Hammer' drove into the gates, causing the wall to shudder with each impact. The screech of iron followed each blow.

*We have to stop it.*

Maximus collapsed behind the cauldron, next to Cassian and the two gasping lads. They were all utterly spent, their faces crimson from effort, sweat streaming off their brows.

"Fetch torches," Maximus ordered the lads, his voice raspy with effort. "And two pairs of smith's gloves. Quickly now."

With nods, the boys scrambled away.

Breathing hard, Cassian crouched next to Maximus. They were currently protected from arrows by the bulk of the pot of smoking pitch, although for their next move the pair of them would be dangerously exposed.

"You think this will work?" Cassian asked, blinking sweat out of his eyes.

"It had better," Maximus grunted. "We're out of Greek fire ... so this is our best hope of sending that battering ram to Hades."

The two men fell silent then, conserving their energy and waiting for the lads to reappear. Maximus's eyes continued to water, and he blinked rapidly.

Cries and shouts filtered over the walls. Maximus didn't just breathe in smoke, but also the tang of fear and desperation. The men who defended Dunnottar were stalwart and brave, yet they'd started to flag under the onslaught, as one by one, the warriors around them fell. It was hard to cling to hope when you watched your friends die. After dusk each day, the castle mourned its dead, but with the rising of the sun, the fighting drove sorrow from their minds.

Maximus frowned, remembering the agony on Draco's face as he'd been carried off the walls earlier. It was just as well the curse hadn't broken—for those arrows looked as if they'd pierced something vital.

A roar went up at the southern end of the wall then. Next to Maximus, Cassian muttered an oath. Following his friend's gaze, Maximus saw that the Wallace had abandoned his spear and blade, and was now fighting the English bare-handed. Beside him, Donnan De Keith did the same.

Red-faced, their eyes wild with fury, the Scots fought savagely, pummeling the faces of two English soldiers who attempted to scale the top of the wall.

And then, as they watched, Wallace and Donnan sent the attackers tumbling backward.

A heartbeat later, the two of them grabbed the top of the ladder and threw their full weights against it.

Maximus's breath caught as he watched the ladder rear back from the wall.

For an instant, it hung there, perpendicular, and then it toppled backward. The men clinging to it let out a collective wail, the sound echoing along the wall—before the ladder collapsed into the defile.

# XXXII

## IN FLAMES

A THRILL PULSED through Maximus. It had to be now, while the men swarming below were distracted. He caught sight of the lads returning then, each carrying a blazing torch and a pair of thick leather gloves. It was hard to run the gauntlet of Welsh archers, keeping as low as possible, while wielding a torch, but the boys managed it.

Maximus favored them with a tight smile. He handed Cassian a pair of gloves and put on his own, before relieving the boys of the torches. "Well done," he grunted. "Keep back now … we'll take it from here."

The lads nodded, their eyes as wide as moons now. Without another word, they both scurried away, leaving Maximus and Cassian with the torches, gloves, and the pot of hot pitch.

Maximus swiveled round, his gaze meeting Cassian's. "Ready?"

Cassian flashed him a feral grin. "Let's rid ourselves of this cursed 'Battle Hammer'."

Maximus nodded, his fingers clenching around the torches while he readied himself to rise to his feet.

Once he did, he would be exposed.

The archers had noted movement above the gates, and so had focused their attention upon the area. Arrows clattered off the surrounding stone and clanged against the iron cauldron.

Maximus swallowed. Having seen Draco brought down by the archers, he was in no hurry to follow him.

However, this had to be done.

Gritting his teeth, he lunged to his feet and rose over the cauldron, lowering the flaming ends to the smoking pitch.

*Ignite, damn you.*

An arrow whistled past his left ear, so close he flinched.

Whoosh.

The pitch burst into flames.

Maximus reeled back, and then Cassian grabbed hold of him, hauling him to safety.

Together the two of them crouched behind the cauldron. A flaming pot of pitch atop the gates would attract attention. They had to act quickly or those below would draw back to avoid being doused.

"Now!" Maximus bellowed.

Together they reached out with their gloved hands and swung the pot hard against the wall. It wavered precariously on its iron frame, but held.

Maximus positioned himself as near to the base as he could, his gloved fingers gripping against the rough iron.

*Mithras, it's heavy.*

Without the aid of the scaffold on which the pot hung, he and Cassian would never have been able to lift it. Leveraging the pot against the ramparts, they shoved hard, their grunts of effort mingling with shouts of alarm from below.

But it was too late.

The pot lurched and then up-ended, spilling its fiery and liquid contents over the wall.

Screams followed, terrible cries that made a man's blood run cold. Yet, lying on his side next to Cassian under the lee of the ramparts, Maximus was too intent on recovering his breath to even notice them. His arms and shoulders burned from the effort it had taken to get that pot over the edge.

The screaming continued.

Dragging himself up, Maximus was greeted by a column of dark smoke. Shielded from the archers for the time-being, he dared lean against the ramparts, his gaze dropping to the 'Battle Hammer' directly below.

Next to him, Cassian muttered another oath.

It was chaos down there. The structure housing the battering ram was in flames, as was the wagon. Men ran around, beating at the flames upon their bodies, while others fell as the fire consumed them.

And as Maximus and Cassian watched, Shaw Irvine's 'Battle Hammer' went up like a beacon, flames roaring high.

Breathing hard, Maximus shot Cassian a victory grin. "I wish Draco could see this."


Gavina didn't leave the infirmary; she didn't leave Draco's side. Around her, she was vaguely aware of Elizabeth, Aila, and the other women moving about the space. And all the while, the boom and shudder of the Battle Hammer's assault rang in her ears.

Gavina waited for the crash of the gates giving way, and the shouts warning that the castle had been breached.

But none came.

And then, the keep went strangely quiet.

Shortly after, a lad rushed into the infirmary, face flushed. "The 'Battle Hammer' is in flames!" he gasped.

Glancing up from where she'd been sponging Draco's fevered brow, Gavina took in the smiling faces of those around her, the gazes gleaming with relief.

The siege wasn't over yet—but with that battering ram dealt to, Edward Longshanks would have to find another means of forcing his way inside the castle.

Warmth suffused Gavina then, relief uncoiling a little of the tension in her chest. Her attention returned to Draco. He lay upon his back before her, his ribs rising and falling shallowly. His eyes were closed, and a light sheen of sweat covered his face.

Gavina's throat constricted. She hated to see him suffer so. Surely, the curse would be working its magic upon him now? Maybe suffering was all part of it. Even so, she couldn't wait for morning to come.

For the first rays of dawn to wash away his hurts.

Body aching, Maximus climbed the stairs in the guard tower, to the quarters he shared with his wife. Dusk settled over Dunnottar now, bringing with it a welcome reprieve—a few brief hours before the fighting started anew.

Stepping inside the main chamber, Maximus's attention went to the glowing hearth and the iron tub filled with steaming water before him.

A sigh gusted out of him.

"I thought ye would appreciate a bath tonight, mo ghràdh." Heather glanced up from where she was kneading bread upon the table in the center of the chamber.

A weary smile stretched across Maximus's face. "You have no idea, just how much, carissima."

Wiping off her hands, Heather crossed to him. He enfolded her in his arms, burying his face in her rosemary-scented hair. Maximus leaned into her; he was a fortunate man indeed, to have a woman like this to return to at the end of each day.

"Ye did well today," Heather murmured against his shoulder. "The whole keep is humming with news of how ye and Cassian brought down the 'Battle Hammer'."

Maximus drew her closer against him, his hands running down her back. "That should slow Longshanks down a bit," he murmured.

His mood shadowed then. Losing the battering ram would be a blow for the English, but no doubt they'd recover soon enough. Longshanks wasn't done.

"Come." Heather drew back from him, her grey-green eyes warm. "Let's get ye into that bath before the water cools."

Maximus didn't need to be invited twice. He longed to soak into the hot water, to let all the day's tension and fury seep from him. Stripping off his filthy leathers, he stepped naked into the tub and sank down into it with a groan of pleasure.

Heather returned to her dough, shaping it into a flat disc and placing it upon the iron griddle that hung above the fire. "Supper will be fresh bread and cheese," she announced. "Sorry it's nothing fancier."

"It sounds good to me," Maximus replied, reaching for the cake of lye soap and the wash cloth she'd left for him. He then began to wash, cleansing himself of the smoke, blood, and grime of battle.

For a short while, husband and wife fell into companionable silence. Then Heather crossed to the tub and lowered herself onto a stool next to it. "Would ye like me to wash yer hair?"

Maximus grinned. "Yes, carissima."

Even without looking her way, he could sense her answering smile. Heather liked the Latin endearment he used with her.

"Ye took a few knocks today," she observed as he handed her the soap.

"Aye ... but not as many as Draco." Maximus paused then. "He'll be loving all the attention though, no doubt."

He glanced down at the red welt on his left flank; a chunk of stone from a catapult had caught him in the morning. His whole body felt bruised and battered. Fortunately for him, the dawn would soothe his hurts and ready him for another day of battle.

His belly contracted at the thought, his good humor fading. "I'm sorry, Heather," he said softly. "I really thought we'd broken the curse."

"Don't apologize for what isn't yer fault," she replied, moving around so that their gazes met. She wasn't smiling either now, and the tenderness in his wife's eyes made Maximus's gut tighten further.

"But I assured you that once we solved the riddle it would be done. I'd be mortal, and we could have a normal life together."

She shook her head, refusing to let him take the blame. "Aye … because that's what ye believed." She paused then, stubbornness lighting in her eyes. "Ye didn't lead me down a path I didn't want to travel, Max … and I refuse to believe all hope is lost."

Their gazes fused, the moment drawing out. Heather reached out, taking his hand, their fingers entwining. She then squeezed tight. "It's not over yet."

# XXXIII

## AWAITING THE DAWN

"WE SHALL BUILD another battering ram."

Edward of England glanced up to see Shaw Irvine standing in the doorway to his tent. His pugnacious jaw was set, his brawny arms folded across his barrel chest.

Edward exhaled slowly, wearily. It wasn't yet dawn, but he was already awake, dressed, and finishing a light meal of bread, butter, and honey in his tent. This hour was the only moment of the day he had to himself. The last person he wanted to see right now was the Irvine laird.

Especially after yesterday.

Edward pulled a face. "Your toy lies in a smoldering heap, Irvine ... there isn't time to construct another."

Irvine's mouth compressed. "With your help, I can ... I just—."

"Enough," Edward growled, cutting the man off. "You aren't getting another battering ram." He raised a pewter goblet to his lips and took a swig of ale. *God's teeth, this man was wearisome.* Irvine never stopped talking. Since the Scot had joined him, they shared supper together every evening. Irvine prattled on and on. He loved that

'Battle Hammer' of his—never stopped talking about the bloody thing.

At least Edward didn't have to hear him boasting about the siege weapon now. Even if its destruction had been a bitter blow to them all.

He'd breach Dunnottar's defenses eventually, but it would just take longer.

Edward set down the goblet on the makeshift table beside him with a thud. *The devil take Scotland.* He was getting too old for this.

Brushing crumbs off his surcoat, Edward rose to his feet. His joints pained him this morning, as they often did before he got moving. Despite his best efforts to ignore his advancing age, today he felt every one of his sixty-two years.

Shaw Irvine backed up a few steps as Edward walked by, stooping to exit the tent.

Irvine, like the vexatious shadow he was, followed him.

Outdoors, a warm breeze caressed Edward's face. Summer was indeed upon them, although in the midst of a campaign, it was easy to forget what time of the year it was. Edward heaved in a deep breath.

*How I miss Margaret.*

It had been months since he'd seen his wife. If only he could click his fingers and find himself standing on English soil, Margaret by his side.

Edward's gaze settled upon the solid walls of Dunnottar, outlined against an indigo sky. Dawn wasn't far off.

Wallace was inside somewhere, waiting him out. England and Margaret would have to keep while the outlaw still eluded him.

Edward turned, his attention spearing Shaw Irvine. The laird had gone red in the face. His lips parted as he readied himself to speak.

However, a shout from behind them interrupted him. "Sire!"

Hugh De Burgh strode through the camp toward them. Dressed for battle in a heavy hauberk, the coif pulled up, the knight was a formidable sight indeed. Hugh had followed Edward through many battles, and the king was pleased to have such a knight at his side.

However, the look on his captain's face as he approached made Edward tense. The man wore a deep scowl.

"What is it?" Edward greeted him.

"Word has just arrived from Stirling, sire … the garrison has fallen."

Edward's breathing caught. "What?"

"It gets worse," Hugh plowed on. "Comyn and Robert Bruce have joined forces against us … their men have slaughtered ours." He paused there, his scowl deepening. "There is a rumor that William Wallace fights with them."

A chill swept through Edward, engulfing him from the crown of his head to the soles of his feet. "A rumor?" he finally managed. "Has he actually been seen?"

Hugh nodded. "A big man with wild dark hair and beard fought alongside Comyn's younger brother … and has helped take back Stirling. Folk say he is William Wallace."

Edward's gut clenched.

Had Lady Gavina De Keith spoken the truth? Had that blacksmith lied to him?

Heat swept through him, dousing the chill of shock. It pulsed in his belly, in time with his heartbeat.

Slowly, he turned his gaze to Dunnottar once more. The De Keiths deserved his wrath, but it was the Wallace he really wanted.

*And the bastard isn't even here.*

Edward's hands balled into tight fists at his side. The blood roared in his ears; Irvine was speaking, but he couldn't hear him.

Nearly two weeks he'd been here. He'd wasted countless soldiers upon the siege, men he could have used elsewhere.

*I'll have Blair Galbraith's guts for this.*

"What do you wish to do now, sire?" Hugh's voice cut through the roar in his ears. "Shall we ready the ladders for the morning's assault?"

Edward unclenched his jaw, tasting blood. He'd accidentally bitten his tongue. Someone was going to pay for this—dearly.

Edward of England wasn't anyone's fool, but right now, he felt as if he'd been played like a lute.

*Wallace is behind this. He wanted me away from Stirling ... this was his plan all along.*

Edward's vision dimmed. When he finally spoke, his voice came out thick, choked. "No ... we pack up this morning and ride for Stirling. Ready the men."

The knight gave a brisk nod, his lantern jaw bunching.

"You can't abandon the attack!" Shaw Irvine stepped into Edward's field of vision, his face as red as raw liver. "You started the siege, and you must finish it."

Edward's gaze fixed upon the laird. "Excuse me?"

A few feet away, Hugh cast Irvine a warning look. Edward had lowered his voice, and all those who'd weathered the king's blistering temper knew what that meant.

But not Irvine. He too had a temper. "But we made an agreement."

"The devil take your agreement. We're leaving."

"Half my men are dead!" Irvine bellowed, spittle flying. "I can't take Dunnottar alone." He halted there, panting as he sought to contain his fury. "Leave me a hundred soldiers, and I'll finish the job you don't have the guts to—."

Edward's fist shot out then, driving into Shaw Irvine's nose.

Bone and sinew crunched under his knuckles. The laird reeled back, sprawling onto the trampled grass, blood streaming from his nose.

"I'll not waste one more English life on this fortress," Edward growled. "You want Dunnottar? Take it yourself."

Gavina had stayed at Draco's side overnight, perched upon a low stool. Toward the end of the night, she kept dropping off—and eventually her fatigue had been so great that she'd lain down on the floor next to his pallet. However, the hard flagstones had been unforgiving.

Draco's sweat-slicked face had grown increasingly pale. After they'd removed the arrows, he'd fallen into a strange fever, one that he hadn't yet awoken from. Elizabeth's quick actions had helped staunch the bleeding. His midsection was now bound up.

But the dawn couldn't come soon enough. She hated to see him suffer.

Rubbing her gritty eyes, Gavina glanced up at the high, narrow window above them. Outdoors the sky was starting to lighten. The castle was still eerily quiet—as it was every morning before the siege resumed. The silence was like an indrawn breath, waiting and watchful.

Any moment now, Draco would heal.

Gavina's breathing quickened. And when he did, she would tell him what lay in her heart. She'd climbed onto the wall yesterday, fully intending to speak to him. However, fate had intervened.

As she watched Draco, watched his body wage its own battle, she wondered how this had actually come to pass. How had this proud, aggravating Moor managed to steal her heart?

The soft pad of footfalls behind her made Gavina turn on her stool.

Elizabeth approached, a mug of something in her hands. "Mutton broth," she said, handing Gavina the mug. "It's a bit weak, but it's hot at least."

"Thanks, Liz." Gavina took the broth with a grateful smile. She hadn't eaten since the morning before, and despite her protesting belly, she had little appetite now. Nonetheless, the hot broth soothed her.

Elizabeth drew nearer, the light of a nearby cresset illuminating the tired yet resolute lines of her face. "Not long now," she murmured.

Gavina sighed. "Aye ... I wish it were dawn already. I hate to see him like this."

A heartbeat passed before Elizabeth met her eye, a quizzical look upon her face. "Ye wed Vulcan for a purpose ... but I didn't think ye actually cared about him?"

Gavina favored her with a weak smile. "I didn't ... not initially. But things are different now."

Elizabeth gave her a long, searching look. "Clearly."

Together the two women waited by Draco's bedside, watching as the sky outside lightened from indigo to pale blue. Strangely, the thunder of battle didn't resume outdoors.

But even stranger still, Draco Vulcan didn't wake from his fever.

# XXXIV

## FADING

"DO MY EYES deceive me?"

"No ... they're leaving."

Maximus stared west, at where the huge army had packed up. It then lifted up off the cliff-top and rumbled south, the clang of iron and thunder of horses' hooves shattering the balmy morning air. "But why?"

"I have no idea."

Maximus tore his gaze from the retreating army, fixing his attention upon the man who stood at his side. In the bright light, Cassian looked tired—exhausted even. Maximus had never seen him appear so weary. Had the siege taken such a toll upon them all?

Maybe it had, for his body still ached this morning—a deep bone ache that cut to the marrow. He felt so weary, he could have slept for a fortnight.

His aches and exhaustion surprised him.

*It's just relief hitting me,* he told himself. *We've all been living on our nerves for too long.*

"Craven bastards, look at them run!" Wallace strode up to the wall, his face creased in a fierce scowl as he glared out at the dark bulk of horses, helmets, and spears that moved away from the fortress. "They couldn't stomach a good fight."

Maximus frowned. He wasn't sure that was the reason for the retreat.

Even with the 'Battle Hammer' destroyed, Edward still had the advantage.

"Longshanks isn't the type to run from a fight," Cassian spoke up then, echoing Maximus's own thoughts. "He'll have a reason for leaving so suddenly ... and it won't be because he's tired of laying siege to this castle."

The Wallace's dark gaze swung around, pinning Cassian. "So why then?"

Cassian shrugged, his own attention returning to beyond the walls. Maximus did likewise, focusing upon the blackened ruins of the siege weapon below. "I'd wager that things have soured between Edward and Shaw," he murmured.

"With any luck, one of them is dead," Cassian replied.

"I wanted to be the man to end Shaw Irvine's life," Wallace muttered, "right before I slammed my dirk into Longshanks's belly." Bitter disappointment laced the outlaw's voice. He'd remained at Dunnottar, not only to defend the fortress, but in order to have his reckoning with Edward of England.

But the English king was now riding away.

"Something must have drawn his eye," Cassian murmured, watching the last of the red and gold Plantagenet banners flapping in the morning breeze. "I'd say he's returning to Stirling."

"You think the castle is under attack?" Maximus asked.

Cassian turned to him, running a tired hand over his face. "Maybe."

William Wallace said nothing at that—instead, his gaze remained focused upon the retreating English army. An army that had been so close to taking them.

"Maximus ... Cassian ... ye are needed in the infirmary."

Hearing Heather's voice, Maximus swiveled around to find his wife standing behind them. Her eyes widened when she realized what the men on the wall had all been staring at.

The retreating enemy.

"What?" she gasped, rushing forward. "Why?"

"Yer guess is as good as ours, lass," the Wallace grumbled.

"What's this about the infirmary?" Maximus cut in.

Heather jolted, her attention snapping back to her husband. Her throat bobbed. "It's Draco ... he's dying."

"His wounds haven't healed ... see for yerselves." Elizabeth drew back the bloodied bandages and allowed Maximus and Cassian to draw close to the pallet. Sunshine filtered into the crowded infirmary, pooling on the bed where Draco lay.

Following the centurions' gazes, Gavina looked upon the twin arrow holes. They were swollen, red, and weeping.

The dawn had long risen, and with it those terrible wounds should have vanished.

But they hadn't—and Draco hadn't yet awoken. A worrying pallor lay upon his skin, and his breathing was shallow, labored.

Elizabeth straightened up from examining Draco's wounds. "He's fading."

*Fading.*

Gavina's throat closed, an ache rising deep in her chest.

"So, it's broken then." Maximus's voice was soft, awed, his peat-brown eyes glittering. "We can all die."

Elizabeth nodded. "It seems so."

"I thought I felt different this morning," Cassian murmured. He too hadn't taken his gaze from Draco. "My limbs are heavy ... I feel ... *old*."

Hysterical laughter bubbled up within Gavina, yet she forced it down. They'd wanted this for so long, and yet neither Cassian nor Maximus looked overjoyed right now.

Next to Cassian, Aila placed an arm around his waist and squeezed tight. "That's because ye are, my love," she whispered. Her attention shifted to Gavina then, realization dawning. "This means the pair of ye are ..." Her voice trailed off there.

Gavina's hands fisted at her sides, her nails digging into her palms. "Aye," she whispered. "It does."

She couldn't believe it. Despite that he'd told her he wasn't capable of it, Draco loved her too.

Gavina's vision blurred. Life was cruel indeed.


They moved Draco up to Gavina's bed-chamber, where he would be more comfortable. Although Maximus and Cassian were as careful as possible, their friend groaned every time the litter jolted.

Draco was in a strange state—halfway between waking and sleeping. He didn't appear to notice his surroundings, yet he was clearly suffering.

No one spoke when Maximus and Cassian eventually got Draco onto the bed. Instead, they merely stood over him, their brows furrowed, their faces strained.

"I can't believe it," Maximus finally muttered. "All these years the bastard chased death ... and now it's standing over him with its scythe."

"Yesterday on the wall ... do you think he knew?" Cassian asked.

Standing behind them, Gavina tensed. She hoped not—the thought that Draco might deliberately throw himself into the sights of Edward's archers made her belly churn.

Surely, loving her wasn't so terrible?

"I don't think he did," Maximus answered with a sigh. "He was just doing what he always does ... playing the idiot."

The centurions eventually left the bed-chamber, exhaustion and worry etched upon their faces. The breaking of the curse had made both men weary; they needed to sleep, needed to come to terms with how their bodies had changed.

Breaking the curse should have been a moment of great relief—and Maximus and Cassian would soon be able to celebrate with their wives—but Draco's grave injuries had soured everything.

Watching them go, Gavina realized that these three were far more than just friends. They'd weathered the centuries together. They were closer than brothers.

Alone in the bed-chamber with Draco, Gavina approached the bed. His leathers were sweat-stained and dirty. He needed to be undressed and washed, and then she'd tend his wounds. She carried a small basket with some healing herbs Elizabeth had managed to salvage for her.

Setting down the basket on the bedside table, Gavina moved to Draco. She pulled off his boots and started to unlace the ties on his braies.

Draco groaned in his sleep, his long dark eyelashes fluttering against his cheeks. The sheen of sweat upon his skin worried her. If the wounds soured, he would surely die, for he was in a weakened state after losing so much blood.

A soft knock on the door behind her sounded, and a moment later, Aila entered carrying a large bowl of warm water, and clean cloths.

Aila's shadowed gaze took in Draco's prostrate form. She then placed the bowl and cloths down on the table and drew close to the bed. "Can I help ye, My Lady?" she asked.

Gavina shook her head. "Not at present ... but thank ye, Aila. I shall tend to my husband."

*My husband.*

Aye, he was hers, body and soul.

Six long years she'd been wed to David De Keith, but he'd never once touched her heart or eased the ache of loneliness inside her. If anything, he'd made her feel more alone. But Draco Vulcan had truly *seen* her.

He was the last man she'd have thought to fall in love with—but the heart knew what it wanted. What a terrible irony that he was now dying.

Tears blurred her vision then, obscuring Aila's pained face. Gavina felt them escape, scalding her cheeks. Heaving in a shaky breath, she placed a hand on Draco's naked chest, over the fluttering beat of his heart. "I won't leave his side."

# XXXV

## TOO LATE

DRACO AWOKE TO pain.

It felt as if a beast were tearing at the left side of his body, rending his flesh with its deep fangs. Yet, when his eyes fluttered open, he saw that he was alone upon a large bed.

A wave of nausea washed over him, and Draco attempted to swallow it down. "Water," he croaked.

"Ye are awake!" Gavina's lovely face hove into view. She was pale, her blue eyes red-rimmed and hollowed, yet he'd never seen a lovelier sight.

"Water," he repeated, desperate now. His tongue felt too big to fit in his mouth.

Great Lord of Light—he felt terrible.

"Of course." Gavina disappeared from view before reappearing with a wooden cup. "Take small sips," she instructed. "In case ye choke."

Draco did as bid. She'd propped him up on pillows, which made drinking easier. But despite the solace of sweet boiled water upon his tongue and throat, the agony in his torso was almost unbearable.

He let out a groan between clenched teeth. "The fiery pits of Hades," he finally grunted. "How far off is dawn?"

He'd suffered many injuries over the years, some of them horrific. But never had he looked forward to the new day like now.

Mortality be damned, he just wanted the pain to stop.

But Gavina now wore an odd expression on her face, her cornflower-blue eyes clouded.

"What?"

"Three dawns have come and gone since ye were injured, Draco," she said softly. "But ye have remained close to death. The curse is broken."

Draco stared up at her, shock distracting him momentarily from the fiery pain that pulsed down his left-hand side. It rose and fell like lapping waves. It was hard to bear, but Gavina's news made the agony ebb just a little.

"You mean ... all three of us are mortal?"

She nodded.

"And the English ... surely they've broken through the gates by now?"

"Maximus and Cassian destroyed the 'Battle Hammer' on the afternoon ye took those arrows. The following morning, the English packed up and left. Word has just reached us that Comyn and Bruce have taken back Stirling ... Edward's gone off to deal with them."

Draco let out the breath he'd been holding—slowly, for it hurt to breathe.

No wonder he felt as if he was on death's door.

He *was*.

A sickening realization filtered through him, chilling his limbs and making the pain return with such force that he groaned. "I'm done for ... aren't I?"

Gavina's throat bobbed. She didn't need to answer him; he could see the truth in her eyes. He glanced down at his bandaged torso, at the dark stains that seeped through the linen.

"Yer wounds have soured," she whispered. "I'm doing my best to tend them ... to heal ye ... but nothing I try does any good."

The pain, the vulnerability in her voice, cut him deeply. It hurt as much as his body did, to see the grief in this woman's eyes, to hear the quiver in her voice.

Reaching out, he entwined his fingers through hers upon the coverlet. "If the curse is broken," he gasped out the words, "you know what that means ... about us?"

"Aye," she whispered.

His fingers tightened around hers. "I'm a fool, Gavina. I should have been honest with myself ... I would have been if I wasn't so bull-headed." He heaved in a pained breath. Mithras, it hurt to talk. He could feel darkness pulling at the edges of his vision, drawing him down, yet he resisted.

He wanted to remain awake a while, to gaze upon his wife.

Draco's throat thickened, a pain rising under his breastbone that had nothing to do with the festering arrow wounds.

There was no numbness in his chest now. Instead, he felt *everything*.

Gavina's mouth trembled. "Dolt," she whispered. "Why did ye have to go and throw yerself in the path of those arrows?"

He drew in a shallow breath, fighting the pain. "It wasn't deliberate ... I was defending the wall ... but I was careless ... I've gotten too used to being invincible."

As he stared up at her, Draco saw tears escape Gavina's glittering eyes and trickle down her cheeks. Her fingers clenched around his. "I love ye, Draco," she whispered, "so much that it hurts to breathe."

"You are the best thing to ever come into my life," he whispered back, his voice cracking. "I never knew true joy ... till I met you." She was right, they had left it too late. All these years, he'd sought the oblivion of death, had dreamed of breaking the curse so that he could finally let nature take its course. But now that he perched on the brink while death's cold hands reached for him, Draco didn't want to die.

He desperately wanted to live.

Maximus and Cassian came to see him, and he saw from the somber expressions they wore, their guarded gazes, that things were indeed dire.

"I'm not a corpse yet," he greeted them, attempting a wan smile and failing. "You don't have to both look so tragic."

Maximus snorted, attempting a tight smile of his own. "Half-dead and you still manage to be aggravating. Some things never change."

Next to him, Cassian's hazel eyes guttered, his throat bobbing. His friend, whom Draco had never seen weep, looked on the verge of breaking down.

"Sit by my side," Draco rasped, patting the coverlet next to him. He was so weak that it was an effort to do even that. Agony pulsed in time with his heartbeat, but while he hurt, he was still alive—and before he died, he had things to say to these two.

Maximus and Cassian did as bid, lowering themselves onto the bed. The mattress dipped beneath their weight, causing a jolt of hot fire to lance through Draco, and his vision speckled. He needed to say this fast; he could tell he didn't have much time left.

"You know I was the youngest of five brothers," he said weakly. It frustrated him just how feeble his voice sounded, but he pressed on nonetheless. "All the same, my father ... the proudest Moor in Valentia ... was furious when I enlisted in the Roman army. In one afternoon, I gave up my heritage and became a Roman citizen." Draco swallowed then, wetting his parched lips. "Despite everything, it was the best decision I ever made. You two are kin to me."

Maximus stared down at him, his proud face all taught angles. Tears shone in his eyes. "Don't try to speak," he rasped. "It's taking its toll on you."

"I must ... say this," Draco countered. "I don't have much longer ... and I want you both to know about what happened to me ... why I turned into such a bitter bastard."

"You lost Magda," Cassian replied gently. "In that raid ... we know."

Draco shook his head. Weakness was suffusing his body now. The soured wound was spreading its poison through him. "No," he gasped. "That's not the reason."

Seated outside the bed-chamber in her solar, Gavina stared sightlessly at the flickering hearth. It was a warm day, yet she felt chilled to the marrow. Outdoors, through the open window, she could hear the cry of gulls, the clang of metal, and shouts of men as they worked on repairing the damage to the fortress.

Work would continue on Dunnottar for a long while, before all signs of that attack were erased. Huge chunks had been ripped out of the western curtain wall, the grey stone blackened from Greek fire.

Nearby, Heather and Aila sat silently. All three women had taken up sewing or knitting projects, but none had touched their work.

Their thoughts were on other matters.

The faint rumble of male voices filtered through the closed door. Maximus and Cassian had been in there for a while—and although Gavina knew Draco needed to say a proper farewell to his friends, she felt robbed of him.

They had such a short time left together.

She didn't want to waste a moment.

Gavina glanced right, toward the window. The sun blazed down from a clear blue sky. It was a bright summer's day, but winter lay in her heart. She felt as if she would never feel warm again.

Her unfinished tapestry sat near the window—the panorama of Dunnottar only needed a few more rows before it would be completed. Gavina's throat closed, grief swelling within her so fiercely that it hurt to draw breath. She never would finish it now.

"Gavina!" Elizabeth appeared in the doorway, her cheeks flushed from what must have been a rapid climb up the stairs. Ever since the English had retreated, Gavina had handed over charge of Dunnottar to her sister-by-marriage.

Now that she had wed Draco, she could no longer continue as laird.

Not that she wanted to.

She wanted nothing other than for her husband to live, but with each passing hour, she knew her prayers wouldn't be answered.

"A woman is here to see ye ... from Stonehaven."

Gavina frowned. Right now, she didn't want to see anyone. "Who is it?"

"It's Nessa ... the wise woman."

Gavina stiffened. "What does she want?"

As she spoke, a figure appeared in the doorway behind Elizabeth—a tall woman with a mane of red-gold hair. Nessa was dressed in the same blue kirtle she'd worn when Draco and Gavina had visited her. However, this afternoon, she also wore a sky-blue cloak about her shoulders. And she carried a small wooden basket hooked over one arm.

"I'm here to tend Draco," the wise woman greeted Gavina with a half-smile, her pine-green eyes glinting as their gazes met. "The folk of Stonehaven know me as a wise woman ... but I am also a skilled healer."

Gavina shoved her sewing to one side and rose to her feet. "But I didn't send for ye ... how did ye know he was injured?"

Nessa held her gaze, before she inclined her head. "I cast the bones this morning," she replied, "and they warned me that yer man lies gravely ill. If I don't tend him, he will die."

A shocked silence settled over the solar as the four women surrounding Nessa stilled.

Gavina was the first to recover. "But he *is* dying?"

Nessa patted the basket she carried. "A man isn't doomed until he draws his last breath. Will ye take me to him?"

Around her, Gavina heard the sharp intake of breaths from Elizabeth, Heather, and Aila. However, she didn't look their way; instead, her gaze remained upon Nessa.

Whatever she was—seer, wise woman, witch, healer—it didn't matter. Nessa claimed she could help Draco, and that was enough for Gavina.

The woman had been right once before, about how the curse would be broken.

Gavina moved toward the bed-chamber door, beckoning for Nessa to follow. "This way."

# XXXVI

## SECOND CHANCES

DRACO STARED UP at the woman who set her basket down by the bed. Nessa ran an appraising eye over him.

"I didn't expect to see you again," he greeted her weakly. Hades, it was such an effort to speak.

The wise woman arched an eyebrow. "No … neither did I. But ye seem to have a knack for requiring my help."

Nessa turned, her gaze sweeping over the four women and two men who stood behind her. "I can't work with an audience," she informed them. "I need to be alone with Draco for a short while."

Maximus and Cassian hesitated, their gazes narrowing, but Draco nodded. "All will be well," he reassured them.

The others filed out, although Gavina hovered.

"Ye too, Gavina," Nessa said, although there was compassion in her voice. "Please."

Gavina's heart-shaped face went taut, and her lips parted as if she would argue, but then she thought better of it and nodded. Picking up her skirts, she turned and swept from the chamber, closing the door after her.

Draco watched as the wise woman turned back to him. "So, you're a healer as well?"

Her mouth quirked. "Of a sort." She moved close to him then, drawing a sharp knife from her belt. Deftly, she cut away his bandages, her face wrinkling when she saw the state of his injuries.

The putrid odor, despite that Gavina had cleaned and dressed the wounds earlier in the day, made Draco's belly churn. There were few smells worse than rotting flesh.

"The bones were right ... it's a real mess we have here," she muttered under her breath.

"The bones?" he managed between gritted teeth.

"Aye ... I cast them this morning, and they were quite adamant."

Draco's brow furrowed. The woman wasn't making any sense—although it probably had more to do with his fever-addled brain.

However, he didn't answer her. Quite frankly, he lacked the energy to do so. He wanted Gavina back in here at his side, to interlace his fingers through hers one last time before oblivion took him.

He needed for this woman to get on with things.

But instead, this witch, in her blue kirtle, smelling of dried herbs and summer, was digging through her basket. She produced a small clay pestle and mortar and proceeded to add herbs and powders to the mortar.

Draco watched her mash them. She was frowning in concentration now, and there was something about the woman that made him uneasy—as it had back when they'd visited her hovel in Stonehaven.

Now, just like then, the hair on his arms prickled.

Nessa wasn't what she appeared—this woman's young and pretty appearance perhaps fooled many. Yet Draco sensed she wielded real power.

She finished mixing the herbs before adding a few drops of something from a clay bottle. And then, as Draco continued to observe her, Nessa's eyelids fluttered closed. Flexing her fingers over the mortar, she murmured a few words.

Draco's skin prickled once more. *Ancient words.*

Suddenly, he was back in that bandruì's hut, watching her paint a sickle on Maximus's forehead with crow's blood.

This woman was truly a witch. Not just a wise woman who dabbled in ancient arts—but a real witch. Energy vibrated off her.

"Who *are* you?" he asked as she picked up the mortar and turned to him. It was the same question he'd asked her in her hovel. And now, just as then, she didn't answer him directly. "Someone who's about to save yer life," she replied, her full mouth lifting at the corners.

"But—"

"Lie still, man. Save yer strength." The firmness in her voice warned him from pressing further.

Sinking back against the pillows, Draco took a shallow breath, and then another. He hated feeling this weak.

"Fortunately for ye, the power of the Mead Moon still dominates," Nessa murmured. "The tides are high, and healing energy is at its strongest."

Draco listened, not understanding half of what she'd just uttered. She mentioned the Mead Moon when he and Gavina had visited her in Stonehaven; clearly, the moon's cycles were linked to Nessa's power.

Pouring some vinegar onto a piece of linen, Nessa leaned over him and cleaned his wounds.

Draco sucked in a breath, biting down to prevent himself from crying out.

Oblivious to his pain, Nessa reached into the mortar, took a handful of the paste she'd just mixed, and then spread it over his wounds, pushing it into the holes.

Draco arched off the bed, letting out a howl of agony.

The door to the bed-chamber flew open, and Gavina appeared. "Draco!" she gasped, her gaze snapping to the wise woman. "What are ye doing to him?"

"Attempting to help him," Nessa replied, not glancing Gavina's way, her tone clipped. "Now ... please leave us alone."

Gavina placed her hands upon her hips, scowling. She didn't intend to go anywhere.

"It's fine, Gavina," Draco gasped, collapsing back onto the bed. "Do as she says."

He closed his eyes then, gritting his teeth as the agony subsided. An instant later, the door thudded shut.

"You could have warned me," he said weakly, "before you did that."

"Better I didn't," Nessa replied. "Ye were never going to enjoy it."

Draco opened his eyes to see that she was now spreading the rest of the ointment upon his wounds. Heat suffused his side, and then it started to burn.

Draco growled a curse. "What have you treated me with, woman? It feels like my insides are on fire."

"Best ye don't know." Nessa stretched a hand over his flank, her fingers flexing once more. "Folk get squeamish about such things … quiet now … I'm almost done."

Draco clenched his jaw, tensing as the ointment burned into his flesh. He was now riding a wave of pain—agony pulsing in time with his heartbeat, with each ragged breath. Sweat ran down his face and neck. He wasn't sure how much more he could endure before he wailed like a babe.

Ignoring his suffering, the witch closed her eyes and started to murmur.

Words slipped from her tongue, rising and falling in the bed-chamber. Draco paid them little mind now though; he was fighting his own battle.

One he was slowly losing.

Bile crept up his throat. He was going to be sick.

His world shrank. Heat. Pain. A woman's whispers. Nothing else existed.

And despite that he clung to life like a drowning man on the end of a rope, Draco Vulcan wished for his suffering to end—even if that meant death claimed him.

Time lost all meaning, and he blacked out for a spell. When he came to, the heat had turned to a numb chill down his side, and Nessa was no longer speaking.

Instead, she perched upon the edge of the bed, her piercing green stare upon his face.

"I always wondered if the legend was true," she greeted him solemnly.

Draco licked his parched lips. "Legend?"

"Aye." She reached for a cup of boiled water and shifted forward, helping him to take a sip. "The women of my coven all know about Maximus, Cassian, and Draco ... the three immortal centurions."

Draco went still, his weakness and pain momentarily forgotten. "You know of us?"

Nessa nodded. "The bandruì who founded our coven ... was the one who cursed ye."

Draco stared at her, shock rendering him speechless. *Coven?*

Seeing his confusion, Nessa's full mouth curved. "Her name was Bedelia ... and she was the most powerful of us all. The tale of her greatest deed ... cursing the hated Roman invaders ... has been passed down through the centuries." Nessa paused there. "Some of us believed it just a myth, but the moment ye told me yer tale, I knew who ye were." Her features softened. "Truthfully, I pitied ye and yer friends. Ye have wandered lost for far too long."

Draco drew in a slow, pained breath. "So, is that why you helped us break the curse?"

She nodded. "Bedelia had her reasons for cursing ye ... and the coven she established has protected this land from invaders for many years. But ye have suffered enough."

Their gazes fused.

"And that's why you're treating me now?"

A smile crept across her face. "Everyone deserves a second chance, Draco Vulcan ... even ye."

# XXXVII

## THE BEST GIFT OF ALL

"YE ARE THE canniest bastard I've ever met."

William Wallace's gruff voice echoed through the bed-chamber.

Draco cocked an eyebrow. "Does that mean you're pleased to see me alive?"

"Those injuries would have killed most men," Wallace rumbled with a shake of his head. "Ye have nine lives, lad."

Draco's expression sobered. "I did once," he murmured. "But not anymore. I think I just used my last one."

He sat propped up on a nest of pillows. On his insistence, the servants had left the shutters open, letting in a crisp sea-breeze. Outdoors, the sound of industry—hammering and shouts—filtered in. Dunnottar had undergone a battering indeed.

Draco's gaze wasn't on the view out the window though, but on the big man whose presence dominated the chamber. They were alone. Maximus and Cassian were helping repair the curtain wall, and Gavina had ridden out to Stonehaven with Aila and Heather to bring a basket of gifts to Nessa, in thanks for all she'd done.

The wise woman had saved his life.

Four days had passed since her visit. She'd left him still in pain and fevered, but the fever had broken that night, and he'd healed quickly since.

Gavina had wept the following morning, when it had become clear that he would indeed live. They had wept together.

Draco had laughed in the face of death many times—but he'd never come so close to dying. One day he would breathe his last, but now that he'd been given a mortal life once more, he wanted to savior it.

Meeting the Wallace's eye, Draco smiled. "So, what now, William?"

He'd followed the Wallace for a while, and knew that restless look on the man's face; impatience vibrated through his huge body. Dunnottar had become a cage.

"We've helped with the repairs," Wallace grunted, "but my time here is coming to an end. I need to move on … and rally more warriors to my side once more. The cause cannot be abandoned."

The outlaw's gaze guttered then. It occurred to Draco that William Wallace carried his own curse—the curse of a wanted man. He would be hunted forever—they both knew it. The man wore an expression of grim resolve, of fatalism.

"When then?" Draco asked.

"Tomorrow," Wallace replied. "The lads and I will depart with the dawn." His gaze roved over Draco then. "And I take it ye won't be joining us?"

Draco shook his head. "I'm a wedded man now. Gavina would never forgive me if I rode off into the wilderness with you."

"Fair enough," Wallace grunted, his features stretching into a grin. "You're a lucky one, Draco. Gavina is a jewel among women."

Draco raised his eyebrows. It was rare to hear Wallace use such language.

Seeing his incredulous look, the Wallace snorted. "It's true."

Draco smiled. "It is. I don't know what I did to deserve Gavina … but now she's mine, I'm not leaving her side."

Wallace grinned. "Good lad."

Gavina gently opened the door to the bed-chamber, peeking inside. Draco was propped up, his hands wrapped around a cup. He wasn't looking her way; instead, his gaze was trained out of the window.

He wore a gentle expression—one she'd rarely seen upon his face before the curse was broken.

Her breathing hitched. He still looked drawn from his brush with death, yet her husband was a sight to behold all the same: his face all lean planes, his bearing lordly. She would never tire of looking upon him.

"Are ye taking more visitors?" she asked softly, cutting into his reverie. "I know folk have been tramping through here since dawn like it's harvest market."

He glanced her way, a slow smile creeping across his face. "You aren't a visitor, Gavina. You're my wife." He patted the bed next to him. "Come here, love."

*Love.*

She never tired of hearing him say that. Even a week after they'd professed their feelings for each other, she still reeled from the fact that things had worked out.

She was no longer laird of Dunnottar, but frankly that was a relief. Instead, she was wed to a man she loved, and they were about to embark upon a wonderful new life together.

Crossing to the bed, she lay down upon the blankets and snuggled up to him, placing her cheek upon his shoulder.

"Did you find the wise woman well?" Draco asked after a moment. "I hope she appreciated your gifts."

"She wasn't there," Gavina replied, disappointment creeping into her voice as she recalled the deserted hovel and the fowl—freed from their coops—scratching in the overgrown garden. "She's gone, Draco. I asked around in Stonehaven ... but no one knows where she went."

His body stiffened against hers.

Propping herself up, Gavina angled up her chin to meet his gaze. He'd said little of what had passed between him and Nessa. The wise woman had tended to him, and after she left, Draco had fallen into a deep slumber. When he'd awoken the following morning, clearly on the mend, Gavina had been too relieved to question him about what the healer had actually done to him.

"There's something ye aren't saying," she murmured. "Will ye share it with me?"

He grinned. "I was wondering when you'd bring this up."

Gavina arched an eyebrow. "Keep yer secrets then," she huffed.

Draco's grin faded, his gaze growing soft as he lifted a hand and stroked her cheek. "Not anymore ... and never with you." He paused then. "You realize that Nessa is much more than she appears, don't you?"

Gavina inclined her head. "Ye mean, she's a *witch*?"

He nodded. "That's why she has disappeared. Folk tolerate having a local wise woman living amongst them ... someone to lance their boils and bless the harvest ... but if they learned who she really was, they'd turn against her."

Gavina sucked in a breath. "She healed ye with magic then?"

"That and some healing herbs that nearly dissolved my flesh." Draco cringed at the memory, and Gavina found a smile curving her lips. She'd known he was feeling better when he started to complain about the pain.

When he'd been on death's door, he'd barely uttered a word.

"We owe Nessa yer life," she said after a pause. "I wish I could have thanked her properly."

Draco smiled, his thumb tracing Gavina's lower lip. As always, his touch sent shivers of need through her. They hadn't lain together since his recovery, but she could tell from the glint in her husband's eyes that tonight they'd rectify matters. "As do I ... when she helped me, I was distracted." His mouth twisted. "I was also reeling from her admission that she's part of a coven that dates back to ancient times." His gaze held Gavina's. "The witch who founded the coven ... was the one who cursed me, Max, and Cass."

Gavina drew back. "Really?"

Draco gave a rueful laugh. "You can imagine my surprise."

"Do Maximus and Cassian know?"

"Yes, I told them yesterday." He paused then, his expression turning wistful. "It's like everything has gone full-circle. The riddle has been solved ... and ironically, the bandruì who cursed us also had a hand in freeing us."

"The Broom-star has gone from the night sky," Gavina confirmed. "So ye figured everything out just in time."

"We did," Draco replied, interlacing his fingers through hers. "But we wouldn't have done it without your resolve ... your courage."

The intensity of his gaze made her breathing quicken, heat flaring across her chest. "I'm no braver than ye," she murmured.

His fingers tightened around hers. "When the witch spoke that riddle all those centuries ago, she was making a prophecy," he replied. "Of the White Hawk and the Dragon. I never knew it ... but I've been waiting a long time to meet you."

The heat spreading across Gavina's chest intensified, and tears pricked her eyes. It was hard to believe that she was part of a foretelling, one that been made back in the mists of time.

"I have something for you," Draco said finally, shattering the moment. A boyish smile lit his face as he reached under the pillows. "Sit up, and close your eyes."

Gavina inclined her head. "A gift ... really? What is it?"

"You'll find out soon enough. Hold out your hand." His smile widened to a grin. "You're not getting it until you close your eyes."

Gavina gave a snort, but complied, holding out a hand as bid.

A moment later, something solid landed upon her palm.

"You can open your eyes now."

She did, her gaze fastening upon a small wooden figurine—of a beautiful naked woman with long hair tumbling down her back.

Gavina stifled a gasp. "That's me?"

"It doesn't even begin to do you justice, love," he murmured, his voice spilling over her like warmed honey. "But I've been working on it for the past weeks. I found a large piece of rosewood a while ago and wasn't sure what to whittle out of it. Before I knew it, I was carving your likeness."

Gavina traced a fingertip over the intricate carving. "This is lovely ... ye have great talent."

"I've had centuries to hone my craft," he replied, a smile in his voice. "Max and Cass both have religious figurines made by my hand."

Gavina glanced up, her throat thickening. "I will treasure this always," she murmured. Their gazes locked, and the tenderness she saw in his eyes robbed her of breath. Her fingers wrapped around the figurine. "No one has ever gifted me something so special."

His mouth quirked, and he leaned forward, cupping her cheek with his hand. "I received the best gift of all," he whispered. "A beautiful, bold-hearted Scotswoman in flesh and blood." He paused then, his gaze searing. "You have taught me what love is, Gavina ... and I will never forget it."

# EPILOGUE

## ALL I'LL EVER WANT

GAVINA STEPPED OUT of the cottage, bracing herself against the chill wind that gusted in from the north.

Samhain had come and gone, and now they'd entered the last moon cycle before Yule. Winter had arrived, after a long, tumultuous summer and tense autumn.

Much had happened since Edward's departure from Dunnottar. He hadn't managed to take back Stirling, but instead, he'd unleashed his wrath upon the south, and in early autumn had taken Robert Bruce's Turnberry Castle. Longshanks and his son—and their armies—were now wintering in West Lothian.

Unfortunately, Scotland hadn't yet rid itself of Edward of England. While William Wallace was still at large, and the Scottish clan-chiefs resisted the English, Edward wouldn't rest.

Shrugging off such grim thoughts, Gavina drew her fur mantle about her shoulders. Thank the Lord that Edward had let Dunnottar be. She cast a glance then over her shoulder at the doorway behind her. The midwife had confirmed what she'd already suspected.

She was at least two moons gone with bairn.

A smile spread across her face, and she made her way over to where her palfrey stood nearby, obediently tied up to a rail outside the midwife's cottage.

Excitement fluttered deep in her belly—or perhaps it was the bairn—as her smile widened.

*Draco will be beside himself.*

And he would be. All three of the centurions hadn't been able to father children since the day of their cursing. But Heather and Aila were both now carrying their husband's babes—Heather was due in late winter, Aila in early spring.

Gavina's bairn would be a summer child.

The last lingering shadow of that terrible curse had finally faded. It had taken a while, for the curse was like a deep bruise that left a mark long after the original injury healed. Maximus, Cassian, and Draco were free, but all three men were still coming to terms with what freedom actually meant.

Untying her palfrey from the rail, Gavina mounted and turned the horse toward Stonehaven's market— where the weekly event was taking place upon the docks.

She'd slipped away while Heather and Aila bickered over which cloth to buy, their long-suffering husbands looking on.

Even Draco hadn't seen Gavina leave, for he'd been haggling with an iron monger. But he'd be looking for her now.

Returning to the busy quayside—where gulls screeched at each other as they fought for scraps, and the cries of vendors rose against the whistling wind and the rumble of surf—Gavina hurried back to the market.

Draco spied her from a distance. He strode toward her. The others hurried close behind him.

Seeing their worried faces, guilt speared Gavina. She hadn't been away that long—but she now realized they'd all been searching for her.

Even with his face creased with concern, the sight of her husband—tall and swarthy, a fur cloak around his broad shoulders—made Gavina's belly tighten with excitement. He'd made Dunnottar his home, but he was still a warrior, and he stalked toward her like one.

"Gavina!" he greeted her, his voice tight with relief. "Where in Hades have you been?"

"To see the midwife," she replied.

Draco stopped, halting so abruptly that Maximus ran into him. His dark eyes went wide, before his throat bobbed. "Why? Are you …?"

Gavina nodded. "The bairn will be born just after Beltaine."

"I knew it!" Aila squealed, her face alight with joy. "Ye have been off yer bannocks for days now." Beside Aila, Heather was beaming, a hand upon her swollen belly. Likewise, Aila's stomach appeared rounded under her kirtle. Gavina's, however, had yet to curve.

Standing behind their wives, both Maximus and Cassian were smiling. Their gazes gleamed. They knew how much this meant to Draco and Gavina.

She'd feared she was barren, for although she hadn't lain with David often, her womb had never quickened nonetheless. And when both Heather and Aila fell pregnant and she didn't, she began to worry. Draco had been given his mortality, and should be able to father a child. But what if she couldn't give him one?

Gavina's gaze met Draco's. His worry had faded. He approached her now, his hands cupping her face. "That is fine news, my love," he murmured, gazing into her eyes. "But even if you weren't with child, you know I'd adore you all the same." Perhaps seeing the tension upon her face, his gaze narrowed. "I mean it. Having a bairn together is wonderful." His voice had lowered, growing intimate, as if they were alone and not standing in the midst of a jostling crowd with their friends looking on. "But it's you I want … all I'll ever want."

Gavina stared up at him, and something deep inside her—a tension she hadn't realized she'd even been carrying—unknotted. He had no idea how freeing his words were.

Throwing her arms around Draco's neck, she pressed her lips to his, clinging to him. She heard one of the men whistle, while one of the women—Aila most likely—giggled.

Gavina and Draco paid them no mind.

The kiss deepened, and Gavina's surroundings faded. She too had everything she would ever want. Right here in this moment. This man in her arms—who kissed her as if they were newly-weds standing at the doorway of the chapel—was the only thing she needed.

# FROM THE AUTHOR

I hope you enjoyed the final installment in THE IMMORTAL HIGHLAND CENTURIONS.

DRACO was a story full of surprises for me—there were a few developments I didn't expect at all! When I planned the book, I was thinking more of a typical 'enemies to lovers' story, but this tale developed into something much more complex. Draco was more troubled and damaged, and Gavina more mature in her thinking than I'd expected. It's one of the joys of being a writer—those times when your characters 'take over'.

There were quite a few things to tie up, including the tense situation with Edward of England and breaking the curse. I often find it hard to say goodbye at the end of my trilogies—so to that end, I've written a novella that tells Elizabeth and Robert De Keith's story. It's a festive novella, just in time for Christmas. Look out for it a couple of days after the release of DRACO!

Once again, there's quite a bit of historical background that went into this novel (read my historical notes below for details on it).

Jayne x

# HISTORICAL NOTES

Once again, these notes are lengthy—but worth the read if you like a bit of historical background insight!

As those of you who've read the entire series will know, this story hinges around the story of the Ninth Legion—a legion of around five thousand men who marched into the wilds of Caledonia in around 118 AD and were never seen again.

The Ninth legion was also called 'the Hispana', or Spanish legion. The generals and commander would have all been Roman, but most of the legion was made up of soldiers from Hispania (Spain). Draco comes from what is now southern Spain, and the Roman fort of Valentia, now the town of Valencia.

An important thing to note here, regarding Draco's Moorish origins, is that I have taken a bit of 'creative license' with history in this series (considering it's all about immortal Roman centurions that shouldn't come as too great a surprise!). The Moors weren't established on the Iberian Peninsula during the time of the Roman Empire—although there was quite a bit of existing trade between the Berbers of North Africa and the continent. However, I really wanted to show the breadth of cultural diversity within the Roman Empire, and as there were North African colonies too, I decided to shift the Moors' arrival forward a few centuries. Draco's original name, Amestan, is of Berber origin. It means 'Protector, defender', which is perfect for his character, and ties into what would have been his actual heritage.

Halley's Comet is a prominent feature in the whole series. Back in the Dark Ages and Medieval period it didn't go by that name (as it was named after the scientist who 'discovered' it in 1758). Instead, there are

references to it being called 'the fire-tailed star'.
Maximus calls it 'the Broom-star', which was actually a
name that Chinese astronomers attached to the comet.
Halley's Comet appears in our skies every 75-76 years,
and in ancient times it was often heralded as an ill omen.
The comet actually appeared in the night-sky in the
months preceding the Norman invasion of England,
something that the English blamed for their defeat. The
Bayeux tapestry even shows the comet! The year in
which this series takes place, 1301, was a year in which
the comet was sighted.

At the beginning of the novel, I mention the Chapel of
Saint Margaret of Scotland in Edinburgh Castle—this
place is real, as is the saint herself. She was a pious
Scottish queen, married to King Malcolm III. She
famously died in 1093 just days after hearing of her
husband's death in battle. Her saint's day is actually 16
November, although for the purposes of my novel, I shift
it to June!

Dunnottar does mean 'fort on the shelving slope' in
Scottish Gaelic: Dùn Fhoithear. The castle is a mighty
stronghold perched on cliffs on the north-eastern coast
of Scotland. As I mention in my story, the castle was
taken by the English in the final years of the 13th Century
and then liberated by William Wallace and his men.
When the English garrison realized they were doomed,
they locked themselves inside the chapel, hoping to find
sanctuary there. However, Wallace showed them no
mercy and burned the lot of them to death inside it.

William Wallace, of course, is the famous Scottish
freedom fighter. My depiction of Wallace isn't the Mel
Gibson, *Braveheart* version (sorry!). Instead, I followed
the historical records of him as a huge giant of a man
with thick dark hair and beard. He was also reputed to
have had a terrible temper. Not a man to mess with!

The year 1301 is also in the midst of the Scottish Wars of Independence (although they weren't called that at the time). When this series begins, there was a period of unstable peace although later that year Edward I of England resumes his campaign. The laird of Dunnottar, Robert De Keith, was an English prisoner as I describe, and he did have a wife named Elizabeth. However, his brother, David, is fictitious, as is Lady Gavina.

While it's true that Edward's son did occupy the south-west of Scotland as his father focused on the other territories, I couldn't find any mention of Edward residing in Stirling at this time. However, that doesn't mean he didn't!

I did a bit of research into Edward of England. Indeed, he went by the name of Longshanks (due to his considerable height), and did have the moniker: The Hammer of the Scots (something that ties nicely into our curse). He was tall with dark-blond hair and 'icy blue' eyes. He was also reputed to be quite handsome, although a drooping left eyelid marred his looks slightly. Edward was said to have a powerful voice, despite a slight lisp, and a terrible temper when riled. He was clever and a good fighter. He also hated William Wallace.

In 1301, Edward was 62 years old—getting on in years to be campaigning so heavily in Scotland. Nonetheless, he was still a force to be reckoned with. Edward was a formidable man and a great leader, and he was lucky in love. He was happily married to his first wife, Eleanor (who bore him fifteen children!), and when she died, he grieved her terribly. In her memory, Edward ordered the construction of twelve elaborate stone crosses marking the route of her funeral procession between Lincoln and London. His second wife, Margaret, was around forty years his junior! However, despite the age gap, their union was also a happy one.

As a bit of historical background, in July 1301, Edward launched his sixth campaign into Scotland (I bring his campaign forward by a few months in this series), aiming to conquer Scotland in a two-pronged attack. One army was commanded by his son, Edward, Prince of Wales, the other, the larger, was under his own command.

Just as there isn't any historical mention of Edward being in Stirling, there isn't any of him attacking Dunnottar during 1301. His siege on the castle is entirely a figment of my imagination. However, his hatred of William Wallace was real—and I like to think that if he'd known where the Wallace was hiding out in this period, he would have marched off to try and capture him!

Later in 1301, in the months after this novel concludes, Scot forces attacked Prince Edward's army at Lochmaben in early September and also threatened Robert Bruce's Turnberry Castle, which Edward had taken earlier in the year. Scottish rebels also threatened the king's army at Bothwell in the same month. Despite over six months of hard campaigning, Edward was having difficulty keeping control over southern Scotland. The two English armies met to winter at Linlithgow, but in January 1302, Edward agreed to a nine-month truce.

John Comyn has a small role in this novel. He was a leading Scottish baron and magnate who played an important role in the First War of Scottish Independence. He served as Guardian of Scotland after the forced abdication of his uncle, King John Balliol, in 1296, and for a time commanded the defense of Scotland against English attacks. I couldn't find out if he was actually in Stirling in 1301, but since he was Guardian, I thought it probable. In later years, his relationship with the Bruce was strained (Robert the Bruce famously murdered him), but in this series I have him enlisting Bruce's help to win back Stirling while Edward is distracted.

In this series, I have most definitely bent and shaped historical fact to suit the story I'm telling. However, I've done so with respect to the historical figures and events involved—and whenever possible, I've tried to stick as close to the 'truth' as I can. When it comes to events that aren't recorded, I like to think that I'm merely 'filling in the blanks' of history. So many historical events were never written down ... who's to say Edward I of England didn't make a wee trip to Dunnottar in 1301!

It's easy to get carried away with the fascinating history, but this series is first and foremost a work of fiction. As much as I love research and incorporating fascinating details, they can never overshadow the love story.

# CHARACTER GLOSSARY

**The three immortal centurions:**
Maximus—from Ostia, Italia
Cassian—from Brigantium, Hispania
Draco—from Valentia, Hispania

William Wallace—Scottish freedom fighter

**The De Keiths**
Robert De Keith (former laird of Dunnottar, currently imprisoned by the English)
Elizabeth De Keith (Robert's wife)
Robbie De Keith (Robert and Elizabeth's young son)
David De Keith (Robert's younger brother—former laird of Dunnottar Castle, now deceased)
Gavina De Keith (David's wife, née Irvine)
Donnan De Keith (Steward of Dunnottar)
Iona De Keith (Donnan's wife)
Heather De Keith (Donnan and Iona's eldest daughter)
Aila De Keith (Heather's younger sister)

**The Irvines**
Shaw Irvine (laird of Drum Castle—brother to Gavina De Keith)

**The Galbraiths**
Logan Galbraith (laird of Culcreuch Castle)
Lena Galbraith (Logan's wife)
Cory Galbraith (Logan and Lena's son—the eldest of four sons: Rory, Aran, and Duglas)
Iain Galbraith (cousin to Cory, former blacksmith of Fintry)
Blair Galbraith (Iain's younger brother, smith at Dunnottar)

**The English**
Edward I, King of England
Hugh De Burgh (Edward's commander)

# ACKNOWLEDGEMENTS

Thanks so much to my wonderful readers. Your emails and social media messages mean the world to me—it's such a thrill to know that my stories touch you. I took a bit of a risk with this series, and it's great to see that you love it!

Thanks as well to the wonderful Otago/Southland Chapter of RWNZ (Romance Writers of New Zealand). It would be difficult to find a more supportive group anywhere!

And a huge thank you to my husband, Tim, whose tireless work helped make this series rock!

# ABOUT THE AUTHOR

Award-winning author Jayne Castel writes epic Historical and Fantasy Romance. Her vibrant characters, richly researched historical settings and action-packed adventure romance transport readers to forgotten times and imaginary worlds.

Jayne is the author of the Amazon bestselling BRIDES OF SKYE series—a Medieval Scottish Romance trilogy about three strong-willed sisters and the men who love them. An exciting spin-off series set in the same story-world, THE SISTERS OF KILBRIDE, is now available as well. In love with all things Scottish, Jayne also writes romances set in Dark Ages Scotland ... sexy Pict warriors anyone?

When she's not writing, Jayne is reading (and re-reading) her favorite authors, cooking Italian feasts, and taking her dog, Juno, for walks. She lives in New Zealand's beautiful South Island.

**Connect with Jayne online:**
www.jaynecastel.com
Email: contact@jaynecastel.com

www.ingramcontent.com/pod-product-compliance
Lightning Source LLC
Chambersburg PA
CBHW021107110726
47900CB00007B/2067